celg

Six-Gun Law

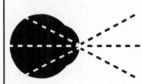This Large Print Book carries the
Seal of Approval of N.A.V.H.

WIND RIVER SERIES

SIX-GUN LAW

A WESTERN DUO

JAMES REASONER AND
L. J. WASHBURN

THORNDIKE PRESS
A part of Gale, a Cengage Company

GALE
A Cengage Company

GALE
A Cengage Company

LIBRARY OF CONGRESS CIP DATA ON FILE.
CATALOGUING IN PUBLICATION FOR THIS BOOK
IS AVAILABLE FROM THE LIBRARY OF CONGRESS

ISBN-13: 978-1-4328-5722-6 (hardcover alk. paper)

Published in 2020 by arrangement with James Reasoner/L. J. Washburn

Printed in Mexico
Print Number: 01   Print Year: 2020

CONTENTS

CONTENTS

■ ■ ■ ■

RANSOM VALLEY

■ ■ ■ ■

CHAPTER 1

The wind sweeping down from the north over the settlement of Wind River brought with it a faint chill that promised the arrival of winter in a month or two.

It also carried the sound of gunshots to Marshal Cole Tyler's ears.

He had just stepped out of the Wind River Café, where he had stopped in for a mid-afternoon cup of coffee . . . and a visit with the café's pretty, strawberry blond proprietor, Rose Foster. Cole and Rose had been keeping company for a couple of months now, although things hadn't gotten too serious between them. Both of them possessed a natural reserve that tended to make them go slow about such matters.

Cole put any thoughts about Rose out of his mind as he broke into a trot toward the southern end of Grenville Avenue where most of the settlement's saloons were located. He figured the two shots he'd heard had come from the Pronghorn, which had a history of violence.

The marshal was a powerfully built man of medium height with square-cut brown hair that fell to his shoulders. His brown hat usually hung from its chin strap on the back of his neck, as it did now. A five-pointed tin star was pinned to his buckskin shirt. Cole had been the law in Wind River for almost two years, and in that time he had seen it grow from a brawling, end-of-track hell on wheels to an established community that still had plenty of rough edges.

Proof of that was the fact that hearing gunshots didn't really surprise him. Folks still resorted to violence to solve their problems all too often.

Cole angled across the wide dirt street and bounded onto the saloon's front porch. His right hand rested on the butt of the Colt .44 holstered on his right hip as he shouldered through the batwings. As he came into the big barroom, he saw that the Pronghorn's patrons had scrambled for cover when the shooting started. Some of them hunkered behind overturned tables while several others tried to crowd behind the piano.

One man crouched at the end of the bar, using the angle of it for shelter as another man stalked toward him brandishing a revolver. The gunman let out a harsh laugh and said, "All right, mister, no place left to run. I'm gonna pin your ears back with lead now."

Cole drew his .44 and was about to warn the gunman to drop his weapon when another man stood up from behind an overturned table and rapidly went into action. He held a gun in his hand, too, but it was reversed, so when it rose and fell, it was the butt that came crunching down on the gunman's black hat.

The gunman grunted in pain and stumbled, then fell to his knees. The revolver in his fist went off with a roar, but the bullet smacked harmlessly into the floor in front of him. He pitched forward onto his face, evidently out cold.

The man who had struck him down glanced at Cole and said quickly, "Hold your fire, Marshal. No need for any more shooting."

This man, like the one who'd been shooting up the place and threatening the hombre at the end of the bar, was a stranger to Cole. They must have ridden into Wind River, because Cole made a habit of meeting all the Union Pacific trains when they pulled into the depot and he hadn't seen either of them get off a train in recent days.

"I'm obliged to you for your help," Cole told the man with a curt nod, "but I'd appreciate it if you'd pouch that iron now."

"Sure, Marshal." The man slid his gun back into leather and smiled. "Always glad to cooperate with the law."

He was in his late twenties, slightly lantern-jawed but still handsome, with crisp black hair under a pushed-back black hat. He wore a black leather vest over a faded red shirt. He might have been a cowboy riding the grub-line or just a drifter . . . something that Cole himself had been at one time in his life.

"Friend of yours?" Cole asked as he nodded toward the man lying unconscious on the floor.

"What? Him?" The stranger shook his head. "Never saw him before today."

"Why did you step in, then?"

"Well, you had the drop on him, but he was drunk and on the prod, and I figured that if you called out to him and told him to drop his gun, there was a good chance he'd turn around and try to shoot you. Then you'd kill him."

"Might well have happened that way, all right," Cole said.

"I didn't think anybody deserved to die

12

just for taking on a snootful. Figured he'd rather have a headache when he woke up than be dead."

"He's going to have to pay a fine for disturbing the peace."

"Still better than being dead," the stranger said with a grin. He put out his hand. "I'm Adam Maguire."

"Cole Tyler." Cole holstered his gun and gripped Maguire's hand. "Thanks again for your help. You're new in Wind River, aren't you?"

"That's right. Just rode in today."

People in the saloon were starting to come out of hiding now that it was obvious the shooting was over. The two bartenders stuck their heads up from behind the hardwood. So did Roscoe Hornsby, who ran the Pronghorn for its owner, Brenda Durand.

Hornsby pointed at the man on the floor and said, "You're going to haul him off to jail, aren't you, Marshal?"

"That's right. Can't go shooting off guns in town without paying the price." Rapid footsteps made Cole look toward the entrance as a gaunt, middle-aged man slapped aside the batwings and hurriedly came in toting a shotgun. "Billy can take care of that."

"Take care of what?" Deputy Billy Casebolt asked as he looked around the room. "Somebody you need me to shoot, Marshal?"

"No," Cole said, a faint smile tugging at the corners of his mouth. He gestured toward the man Maguire had knocked out, who was starting to stir a little. "Got a prisoner for you to take to jail, though. Disturbing the peace by discharging a firearm in the town limits." Cole pointed to a couple of the men who'd been drinking in the saloon before the trouble broke out and went on, "You two get this gent on his feet and haul him down to the jail so Deputy Casebolt can lock him up. Keep an eye on him, Billy. I think he's too groggy to start any more trouble on the way, but you never know."

Casebolt nodded. He kept the scattergun leveled as the two townsmen picked up the prisoner and half-carried, half-dragged him to the door and outside.

Cole turned back to Maguire and went on, "Let me buy you a drink."

"I won't say no to that offer," Maguire responded with a chuckle.

All around the room, the Pronghorn's customers were going back to their drinking, gambling, and flirting with the saloon girls in their spangled, low-cut dresses. Cole and Maguire took hold of the table the newcomer had been using for cover and set it upright again, then took chairs on opposite sides of it.

Roscoe Hornsby himself came over to the table and asked, "What can we get for you, Marshal?"

"A couple of beers," Cole said. "What started the ruckus here, Roscoe?"

Hornsby was a man in his forties, short and stocky with graying dark hair and a mustache. His beefy face was starting to develop jowls. He wore his brown tweed suit well, but he didn't strike Cole as a man who had spent his life in a suit.

Cole didn't know much about Hornsby's life before he had come to Wind River. Hornsby had mentioned St. Louis a few times, giving the impression that he had lived there. That was about all. He had done a decent job of running the Pronghorn since Brenda Durand had hired him. Brenda had bought the saloon at auction after the death of its previous owner, Hank Parker, some six months earlier.

"That stranger came in a little while ago," Hornsby said in reply to Cole's question, "and I think he'd been drinking before he ever got here. He was pretty obnoxious, but he didn't really give any trouble until that

15

freighter Bart Wilcox bumped into him. The stranger yanked out his gun and fired a couple of shots at Wilcox, chased him down the bar, and was going after him when you came in."

The gunman's intended target had been vaguely familiar to Cole, and now that Hornsby had named him, Cole remembered the freighter who passed through Wind River from time to time. Wilcox was now sitting at one of the tables with some friends of his, still looking a little shaken from being shot at.

"I'll send those drinks over," Hornsby promised.

While they were waiting for their beers, Cole looked across the table at Maguire and asked, "What brings you to Wind River?"

"A jug-headed roan," Maguire answered. He laughed again. "Seriously, Marshal, I'm just passing through on my way to Cheyenne."

"Got business there?"

"I hope to. But I've never been there before, so either way it's worth the trip, I expect. I've always been fond of going places I've never been. How about you?"

Cole grunted and said, "I used to be."

"Wearing a badge makes a man put down roots, eh?"

Cole shrugged. Earlier this year, he had taken off that badge and tried to resign as marshal, having had enough of the job. Wind River's newly elected mayor, Dr. Judson Kent, had refused his resignation. Cole might have ridden on anyway if he hadn't unexpectedly found himself the owner of the Territorial House, the biggest and best hotel in town, the Wind River Land Development Company, and a house on Sweetwater Street that was damned near a mansion.

He hadn't wanted any of those things, but he had inherited them from Simone McKay, who before that had inherited them from her husband, one of the co-founders of the town, anyway. He could have sold those holdings — he might yet, he thought frequently — but for now they sort of tied him to the town, along with the friendships he had made here.

One of the girls brought over a tray with their beers on it. She bent over as she placed the mugs on the table, giving the men a good view down the daringly cut bosom of her dress, and said, "Mr. Hornsby wanted me to tell you gentlemen that these are on the house."

"The drinks, you mean?" Maguire asked with a seemingly innocent smile that was

17

anything but.

The girl laughed and said, "Oh, go on with you." She grew more serious as she added, "We can talk more about it later if you want."

"I'll keep that in mind," Maguire promised.

Cole lifted his mug and said, "Thanks again."

Maguire clinked his mug against Cole's. "De nada, Marshal. I'm glad I was around to help."

The two men drank. The beer was good and still the coldest in town, something for which the Pronghorn had a well-deserved reputation. Cole and Maguire continued chatting while they nursed the drinks along, but Cole didn't find out anything more about the man. He didn't worry about it. From the sound of everything Adam Maguire said, he would be moving on soon, and once Maguire rode out of Wind River, Cole didn't figure he would ever see the fella again.

When he had finished the beer, Cole said, "I reckon I'd better get back to work. If you're looking for something good to eat, Maguire, drop over to the Wind River Café for supper later. Best food in town."

"I'll remember that, Marshal. Adios."

Cole stood up, nodded farewell to Roscoe Hornsby, and left the saloon. He had been inside the Pronghorn long enough that the afternoon light was starting to fade. In another hour dusk would settle over Wind River, heralding the arrival of what Cole hoped would be a peaceful night.

As Cole ambled along the boardwalk toward the sturdy building that housed the marshal's office, the jail, and the office of the Wind River Land Development Company, he noticed a couple of familiar figures riding by in the street. One was an older man, dressed all in black, with a deeply tanned face and a shock of snow-white hair under his black hat. His companion was considerably younger, not much more than a kid, with curly brown hair under his tipped-back hat. He gave Cole a grin and a friendly wave as they passed.

Cole wondered what had brought Kermit Sawyer and Lon Rogers to town.

CHAPTER 2

"I ain't sold on this, you know," Kermit Sawyer said as he and Lon reined their mounts to a halt in front of the big, block-long Wind River General Store. "You don't fool me for a second, boy. You're just hopin' to catch a glimpse of that gal and maybe even get the chance to talk to her."

"You're wrong, boss," Lon replied. "I didn't even think about Miss Durand when I said we needed to come to town."

Sawyer just let out a skeptical grunt as he swung down from the saddle.

Lon dismounted, too, and as they started up the steps to the high porch that also served as the store's loading dock, Sawyer said dryly, "If you do talk to her, maybe you should try not to trip over your own tongue this time."

Lon felt his face getting warm. He didn't appreciate the reminder that whenever he had tried to talk to Brenda Durand in the past, it seemed like he stumbled over every other word.

She was just so blasted pretty, Lon thought. Too pretty for an hombre to think straight around her.

Harvey Raymond, the store's manager, was behind the counter. Lon didn't see any sign of Brenda and tried to tell himself that he wasn't disappointed she wasn't here.

Raymond rested his hands on the counter and asked, "What can I do for you, Mr. Sawyer?"

"Ask this young buck here," Sawyer said as he pointed a callused thumb at Lon. "He claims he ordered somethin' special and wants to see if it came in yet on the train."

"Yeah, the, uh, box of books," Lon said.

A woman's voice said behind him, "Books? You ordered a box of books? What are they? Penny dreadfuls?"

Lon jerked around, unable to stop himself. Obviously, Brenda had come into the store behind them, but she moved with such quiet grace that he hadn't heard her until she spoke up.

He tried to answer her question, but it wasn't easy when all he wanted to do was stand there and gape as he drank in the young woman's dark, exotic beauty. She was slender, but the curves of her body in her

21

expensive dark blue gown made it clear she was a woman, not a girl. Her raven hair was piled on top of her head, but several curling strands dangled down artfully around her face. The small, dark beauty mark near her mouth did its job, all right. Brenda Durand was beautiful, no doubt about that.

She was also rich. Through a series of the odd quirks that fate sometimes took, she had wound up owning a large chunk of Wind River despite the fact that she wasn't yet twenty years old. Her grandmother and guardian, Mrs. Margaret Palmer, helped her manage her business holdings, but Brenda wasn't shy about expressing her opinion and demanding that she get her own way. Some people in town considered her little more than a spoiled brat, although of course no one would say that to her face.

Lon had been in love with her from the first moment he laid eyes on her.

"Well?" she demanded now. "Just what is your taste in reading material? Or did you have more in mind taking them to the outhouse with you?"

Lon finally found his voice. He said, "No, ma'am. I mean, I ordered the books to read 'em. They're a, uh, uh, selection of novels."

"Oh. I see." Brenda's tone was cool and mocking. "Perhaps we should start a liter-

22

ary society here in Wind River. We could have meetings and discuss the books you read."

"I, uh, don't think I'd have time for that —"

"No, you wouldn't," Sawyer growled. "There's too much work to do on the ranch for you to be gallivantin' off on such foolishness. And if I'd known that was the errand we were on today, I might've told you to wait until the next time the cook needed supplies."

Lon swallowed hard and said, "Sorry, boss."

Harvey Raymond leaned over the counter. "Actually, I do have that box for you, Lon. It came in on the train a couple of days ago."

"Oh. Well, good."

"I'll get it out of the storeroom for you," Raymond said. "Can I do something for you, Miss Durand?"

"No, I just stopped by to see how the day has gone," Brenda said.

"Good. Profitable."

She smiled. "That's what I like to hear."

She was telling the truth about that, Lon thought. Despite his feelings for Brenda, he wasn't blind to the fact that she liked money. She had made that plain from the moment she'd arrived in Wind River to claim her legacy from a father she had never known, the late William Durand, one of the town's founders.

"I'll leave you to it," Brenda went on. She turned toward the door but paused and looked over her shoulder at Lon to add, "Let me know if you change your mind about that literary society."

He swallowed and nodded, again unable to say anything.

When he looked across the counter he thought that Raymond was having a hard time not laughing. The store manager said again, "I'll get that box."

Kermit Sawyer just sighed and glared at the young cowboy.

Brenda was on her way back to the Territorial House, where she and her grandmother lived in the hotel's best suite, when she noticed the man coming along the boardwalk toward her. He was dressed like a cowboy, as so many of the men around here always were, but something about him was different. He was handsome in a rough-hewn way, and he had a maturity and vitality about him that young punchers such as, say, Lon Rogers lacked.

This stranger was a real man, not a boy like Lon, and Brenda was drawn to him immediately.

As if he could sense that, he stopped and reached up to take off his hat as he nodded politely to her. "Ma'am," he said. "Beautiful day, isn't it?"

"I suppose," Brenda said. "A bit chilly, if you ask me." She drew the shawl she wore a little tighter around her shoulders to illustrate her point.

"I'd say it's brisk and refreshing," he replied. "My name's Adam Maguire."

She hadn't asked him to introduce himself, and she didn't really want to encourage him. There was quite a bit of difference in their stations in life, after all. But she found herself saying, "I'm Brenda Durand."

"It's an honor and a pleasure to meet you, Miss Durand. It is Miss Durand, isn't it?"

"That's right." Brenda was surprised that she would answer such a personal question from a perfect stranger, without even hesitating.

"I was just passing through your town here, but I'm starting to think that might be a mistake. The more I look around, the more reasons I see to linger for a while."

"How do you know it's my town?"

"Ma'am?" Maguire said with a puzzled frown.

Brenda waved that off. "Never mind." She

started to step past him. "I hope you enjoy your stay, however long it is."

He stopped her with a light touch on her arm.

"I'd enjoy it more," he said, "if I could convince you to have supper with me. I was just on my way to the café . . ."

Brenda was actually tempted to accept his invitation. He was good-looking, there was no denying that, and he had a compelling presence about him, but the richest woman in town could hardly share a meal with a man who was more than likely just a saddle tramp. No matter how handsome he was.

"I'm sorry," she said. "My grandmother is waiting for me at the hotel. We always eat in the dining room there."

Maguire shrugged. "Another time, then, maybe."

Brenda didn't respond to that one way or the other. She just said, "Good evening, Mr. Maguire."

He put on his hat and ticked a finger against the brim. "Miss Durand."

As she moved off along the boardwalk, Brenda wanted to look back and see if Adam Maguire was watching her. She forced herself not to give in to that impulse. It seemed to her that the drifter already had a swelled head. She didn't want to give it any reason to get even bigger.

CHAPTER 3

Wind River's justice of the peace was a spare, balding man who wore pince-nez spectacles on his beak-like nose. His name was Edgar Toomey, and he had taken over the job a few months earlier after moving to the settlement from Rawlins to live with his daughter and son-in-law. He had practiced law for a number of years before retiring. Being the local magistrate allowed him to keep a connection with the legal system.

"What's the prisoner's name?" Toomey asked when Cole brought the gunman before him the next morning. The man's face was haggard from a hangover, not to mention the clout on the head that Adam Maguire had given him.

Cole prodded the prisoner's arm. "Speak up."

The gunman winced and cleared his throat. A long, thin mustache hung down on both sides of his mouth. He said, "My name's Lije Beaumont, Your Honor."

"You've been in trouble before, haven't you, Mr. Beaumont?" Toomey said.

"Well . . . I reckon a few times. When I, uh, have too much to drink my head gets sort of muddled . . ."

"Then you know what's going to happen next. I find you guilty of disturbing the peace and sentence you to pay a fine of ten dollars. If you don't have it, you can spend the next ten days in jail."

"He's got it," Cole said. "Deputy Casebolt searched him before he was locked up, to make sure he didn't have a knife or a hideout gun."

"Yeah, I'll, uh, pay the fine, Your Honor," Beaumont said.

"Very well. Give the money to Marshal Tyler, then you're free to go. And I'd suggest that unless you have a good reason to stay in Wind River, your best course of action would be to move on." Toomey rapped the gavel on the table in the town hall where he held court. "We're adjourned."

Cole took Beaumont back to the marshal's office, where the man handed over a couple of five dollar gold pieces from his belongings. Cole gave him back his gunbelt and said, "That Colt's unloaded. Leave it that way until you get clear of Wind River."

"You're runnin' me out of town?" Beaumont asked in a surly voice.

"You heard what the judge said."

"You got no call to run me out. I paid my fine."

"You reckon you can stay sober and stay out of trouble?"

Beaumont hesitated and shrugged. "Probably ain't likely."

"Next time you might wind up dead instead of buffaloed."

Still glaring, Beaumont said, "Yeah, well, you didn't have to hit me so hard. My skull feels like you damned near stove it in."

Cole laughed. "I didn't hit you. Another fella in the saloon took care of that for me. If it had been up to me, there's a good chance I would have shot you."

Beaumont's scowl turned even darker. "Who was it walloped me?"

"That doesn't matter now. Get on out of here. And if you do stay in town, I'll be watching you."

"No need to worry about that," Beaumont muttered. "Wind River ain't a very friendly place."

He left the office. Cole followed and stood on the porch with a shoulder leaned against one of the posts holding up the awning. He watched as Beaumont went down the street to the livery stable. The man emerged a few minutes later mounted on a buckskin. He rode out of town, following the Union Pacific tracks west.

Cole was glad to see him go.

Lije Beaumont rode alongside the railroad tracks until he was out of sight of Wind River. Then he turned his horse and headed northwest, toward a range of low, rocky hills dotted with scrubby pine trees.

He urged his horse to a faster gait and seemed to know where he was going, even though there was no real trail through the desolate country in which he found himself. Some decent cattle range lay further north and west, in the grassy valleys between the foothills of the great snowcapped mountain ranges. That was the area where several big ranches were located. But this semiarid, mostly barren stretch of country not far north of the railroad wasn't good for farming or ranching or much of anything.

Except as a place where men could hide if they didn't want to be found.

Beaumont followed a twisting path into the hills. Sheer rock walls closed in around him, leaving only a narrow passage. Beaumont had to weave around big slabs of rock that had broken off the heights in ages past and tumbled down into the cleft. Because of those obstacles and the looming walls, only two or three men at a time would be able to ride through here. That made the path easy to defend. A few men with rifles could hold off a small army if it tried to come through here.

The trail ran for about half a mile, gradually angling up as Beaumont followed it. It finally ended in a gap that opened into a small valley. A creek flowed from a spring at the head of the valley, maybe a mile northwest of the spot where Beaumont entered it.

The creek petered out before it reached the valley's far end, but along its course it provided enough water for grass and greasewood bushes and a few trees, mostly cottonwoods and aspen, to grow. The vegetation was responsible for a splash of green amidst the brown, tan, and gray landscape. At the moment the green was punctuated with patches of yellow and red as the leaves on the trees had begun to turn with the approach of winter.

Beaumont had ridden only a few yards along the trail leading from the gap down into the valley when a voice hailed him and caused him to rein in. A grin appeared for a second on Beaumont's saturnine face when he saw a man step out from behind a boulder alongside the trail. The grin quickly became a scowl.

"Damn it," Beaumont said, "did you have to hit me so hard? You just about busted my head open with that gun butt!"

"I knew that skull of yours was thick enough to take it," Adam Maguire said as he leaned against the boulder with his thumbs hooked in his gunbelt. "Besides, when I saw how ready that marshal was to shoot you, I figured you'd rather have a sore head than a bullet hole in your brisket."

"Yeah, there's that to consider, I reckon," Beaumont admitted grudgingly. "Anyway, now we know what sort of law they've got in Wind River."

"That we do," Maguire agreed. "And when we make our move, they won't be able to stop us!"

CHAPTER 4

The town council in Wind River met once a month, with the mayor, Dr. Judson Kent, presiding over the meetings in the town hall. The other four men on the council were Nathan Smollet, the manager of the bank; Harvey Raymond, who ran the general store; Duncan Blaisdell, who owned a saddle shop; and the proprietor of the livery stable, Patrick Milligan.

All five men were in attendance at this morning's meeting, their businesses being looked after by others for the moment. Cole was there, too, as was Michael Hatfield, the sandy-haired young editor and publisher of the *Wind River Sentinel.* Michael attended all the council meetings so he could report on them for the newspaper. Cole was there because the council always wanted a report on whether or not there was any trouble brewing in the settlement.

Cole didn't care for the meetings. They

were boring, and he always felt like he could be accomplishing more by being somewhere else. He attended because he considered the councilmen to be his friends and they wanted him here. The fact that they paid his salary had never really entered into it; since he had spent most of his life as a drifter he had never considered himself tied down by the tyranny of wages. And since he'd inherited those holdings from Simone, he certainly didn't need the marshal's salary.

Nathan Smollet was droning on about something. Cole wasn't sure exactly what it was; he had stopped paying attention soon after the bank manager started talking. But then he heard his name mentioned as Kent said, "And how about you, Cole? Do you have anything to report this week?"

Cole looked up at the bearded physician who had come to America from England and wound up in this frontier settlement in Wyoming Territory.

"It's been pretty peaceful," Cole said. "Had to break up a few ruckuses between punchers from the Diamond S and the Latch Hook, and one fella got drunk and tried to shoot up the Pronghorn the other day."

"What happened to him?" Kent asked.

"He spent the night in jail and paid a fine for disturbing the peace the next morning. Then he rode out of town and I haven't seen him since." Cole shrugged. "Good riddance as far as I'm concerned."

"I'm sure we all agree," Kent said. "So, it sounds as if things have been rather tranquil —"

"Which is just what I was talking about earlier," Duncan Blaisdell said as he leaned forward to look at the other men sitting behind the table. "Wind River is civilized now."

"I don't know if I'd go so far as to say that —" Cole began.

"Have you fired your gun since last week, Marshal?" Blaisdell asked. He was a beefy man with shaggy, graying blond hair and a soup-strainer mustache of the same shade.

Since he was standing in front of the table where the council sat, Cole felt a little like a schoolboy who'd been hauled in front of the headmaster for some infraction of the rules. Blaisdell's sharply inquisitive tone reinforced that feeling, and Cole didn't like it.

"As a matter of fact, I haven't," he admitted. "Other than a little target practice, I don't think I've had to fire my gun for a month or more."

"Exactly my point," Blaisdell said to the others. "We're spending money we don't need to on law enforcement."

"Wait just a minute," Cole said. "Are you talking about firing me?"

Hurriedly, Kent said, "No, no, not at all. The town still needs a marshal."

"It's the deputy I think we ought to get rid of," Blaisdell declared.

That blunt statement took Cole by surprise. Judging by Blaisdell's earlier comments, the council had been talking about this before now, and Cole wished that Judson Kent had seen fit to give him a little warning. Maybe Kent had felt that he couldn't do that, ethically. He and Cole were friends, but Kent had a responsibility to the town as mayor, too.

"Billy Casebolt's a good man," Cole said.

"No one is claiming that he isn't," Kent said.

"He's a good lawman, too," Cole went on. "Every time I've needed him, he's been right there to back whatever play I made."

Blaisdell shook a finger and said, "The question is, do you really need him anymore? Based on what's happened in the past month or so, don't you think you could handle any problems that arise, Marshal?"

"Well, that's just the thing of it," Cole

said. "You don't ever know what trouble is going to come up. It's best to be prepared for it, whatever it is."

"That's my thinking, too," Kent said. "Anyway, it's not as if we pay Deputy Casebolt a princely sum. His wages consist of little more than room, board, and ammunition."

"I think we should vote on it anyway," Blaisdell said with a surly frown. "We could put that money to better use. Who'll second the motion?"

None of the other council members said anything.

After a moment, Kent said, "Well, I suppose we should move on to the next order of business. Thank you for your report, as always, Marshal."

Cole nodded, glad for the chance to get out of there while he still had a deputy.

Duncan Blaisdell was a pompous pain in the rear end, Cole mused as he walked back toward the marshal's office, but on the surface, anyway, he wasn't far wrong about Wind River getting civilized. In the early days of the settlement, not a week had gone by without several killings. There had been stampedes, the threat of an Indian war, conflict involving the Chinese members of the community, rogue mountain men, rustling, beatings, a church burned to the ground before it could even finish getting built . . . Back then, it had seemed like hell was breaking loose all the time, and lately, it hadn't been that way.

What Blaisdell didn't understand was that you couldn't tell how long that stretch of peace was going to last. And when it came to its inevitable violent end, Wind River was liable to need both of its lawmen.

Fifteen men rode toward the settlement. Adam Maguire and Lije Beaumont were in the lead. Close behind them came a baker's dozen more, all dressed in rough range clothes except one huge, red-mustachioed man whose bulky muscles strained the fabric of the dusty black suit he wore. The hard-planed, cold-eyed faces of the men marked them as dangerous, as did the veritable armory of guns they carried.

"Just two lawdogs, right?" Beaumont said to Maguire.

"The marshal and his deputy, right," Maguire confirmed. "We've seen them both, and I asked around town enough to make sure there aren't any other deputies."

"That old pelican won't be much to worry about. He likes to run his mouth, but that's about all."

"Don't underestimate him," Maguire warned. "If any of you get a chance, kill him as soon as you can. I'll be looking for the marshal. I did some asking around about him, too. He was a scout and a wagon train guide before coming to Wind River. Rode with Jeb Stuart's cavalry during the war. He's a fighting man."

"A couple of .44 slugs will knock all the fight out of him," Beaumont said.

Maguire smiled and said, "That's true. That's why the first order of business is to put him out of the way. When the shooting starts, he'll come running to find out what's going on. I'll be waiting for him."

When the gang was still a couple of miles from town, Maguire called a halt. "We've been over the plan several times," he said to the other outlaws. "Anybody have any questions?"

A couple of the grim-faced men shook their heads. The others were silent.

"All right. You know your jobs. We'll rendezvous back in the valley to split up the loot." Maguire lifted his reins. "Good luck. Let's go."

The group split up. Four of the men stayed with Maguire as he rode toward the settlement. The others broke into groups of two men each and scattered so they could ride into Wind River at different times and from different directions. The presence of such a large bunch riding into town at the same time stood a good chance of alerting the marshal that something was about to happen. Surprise was an essential part of Maguire's plan.

Along with acting fast and killing anybody who got in their way . . . especially Cole Tyler and Billy Casebolt.

CHAPTER 5

"Marshal, wait up!"

Cole paused and looked over his shoulder to see who had called to him. Michael Hatfield hurried along the boardwalk in his direction. The young editor was hatless, as usual, although he wore a suit and a string tie.

"Council meeting over already?" Cole asked as Michael came up to him.

"They didn't really have any other business to discuss once Mr. Blaisdell spoke his piece about Billy."

"Did you know Blaisdell was going to bring that up about firing him?"

Michael shook his head. "No, not really, but it doesn't surprise me. He's been talking about how he thinks the town should build an opera house, so they'll have to come up with the money for that somewhere."

Cole stared at Michael for a couple of

seconds before he repeated, "An opera house? What in the world for?"

"Why, to have operas in, I guess," Michael said with a smile. "Mainly, though, Mr. Blaisdell thinks it would give the town some culture and help it grow. He says Wind River can become the biggest, most important town in the territory outside of Cheyenne."

"Good Lord! If the place ever gets that big, the council won't have to fire me. I'll quit!"

Shaking his head in amazement over what Michael had told him, Cole walked on toward the marshal's office. When he got there, he found Billy Casebolt pouring a cup of coffee from the battered old tin pot on the stove.

"Anything important happen at the council meetin'?" Casebolt asked.

Cole shook his head and said, "Just the usual hot air and foolishness." He didn't see any point in mentioning what Duncan Blaisdell had brought up and worrying Billy unnecessarily. Cole didn't intend to let anybody fire the deputy.

Hell, he would pay Casebolt's wages himself if he had to, he thought. He could afford that now. The land development company brought in plenty of money.

"When you finish that coffee," Cole went

on, "why don't you take a turn around the town?"

Casebolt frowned, clearly puzzled. "Why do you want me to do that, Cole? We don't normally make rounds this time of day. Besides, Wind River has gotten so plumb peaceful I ain't sure the place even needs a couple of star packers no more!"

Cole looked away and winced. Without knowing it, Casebolt was coming uncomfortably close to echoing what Duncan Blaisdell had said earlier. Cole said, "I think it's just good for folks to see us out and about and be reminded that there's no shortage of law and order in these parts."

"All right," Casebolt said, although his tone made it clear that he considered the idea unnecessary, if not outright foolishness.

Cole poured himself a cup of coffee and sat down behind the desk to drink it. Casebolt left the office a few minutes later. A few more minutes passed before the door opened again and a tall, broad-shouldered figure with arms like tree trunks filled the opening.

"Morning, Jeremiah," Cole greeted the newcomer. "Something I can do for you?"

Jeremiah Newton, Wind River's blacksmith and the pastor of the town's only church, which stood on a knoll just southwest of the settlement, came into the office and said, "I'm not sure, Brother Cole. Something's troubling me, but it seems to me that a man who spreads the Lord's word should always believe the best of people, rather than being suspicious and thinking the worst."

Cole sat up straighter. "If something's bothering you, Jeremiah," he said, "you should tell me. The Lord wouldn't want you to stand by and do nothing if there's trouble in the making."

"That's true," Jeremiah said with a nod. "A couple of men rode past my shop just now, and although it's not very Christian of me to say it, I just didn't like their looks. They reminded me of . . . well, of those hardcases who attacked me and burned down the church the first time we tried to build it."

Cole remembered the brutal assault on Jeremiah all too well. He stood up and said, "We never did round up all those gunnies who worked for Hank Parker. Some of them might have come back looking to settle a score with you."

Jeremiah shook his head. "I don't think these two were part of that bunch. They looked right at me, but I didn't see any sign that they recognized me. They were just the same sort of men, that's all."

"Gunmen. Hired killers."

"We should probably give them the benefit of the doubt . . ."

Cole stood up and came out from behind the desk. He said, "I understand how you feel, Jeremiah, but I want to have a look at those hombres myself. Can you find them and show them to me?"

"They were headed toward the general store. I'd be glad to walk down there with you."

"Let's go," Cole said. As he and Jeremiah left the office, he thought about grabbing one of the shotguns from the rack and taking along a handful of shells, but he didn't do it.

Despite what Jeremiah had said, he didn't really think he would need a scattergun on a beautiful autumn morning like this.

"Where are we going, dear?" Margaret Palmer asked as she walked beside Brenda.

"To the bank," Brenda told her grandmother. "I want to speak to Mr. Smollet."

"Are you sure that's wise? He seems to be doing a fine job of managing the bank's affairs."

Brenda looked over at Margaret and said,

46

"How do you know I'm going to complain about his efforts?"

"You have that look about you, as if you're angry about something."

That was right, Brenda thought. She *was* angry. When she had first come to Wind River, she'd had words with Simone McKay about the large number of people who were behind on the payments they owed for land they had bought from William Durand and Andrew McKay. Simone insisted they were good for the debts and were paying what they could, when they could.

That hadn't been good enough to satisfy Brenda then, and it certainly didn't satisfy her now. She didn't own the land development company — that frontiersman of a marshal did — but she owned the bank and the bank held the notes on many of those land purchases. For the past six months Brenda had allowed things to go on as they were, but now the time had come to bear down. Either people paid what they owed, or they lost the land. Simple as that.

She intended to make sure Nathan Smollet knew how simple it was, too.

Both women were dressed elegantly, Brenda in a green gown and matching hat, her grandmother in a brown outfit that suited her. Wind River had a seamstress who would have been happy to make dresses for them, but Brenda insisted that all her clothes be shipped in from back east. Out here in the wilds of Wyoming Territory it was practically impossible to keep up with the latest fashions, of course, but Brenda did the best she could. She didn't intend to allow herself to start looking like some careworn frontier woman.

Duncan Blaisdell had the right idea. He had mentioned to Margaret, and Margaret had told Brenda, that he would like to see the town build an opera house and become an outpost of culture in this heathen wilderness. That was just a start, Brenda thought. If the town wouldn't make the effort to become more civilized, she might have to finance it herself.

She put those thoughts aside as they reached the bank and went in. Several people were in the lobby, and customers were being waited on at both of the tellers' windows. Nathan Smollet was at his desk behind the railing to the left.

Smollet saw Brenda and Mrs. Palmer come in and immediately stood up. He smiled and said, "Ladies. What brings you here this morning?"

"We need to discuss some banking matters," Brenda told him.

"Of course." Smollet opened the gate in the railing and held it for them. "Please come in."

His tone held that infuriating smugness that always got on Brenda's nerves. He was the sort of man who didn't believe that a woman had any right to involve herself with business. If that woman was young and attractive, as she was, she ought to stay even farther away from any such sordid dealings.

As far as she was concerned, she was just as smart as he was, and since she owned the bank, he would pay attention to what she had to say . . . or else.

"Oh, there's Deputy Casebolt," Margaret said.

Brenda glanced over her shoulder and saw the lawman strolling into the bank. Casebolt caught sight of the two women at the same time and stopped short. For a second he looked like a deer, frozen in the sights of a hunter, unable to bolt no matter how much he wanted to.

For some reason that Brenda had never been able to understand, her grandmother was quite taken with Casebolt. Smitten, actually. She supposed the deputy had a certain crude, rough-hewn charm. And Margaret had been a widow for a long time.

"Go ahead and talk to him," Brenda said,

her voice softening a little. "I don't need your help with this."

"Are you sure, dear?"

Brenda knew that as her guardian, Margaret liked to think that she was really in charge of things. Brenda didn't argue with her about that. It was easier to allow Margaret to believe that she was pulling the strings, whether she really was or not.

"I'm sure." Brenda added with a smile, "You'd better hurry. He might get away."

"I don't know what you mean, dear," Margaret said stiffly. But she started across the lobby toward Casebolt without wasting any more time.

Smollet held the chair in front of his desk for Brenda, then resumed his seat and asked, "What can I do for you this morning, Miss Durand?"

"You can force the people who owe us money to pay their debts," Brenda said.

Smollet winced slightly at the bluntness of her words and the sharpness of her tone. "We've discussed this, Miss Durand —" he began.

His patronizing tone made her angry. "No, you've offered me excuses as to why we have to be patient," she broke in. "Bad weather. Unexpected expenses. Those aren't good

50

reasons for people not paying what they owe."

"If we start taking farms and businesses away from people, then they'll just sit there empty and won't generate any income at all," Smollet argued. "At least this way you're getting something out of the loans, even if it isn't the full amount."

"Wind River is a vital, growing town," Brenda pointed out. "You could turn around and sell those properties again."

And by the bank foreclosing, she would get them away from Cole Tyler, she thought, and that would thwart the intentions of that evil McKay woman. That would be an added benefit.

"I suppose there are a few accounts that are so far behind they'll never be able to catch up . . ." Smollet said.

"Start with them, then," Brenda said crisply. Despite her youth, she knew how to pick her battles, and she knew that she had won this one.

Smollet sighed, nodded, and moved around some documents on his desk. "I'll start going through the paperwork right away," he promised.

"Very good." Brenda smiled as she stood up. "Thank you for seeing it my way."

Smollet got to his feet as well. "Of course.

If there's ever anything else I can help you with —"

"Oh, I'm sure there will be."

Brenda went out through the gate in the railing and started toward her grandmother and Deputy Casebolt, who stood on the other side of the bank lobby, talking. Well, her grandmother was talking, anyway, Brenda thought. Casebolt was listening, and rather nervously at that.

Both doors at the bank's front entrance opened. Several men came in, but Brenda didn't pay any attention to them except for a glance. Then she looked again as she realized that she recognized one of the men. He stopped short as his eyes met hers, but only for a second. Then he came toward her as the other four men spread out behind him.

"Miss Durand," Adam Maguire said. "This is an unexpected pleasure. I didn't suppose I'd see you in here this morning."

"I have every reason to be here," Brenda said. "I own this bank, after all."

Maguire seemed quite interested in that bit of information. "Is that a fact?" he said.

"Do you have business here?"

He nodded and said, "I surely do."

With that he pulled the gun from the holster on his hip, took a quick step forward, grabbed her shoulder, jerked her around so that her back was to him, and looped his left arm around her neck. As his grip on her tightened painfully, he pressed the muzzle of his gun against her temple and shouted, "This is a holdup! Nobody move, or I'll blow the lady's head off!"

CHAPTER 6

A man had to be able to think on his feet, and that's what Adam Maguire was doing now. Fate had dropped an opportunity in his lap — a warm, soft, mighty attractive opportunity, he realized as he pressed Brenda Durand's body against his — and he was damned if he wasn't going to seize it.

Everybody in the bank reacted to Maguire's shout and the sight of his gun. The old woman screamed, the tellers let out startled exclamations, and a couple of the male customers cursed angrily. The skinny gent in a suit who had to be the bank manager started to reach down toward his desk, probably for a gun.

The manager didn't lack for courage, but he had some common sense to go with it. He stopped the motion before he grabbed iron. With Maguire's gun pressed to Brenda's head, he must have realized that he couldn't afford to start a gun battle.

Besides, Maguire's men had their guns out now, and the manager must have known that he'd be riddled with lead before he could get a shot off.

No, the only one they had to worry about was the deputy. Casebolt shoved the old woman to the floor, making her scream again, and clawed at the Griswold & Gunnison revolver on his hip as he tried to dart toward the scanty cover of a marble counter.

Two of Maguire's men fired at the same time, the sound of their guns blending into a thunderous roar. Their slugs smashed into Casebolt. Blood flew through the air and splattered on the counter as the bullets' impact spun him around. Casebolt had cleared leather, but the old Confederate revolver flew from his fingers as he crashed to the floor. He didn't move again.

Maguire's lips drew back from his teeth in a snarl as he said, "Now you know we mean business. You tellers! Start cleaning out your cash drawers. And you, Mr. Bank Manager, you go open the vault."

Brenda trembled against Maguire. "Please," she whimpered. "Please don't kill me."

"Kill you?" Maguire repeated as his snarl turned into a savage grin. "Hell, I wouldn't hurt you, darling. We're going to take you with us!"

Brenda moaned and slumped, and Maguire knew she had passed out from sheer terror.

At the same time, more shots blasted elsewhere in Wind River, telling the boss outlaw that the rest of the raid had begun.

Cole noticed two strange horses tied at the hitch rail in front of the general store as he and Jeremiah approached. There was nothing unusual about that; strangers came and went in Wind River all the time. But Cole nodded at the two mounts and asked Jeremiah, "Are those the animals those hombres were riding when they went by your place?"

Being a blacksmith, Jeremiah had a good eye for horseflesh. He nodded and said, "That's them, all right. The men have to be inside the store."

"You can go on back to your shop if you want, Jeremiah. I'll look them over, maybe ask them a few questions."

"If they're looking for trouble, you might need help."

That was a good point, Cole supposed. And even though Jeremiah didn't carry a gun, in a bare knuckles fight his massive

56

size and strength made him a formidable ally.

"All right," Cole said. "I'm obliged for the help."

They climbed to the porch and loading dock and went inside. Two men stood at the counter in the back, talking to Harvey Raymond. Other than that, the store was empty at the moment. Cole didn't see any guns being waved around, but he thought the storekeeper looked upset about something. He had a hunch that Jeremiah's instincts were about to be proven right.

Before Cole could walk along the aisles of merchandise to the back of the store, guns suddenly went off somewhere else in town. The shots were muffled by building walls but unmistakable despite that.

One of the strangers at the counter glanced around, spotted Cole, and yelled, "It's the marshal!" He clawed at the gun on his hip.

"Jeremiah, get down!" Cole snapped as he reached for his revolver. Swift and smooth, the Colt .44 came out of leather. Cole thumbed back the hammer as the barrel tipped up. The gun roared and bucked against his palm.

At the same time, flame gouted from the muzzle of the other man's gun. Cole felt as much as heard the hot whisper of lead as the slug passed within a couple of inches of his ear.

His shot was more accurate, slamming into the man's chest and throwing him back against the counter. The man was able to stay on his feet, though, and trigger another shot at Cole. This one went low, gouging splinters from the floor.

The second man had his gun out, too. He reached across the counter and smashed the barrel against Harvey Raymond's head. Raymond collapsed. The gunman darted aside and threw himself behind a pickle barrel. As the first gunman pitched to the floor, Cole snapped a shot at the second one. The bullet plunked into the barrel. Brine spewed out through the hole.

Cole ducked as more slugs whipped around his head. From the corner of his eye he saw Jeremiah moving along one of the side aisles toward the back of the store. The big blacksmith crouched low so maybe the gunman behind the barrel wouldn't see him.

Cole wanted to warn Jeremiah to get back, but that would just draw the gunman's attention to him. As Jeremiah advanced, Cole tried to keep the gunman occupied by throwing two more shots at him.

At the end of the aisle, Jeremiah broke

from cover and lunged forward to wrap his long arms around the barrel. It took a lot of strength to budge that barrel full of pickles and brine, but Jeremiah managed, shoving it back hard so that the gunman was crushed between the barrel and the counter. The man groaned in pain and dropped his gun as the barrel trapped him there.

Cole sprinted up to the first man, who lay facedown on the floor in front of the counter. After kicking the man's fallen gun out of reach, Cole hooked a boot toe under his shoulder and rolled him over. The man's sightlessly staring eyes told Cole that he was dead.

Jeremiah picked up the other man's gun. He said, "I think I heard some of his ribs break when I pinned him like that, Cole. He shouldn't be any more trouble."

"Keep him covered anyway," Cole said. "I heard shots somewhere else."

"Go," Jeremiah told him. "I'll check on Harvey, too."

Cole nodded as he thumbed fresh bullets into his revolver. Usually he left one of the chambers empty so the hammer could rest on it, but not this time.

If there was a whole gang of outlaws raiding the town, as seemed likely from the sound of the gunfire, he would need a full wheel in that .44.

As he ran out of the store, one of the townspeople pointed and shouted, "Some shots came from the bank, Marshal!"

"Anybody seen Deputy Casebolt?"

Another man said, "I think I saw him go in there just before the shootin' started."

Cole bit back a curse. It made sense that the outlaws would hit the bank, too, and it sounded like Casebolt might have gotten caught right in the middle of the robbery.

The old-timer was tough, though, Cole told himself as he leaped down from the porch and sprinted along Grenville Avenue. If Billy had any chance at all, he would put up a good fight.

Cole was halfway to the bank when a big man in a brown tweed suit and a derby hat stepped out of an alley and cut loose at him with a rifle. The closest cover was a water trough. He dived behind it and heard bullets thudding into the trough.

At least people had sense enough to get off the street when the shooting started, he thought as he glanced around. The boardwalks had cleared in a hurry.

He stuck his .44 around the end of the water trough and triggered twice, coming close enough with his shots to drive the rifleman back into the shelter of the alley.

60

But when Cole tried to leap up, another round from the Winchester burned past his ear. He hit the dirt again. His mouth filled with grit and the bitter realization that he was pinned down.

He knew he couldn't expect much help from the citizens. The people of Wind River were good, decent folks, but they weren't gunfighters. For once he wished Kermit Sawyer and Sawyer's crew from the Diamond S were in town. Cole and the cattleman might not get along that well, but that bunch of gun-handy Texas cowboys knew how to fight. They would make short work of the outlaws.

It didn't do any good to wish for things, Cole told himself. Besides, he had more trouble right now.

Two men across the street started shooting at him. They had him trapped in a cross fire between them and the rifleman in the derby, and as bullets pounded into the street and kicked more dirt in his eyes, Cole knew there was nowhere for him to go.

CHAPTER 7

Brenda was more terrified than she had ever been in her life. She had tried to struggle against Adam Maguire's grip, but he was too strong. His arm was like an iron band around her body, squeezing so hard she had trouble catching her breath.

Horror at the sight of Deputy Casebolt's bloody body filled her as well. She wanted to close her eyes and make it all go away, but she knew that when she opened them again, all those terrible things would still be there.

"Do like I told you, mister," Maguire snapped at Nathan Smollet. "Open the vault."

"Yes. Yes, I w-will," Smollet stammered. "Just don't hurt anyone else."

"I reckon that's up to you folks," Maguire said. He chuckled. Brenda thought it was an evil sound.

She had to try to talk some sense into her

captor's head. "If you'll let me go," she said, "I'll see to it that you're well paid. I have money —"

"It's in this bank, isn't it?" Maguire interrupted her.

"Well, yes, but —"

"And I'm taking all the money here anyway," he pointed out. "So you don't really have anything to bargain with you, do you, Miss Durand? Unless . . ."

"Whatever you want, I'll do it," Brenda said flatly. "Just don't hurt me or anyone else."

More shots came from outside. It sounded like a pitched battle was going on in Wind River.

"I can't exactly promise that," Maguire said, "but maybe you'll get a chance to strike a deal with me once we're out of here."

A moan of terror welled up in Brenda's throat. He had said that he meant to take her with them when they fled, and obviously he hadn't forgotten about that.

"You can't . . . you just can't . . ."

His grip on her tightened even more, although she wouldn't have thought that was possible, and the gun pressed harder against her head.

"I can do whatever I want," he snarled.

"I've got the gun here, remember?"

Nathan Smollet had the vault door open. One of the robbers crowded past him and started raking bundles of cash into a canvas sack. Over at the tellers' windows, another outlaw was cleaning out the cash drawers. Another man reached down to where Margaret Palmer sat huddled against the counter, a few feet from Casebolt's sprawled body, and ripped the brooch from the bosom of her dress. He held it up and laughed, saying, "A fancy geegaw like this oughta be worth somethin'!"

The man who emerged from the vault said, "I think we got it all, boss."

"Good," Maguire snapped. "Give 'em something to remember you by."

The outlaw who clutched the canvas bag full of cash in his left hand turned and slashed at Smollet's head with the gun he held in his other hand. The vicious blow took Smollet by surprise. He had no chance to defend himself from it. The gun barrel crashed into his head, and the sight raked a long gash above his ear. Smollet cried out and fell.

One of the bank's customers, a man Brenda didn't know, exclaimed, "By God, that's enough!" and leaped toward the outlaw closest to him. The daring move was unexpected enough that the man was able to get his hands on the raider's gun.

But then the killer shoved the weapon into the customer's belly and jerked the trigger. The man's body muffled the shot. He jerked and let go, stumbling back a step. Looking stricken, he pressed both hands to his belly. Crimson blood welled between his fingers. He groaned, fell to his knees, and then toppled onto his side.

Margaret screamed again.

For an awful second, Brenda thought one of the men was going to shoot her grandmother, but then Maguire barked, "Let's go!" and they all turned toward the door. He hauled her along with him, and although she started to kick and struggle again, it was no use.

She was going with them whether she wanted to or not, and she was wracked with the horrible, despairing feeling that she would never come back.

More shots roared from Cole's right, but this time they weren't directed at him. They came from Jeremiah Newton, who crouched in the alcove of a store's entrance and fired the gun he had taken from the outlaw in the store at the two men who had the best angle on Cole.

Jeremiah was no sharpshooter; his bullets flew wildly around the two outlaws. But that was enough to make them forget about Cole for a second. Cole used that opportunity to draw a bead on one of them and fire. The man staggered and howled in pain as the bullet smashed the shoulder of his gun arm. Cole fired again and narrowly missed the second man.

Pounding hoofbeats suddenly competed with the gun-thunder. Cole leaned to the side and risked a look along the street. Several men leading quite a few horses were riding down the center of Grenville Avenue, snapping shots at the buildings to keep everybody's heads down. More men came running out here and there to grab those horses and swing into the saddle. The gang was making its retreat.

Cole rolled to his left, scrambled longways beside the water trough, and came up on a knee. He tracked his Colt from left to right and fired until it was empty as the fleeing desperadoes galloped past him, but he couldn't tell if he hit any of them. None of the horses went down, and no one pitched out of a saddle.

Cole had to dive for cover again, though, as a bullet plucked at the side of his buckskin shirt. He lifted his head to look after the outlaws, and his eyes widened in shock as he spotted Brenda Durand perched on horseback in front of one of them. For a crazy split-second Cole thought that Brenda was one of the gang, then he realized how terrified she looked. She was being kidnapped.

And Cole recognized the man who held her, too.

Adam Maguire.

He didn't have time to think about that now. He leaped to his feet and started reloading as the outlaws reached the southern end of Grenville Avenue. His big golden sorrel, Ulysses, was stabled nearby in Milligan's livery, and Cole intended to get the horse and give chase.

Before he could do that, Margaret Palmer stumbled up to him and clutched at his sleeve. "Marshal, they took Brenda!" she screamed. "You have to go after them!"

"I'm going to, ma'am —" Cole started to say.

"And they killed Deputy Casebolt!"

A wave of dread washed through Cole at those words. Billy Casebolt was more than his deputy; he was Cole's best friend in Wind River. A glance toward the south told him that the outlaws were almost out of sight, disappearing in the cloud of dust raised by their horses' hooves.

With his experience as a scout, he knew he wouldn't have any trouble trailing a group of that size. He gripped Mrs. Palmer's shoulder and asked, "Where's Billy?"

"In the bank," she said. Tears had left streaks on her face. "But you have to go after Brenda —"

"I will, ma'am, and I'll bring her back safe and sound," Cole promised. He didn't know if he could keep that pledge, but he would do his best. For now, though, he had to check on Casebolt.

He ran toward the bank. Jeremiah called from the boardwalk on the other side of the street, "Cole, what can I do to help?"

"Find Dr. Kent. Send him to the bank!"

As much shooting had been going on all over town, the doctor's services would be needed just about everywhere, Cole thought. The raid on Wind River had been a well-coordinated attack, almost like some of the military maneuvers Cole had taken part in, back during the war. It wouldn't surprise him if whoever had planned the raid — Maguire? — had been in the army.

Cole ran into the bank to find Nathan Smollet leaning against the railing and pressing a bloody handkerchief to his head. Two bodies lay on the floor, one belonging to a man Cole didn't recognize right away.

The other was Billy Casebolt.

Cole dropped to his knees beside Casebolt, grasped the deputy's shoulders, and rolled him onto his back. Casebolt's leathery, beard-stubbled face was pale as milk, probably because of the puddle of blood that had formed on the floor underneath him. Casebolt's shirt and vest were soaked with blood. Cole couldn't tell how many times he'd been hit. He pulled the vest aside and ripped the deputy's shirt open.

Casebolt had a deep graze on his right side, a messy but not life-threatening wound. The same couldn't be said about the puckered bullet hole in his left side. Cole hadn't seen an exit wound on Casebolt's back, so that slug was probably still somewhere inside him.

Casebolt was breathing, though. His scrawny chest rose and fell in a jerky, irregular motion. But at least he was still alive and fighting to hang on.

"Cole!"

That was Judson Kent's voice. Cole looked up as the doctor rushed into the bank.

"Look after Billy," Cole said as he got to his feet. "I have to check on the rest of the town."

"Good Lord," Kent muttered as he knelt beside Casebolt. "What's happened here today?"

"Looks like Wind River's not as civilized yet as some people thought it was," Cole said.

CHAPTER 8

The scene in town really did look like the aftermath of a battle, Cole discovered over the next half-hour.

Three people had been killed by all the bullets flying around, including the man in the bank, whom Smollet identified as Simon Hartwell, a fairly new arrival to the area who had a farm outside of town. Eight more citizens had been wounded. Billy Casebolt's injuries were the most serious, but for now at least, the deputy was clinging stubbornly to life. He had been carried carefully on a stretcher to Dr. Kent's residence.

The outlaws had cleaned out the bank, which was the biggest loss financially, but they had also hit the store, the hotel, and even the office of the land development company, which was in the same building as the marshal's office. That was a bitter pill for Cole to swallow, knowing they had gotten in there after he and Jeremiah ran out.

They had blown the safe open with blasting powder and taken all the money in it.

Once Cole was sure about the extent of the raid's damage, he started rounding up a posse. The pickings were sort of slim, he discovered quickly. Plenty of men in town were willing to ride after the outlaws, but few of them had much experience with such things. Going up against such a potent force of hardened thieves and murderers would just get some good men killed, Cole thought bleakly.

But the thought of letting the outlaws get away never entered his head. They had to pay for what they had done. Losing the money they had taken would severely cripple the town's business.

And most importantly, they had carried off a young woman, and Cole had promised her grandmother that he would get her back. He intended to keep that promise.

One of the thoughts that had crossed his mind earlier came back to him when he saw Michael Hatfield hurrying around town asking questions of the people who had been caught up in the raid. Michael wanted quotes for the paper, but Cole thought there was something more important the young editor could be doing right now.

"Michael, I've got a job for you," Cole

called. He beckoned Michael over to him on the boardwalk in front of the marshal's office.

"What can I do for you, Marshal?" Michael asked.

"I want you to ride out to the Diamond S."

"Mr. Sawyer's ranch?" Michael looked as surprised as he sounded. "What in the world for?"

"I need men for a posse. Sawyer and Frenchy LeDoux and that bunch are the saltiest crew around here."

"But it might take several hours for me to get out there and them to ride back here," Michael objected. "You can't mean to wait that long to start after the bandits."

"No, but Sawyer and his bunch can catch up to us. I'd be willing to bet that he's got several men who are good trackers. They'll be able to pick up the trail at the edge of town and follow it just like I plan to."

"I thought I would ride with you and the rest of the posse."

Cole shook his head. "You can do more good for the town, and for Miss Durand, this way."

Michael had acquitted himself fairly well when they went after the men who had kidnapped his wife, Delia, along with Simone McKay, not long after the town was founded. Normally Cole would have let him come along. But in this case, he was right about Michael being more valuable in other ways. For somebody from Cincinnati, he was a good rider and had a speedy horse.

Michael must have seen the logic in that. He sighed and said, "All right. When do you want me to leave?"

"The sooner the better," Cole told him.

"You'll be gone by the time I get back?"

"More than likely." Cole's face was grim as he turned toward the door of the marshal's office. "There's just one thing I've got to do first."

Michael hurried off toward the livery stable as Cole went into the office. The room seemed oddly empty without Billy Casebolt in it.

A groan came from the cellblock. Earlier, Jeremiah had brought the outlaw whose ribs he had broken down here and locked him in one of the cells. Cole went into the cellblock now and looked through the bars at the man who was stretched out on a bunk with a threadbare blanket.

The outlaw realized Cole was there and gasped, "Marshal, I'm hurt bad! You gotta get the doc in here to tend to me. Every time I take a breath, it . . . it feels like I'm bein' jabbed inside by cavalry sabers!"

"Those are broken ribs," Cole said. "If you're lucky, none of 'em will poke a hole in your lungs."

"You gotta help me!"

"The doctor's busy taking care of innocent folks who were hurt by you and your bunch. He'll get to you when he can, and if you die before then, that's just too damned bad." Cole drew his .44. "Of course, I can put you out of your misery right here and now if you want me to."

The man's eyes widened with fear. Instinct made him shrink back on the bunk, and that movement caused him to blanch as a fresh wave of pain went through him.

"You . . . you can't do that," he whined. "You're a lawman."

"A lawman whose deputy was cut down by you varmints." Cole pulled back the gun's hammer. "At least three people were killed out there today. As far as I'm concerned you're all equally guilty. I can save the town the expense of a trial and a hang rope."

"Please . . . please, mister . . ."

Cole's eyes were like chips of ice as he stared at the outlaw over the barrel of his gun. "Answer some questions for me."

"Anything! Anything you want to know!"

"Is Adam Maguire the leader of your gang?"

"Yeah. Yeah, Maguire put the bunch together. Him and Beaumont. They're friends. Rode together in the Union cavalry durin' the war."

"Lije Beaumont?"

"Yeah."

Cole hadn't seen Beaumont during the raid, but that wasn't surprising, considering all the dust and gunsmoke that had filled the air. He realized now that the little fracas involving Beaumont a few days earlier had been a ruse, a show designed to let the two outlaws know how many lawmen were in Wind River and how much of a fight the town would put up.

Not enough, Cole thought bitterly. Not nearly enough.

"Why did Maguire kidnap that young woman?"

The outlaw blinked at Cole in what appeared to be genuine confusion. "Woman?" he repeated. "What woman?"

"The plan didn't include taking any prisoners?"

"All we planned to do was clean out the town and then light a shuck away from here, Marshal. You gotta believe me. I don't know anything about kidnappin' a woman."

The decision to carry Brenda away with them must have been a spur of the moment thing on Maguire's part, Cole thought. Either Maguire was taken with her looks and wanted her for himself, or he planned to use her as a hostage. Maybe both.

Cole's eyes narrowed as another possibility occurred to him. If Maguire had found out somehow that Brenda was the richest person in town, he might be planning to hold her for ransom. If that was the case, it was a double-edged sword. He would have to keep her alive for her to be worth anything to him . . .

But he didn't necessarily have to keep her in the same condition she was when he carried her off.

"All right, last question . . . and it's the most important one. Where's the hideout?"

The outlaw gave a weak shake of his head. "I can't tell you that, Marshal. You don't know Maguire. He acts all friendly-like, but he's really loco from all the killin' he saw in the war, and he's meaner than a whole band of Comanches! He wouldn't just kill me, he'd make sure I was a long time dyin', screamin' all the time."

"Yeah, and I'll just put a nice quick bullet through your brain," Cole said. "Maybe you're smart not to tell me."

His finger started to tighten on the .44's trigger, and at that instant he couldn't have said beyond a shadow of a doubt that he wasn't going to kill the outlaw. The man must have seen that, because he screamed, "No! Don't shoot! I'll tell you, for God's sake, I'll tell you, but you gotta protect me from Maguire."

"If I catch up to Maguire, you won't have to worry about him. Spill what you know."

"There . . . there's a valley about five miles west of here, a couple of miles north of the railroad tracks. You gotta go through a little gap in the hills to get to it. Nobody lives there. Maguire says nobody even knows about it."

Cole frowned. He wasn't familiar with the valley the man was talking about, but he didn't doubt that it was there.

"Is there more than one way in and out?"

The outlaw shook his head again. "No, the hills are too rough and steep around it. You couldn't get a posse in there. It's like a fortress, and Maguire's got the only way in."

"We'll see about that," Cole said. He let down the hammer of his gun and slipped the weapon back in its holster.

"I . . . I told you what you wanted to know, Marshal. You'll get the doc to come see about me now?"

"He knows you're in here," Cole snapped. "He'll get to you when he can."

"You promised you'd help me —"

"I didn't shoot you in the head," Cole said. "That's about all the human kindness I got in me right now."

see about it, too."

"He knows you're in bad—" Cole warned.

"He'll get to you when he can."

"Cole, please, you'd help me."

"Cole," about you or the boy? Cole was that it's about all the people in—

I need me—

CHAPTER 9

Wind River had been founded because two unscrupulous men, Andrew McKay and William Durand, had been able to spread around enough bribe money to find out the exact route of the Union Pacific railroad. Armed with that knowledge, they had bought up all the land at a certain spot in southern Wyoming and planned out the town they would build there when the steel rails arrived. In fact, some of the settlement already existed before the railroad ever got there.

Since then Wind River had done nothing but grow and prosper, even after the railhead moved on. Unlike some hell on wheels towns, it hadn't faded away, due in large part to the efforts of Simone McKay, Andrew McKay's widow, after her husband was murdered. When McKay's business partner was killed as well, Simone had found herself running things, at least until

Durand's daughter, Brenda, showed up.

Then Simone, too, had lost her life under tragic circumstances, and with a few exceptions such as the hotel, the land development company, the newspaper, the blacksmith shop, and the café, Brenda now owned most of the town. That made her one of the richest women in the territory.

And it was one more reason she would never have anything to do with him, Lon Rogers reflected as he rode up a brushy draw on Diamond S range, searching for any of the rangy longhorns that might have wandered up here. With winter coming on, Kermit Sawyer's crew of Texas cowboys was scouring the hills for stock so the cattle could be gathered and moved to better pasture where they would be more likely to survive the coming months.

Lon was looking at the piles of rocks and thick clumps of brush, but he was seeing Brenda's face, as hauntingly lovely as ever. He had thought about her a lot since his latest encounter in town with her, several days earlier.

He had even found his mind wandering to her when he tried to read one of the books he had sent for. He really did have a love of reading, fostered by Mr. Sawyer's late wife, Amelia, while Lon was growing up on the Sawyer ranch in Texas, but it was hard to concentrate on the printed word or anything else when he kept thinking about the beautiful young woman.

That was probably why he didn't notice when the old bull burst out from behind some rocks and charged him and his horse, its long, dangerous horns held low and ready to rip upward into them. Lon didn't see the longhorn until somebody yelled, "Look out, kid!"

His head jerked up and fear shot through him as he saw the maddened critter barreling toward him.

A rifle cracked, the echoes of the report bouncing back from the surrounding hills. The bull stumbled, then its front legs gave way and folded up. One horn dipped, dug into the ground, and caused the bull to spill over in a spectacular fall that left it quivering and dying on the dirt only a few yards from where Lon had yanked his horse to a halt.

Hoofbeats pounded up behind him. Frenchy LeDoux, the Diamond S foreman, reined in sharply as he came alongside Lon. He still held his Winchester in one hand as he demanded angrily, "What the hell were you thinkin', Lon? You know you can't go around wool-gatherin' when you're dealin' with these loco varmints!"

Lon gulped. "Sorry, Frenchy," he said. "You're right, I wasn't paying close enough attention. You saved my life!"

"Maybe," Frenchy said as he thumbed a fresh cartridge through the rifle's loading gate to replace the round he'd fired. "Mainly, though, I was savin' myself the trouble of havin' to explain to the boss how you wound up with your guts ripped open by that old mossyhorn. He won't be happy about losing that steer for no good reason, but he'd have been more upset to lose you."

"Well, I'm sure obliged to you, no matter what the reason."

Frenchy snorted. He was a lean, dark-complected Cajun originally from Louisiana, although he had spent most of his life in Texas. He had started out as a puncher on Kermit Sawyer's ranch sprawled on the Brazos and had risen to the job of foreman, so when Sawyer had decided a couple of years earlier to relocate to Wyoming Territory, it was just natural that Frenchy had come along, too.

"Get the hide off that steer," he ordered Lon. "Might as well get some use out of it, now that it's dead."

Lon tried not to wince. Skinning the longhorn would be a hard, ugly, messy job,

83

but he supposed he had it coming. The only good thing about the chore was that it would take place far from town, so there was no chance Brenda would see him covered in blood.

Just like that she was back in his head. He had it bad, no doubt about that. But there was nothing he could do about it. A man couldn't help what was in his heart.

Frenchy slid the Winchester back in the sheath strapped to his saddle. "When you're done with that," the foreman told Lon, "get back to work."

"Sure, Frenchy." Lon didn't point out that skinning the longhorn ought to be considered work, too.

He sure as blazes wouldn't be doing it for fun.

Before either of them could say anything else, the sound of rapid hoofbeats came to their ears and made them look around. One of the hands, a big blond man called Swede, was riding up the draw toward them, and he was coming hell for leather, too. Red-faced from effort, he hauled back on the reins and brought his mount to a skidding stop a few feet away from Lon and Frenchy.

"Mr. Sawyer wants everybody back at the house right away!" Swede reported. "Big trouble in town!"

"What sort of trouble?" Frenchy asked. "And why is it any of our business?" There had been a certain level of animosity between the townspeople and the cowboys ever since the Diamond S crew had arrived from Texas.

"That newspaper fella from Wind River, he rode out and told the boss a bunch of outlaws attacked the town this morning. Killed some folks, cleaned out the bank and some of the other businesses, and carried off a young woman as a hostage!"

The foreman cursed softly in French, one of the rare expressions of his Cajun heritage. "Mr. Sawyer put some of his money in that bank," he said. "I reckon that's why he wants to go after that bunch. That's what he wants, isn't it, Swede?"

"Well, he didn't exactly say," Swede replied, "but I'll bet that's what he's thinkin', yah."

"All right, come on, Lon," Frenchy said. A grim smile played around his lips. "I guess you got out of skinnin' that ol' mossyhorn after all."

"I'd rather not get out of it this way," Lon said.

"I know. Swede, the rest of the boys are over yonder." Frenchy waved to indicate the direction Swede should take to look for the other Diamond S punchers. "Lon and I will see you back at the ranch."

The two young men headed one way while Swede rode the other. After a few minutes, Frenchy commented, "Things must be pretty bad for Marshal Tyler to ask the old man for help."

"Yeah, I guess so," Lon said. "We've got some experience trading shots with owl-hoots, though. Most of the people in Wind River don't."

"I reckon that's true. Better grab some provisions and plenty of ammunition when we get back to the bunkhouse. This is liable to be a pretty long chase. You never know."

Kermit Sawyer already had men saddling fresh horses when Lon and Frenchy reached the ranch headquarters. The rugged old cattleman nodded to them as they dismounted and said, "I reckon Swede told you what happened."

"That's right," Frenchy said.

Lon saw Michael Hatfield standing on the front porch of the ranch house. The young newspaperman looked tired, and he was covered with trail dust from the hard, fast ride he had made out here. Lon went over to him and nodded.

"How bad is it in town?"

"Pretty bad," Michael said. "Several

people were killed, and more were wounded. Those outlaws hit town like . . . like a cavalry raid, I guess, although I wasn't in the war so I don't know firsthand. But I know they struck several places at once, including the bank. That's where they shot Deputy Casebolt."

"Good Lord!" Lon exclaimed. "The deputy was shot?"

"Yes. He was still alive when the marshal sent me out here to fetch Mr. Sawyer, but he was hurt pretty bad. I don't know if he'll make it."

"That's a shame. I liked Deputy Casebolt."

Michael looked at Lon and said, "You like Miss Durand, too, don't you?"

The question made alarm shoot through Lon. "What?" he said. "What about Brenda? Was she hurt, too?"

"She was in the bank when the outlaws robbed the place," Michael explained. "They took her with them."

Lon took an involuntary step back. He felt like a mule had kicked him in the gut. Swede had said that a young woman had been taken hostage, but it had never occurred to Lon that the captive might be Brenda Durand.

"From what I heard, she was all right

when the outlaws rode off with her," Michael went on, "but God knows what's happened to her in the meantime."

Lon turned quickly, forgetting all about Frenchy's advice to gather up some supplies and ammunition. Instead he bounded down from the porch and ran toward the corral where the fresh horses waited. Sawyer and Frenchy saw him coming, and the cattleman lifted a hand, saying, "Lon, what are you —"

Lon bolted past them, jerked the corral gate open, and leaped into the saddle. He jerked the horse around and jabbed his heels into its flanks.

"Lon, wait!" Frenchy called.

Lon ignored the order. As the horse lunged out of the corral, Frenchy and Sawyer had to scramble to get out of the way. Lon raced past them, kicking the horse into a hard gallop as he headed for town.

Earlier, when he was riding up that draw, Brenda had filled his thoughts, and now once again she was all he could think about.

This time, though, he was filled with fear for her safety.

If those outlaws hurt her, he would track them down, every last one of them, and he wouldn't stop until either they were all dead . . . or he was.

CHAPTER 10

Less than an hour after the raid, Cole had a posse of ten men ready to ride out of Wind River with him. His best estimate was that the gang contained about a dozen men when the outlaws made their getaway, so the odds weren't really that uneven.

Such things couldn't be measured solely in numbers, though. Jeremiah was going along, and the blacksmith was a good man but not much of a hand with a gun. Monty Riordan, the biscuit-shooter at Rose Foster's café, had volunteered as well, and while he had experience as an Indian fighter, he was old and about half crippled. The only fighting he'd done in recent years had been with pots and pans.

Nathan Smollet insisted on coming along, too. Dr. Kent had cleaned the gash on the side of his head and wrapped a bandage around it. Smollet had good intentions, but

Cole didn't expect much fighting ability out of him.

The other volunteers were an assortment of townsmen and farmers. Cole didn't know any of them that well. Some of them might be able to hold their own in a fight, but he couldn't really count on that.

He wasn't going to wait for the men from the Diamond S to arrive, though, especially since he knew where the gang's hideout was located. By heading directly for that hidden valley instead of following the false trail that the outlaws had laid to the south, there was a slim chance Cole and the posse might be able to head them off before they reached their stronghold.

"Mount up!" he called to the men who had gathered in front of the livery stable. He swung into the saddle on Ulysses's back and looked around at the others. "Everybody got plenty of ammunition?"

Several of the men answered in the affirmative. The others nodded.

Cole nodded toward the blacksmith and went on, "If anything happens to me while we're out there, Jeremiah's in charge."

Jeremiah looked surprised by that decision. He said, "But Brother Cole, I'm a preacher, not a lawman."

"You're all lawmen today," Cole said.

"Let's ride!"

He led the posse out of Wind River, riding north along Grenville Avenue to the railroad station, then cutting around the depot, crossing the tracks, and heading west. Quite a few of the citizens had turned out to watch them depart. Enthusiastic cheers went up from the crowd.

Cole hoped they would still be cheering when the posse got back.

He urged the big golden sorrel into a ground-eating lope. The others trailed behind, some of them struggling to keep up. The settlement soon dwindled into the distance behind them.

Cole followed the railroad tracks and kept his eyes on the hills bulking to the north. The farther west the posse rode, the closer those hills came to the railroad, slouching across the terrain like great, gray, prehistoric beasts.

At the same time, he watched to the south, searching for a dust cloud that would mark the location of the outlaw gang if Cole and the posse had managed to get between them and the hideout. Realistically, Cole considered the odds of that unlikely, but there was an outside chance and he couldn't afford to overlook it.

Before leaving Wind River, he had stopped

at Dr. Judson Kent's office to see how Billy Casebolt was doing and to ask a favor of the medico.

"Deputy Casebolt is an extremely stubborn man," Kent had said, "and that works in his favor. Even though he hasn't regained consciousness, I get the feeling that he's determined to hang on to life. That can only help him."

"Were you able to get that bullet out of him?" Cole had asked.

"Fortunately, yes," Kent had replied with a nod. "I don't believe it damaged any vital organs, but the shock of being wounded, along with the blood that he lost, is the real threat now. I'll do everything I can for him, Cole."

"I know that. I've got a favor to ask of you, as mayor, I guess you'd say, instead of as a doctor."

"As mayor, I'm devastated as well as furious about what happened to our community this morning, so go ahead."

"I sent Michael Hatfield to fetch Sawyer and the Diamond S crew," Cole had explained. "I think there's a good chance they'll come. Sawyer's got no love for outlaws, and I'm pretty sure he had some money in the bank, so he'll want to get it back. When they show up, tell them not to follow the trail that the gang left." Cole had gone on to explain what he had found out from the prisoner about the location of the outlaws' hideout. "Send them that direction instead. They can follow the tracks the posse will leave, because that's the way we're going."

"You'll be taking a chance by not following their trail," Kent had pointed out. "What if that prisoner was lying to you?"

"I think he was too scared to do that. He knew I was about to shoot him if he didn't tell me the truth."

"You mean you threatened to shoot him."

Cole had just smiled grimly at that.

As he thought back over the conversation now, he knew that Kent would do what he had asked. The Texans ought to be an hour or two behind the posse. Maybe the fireworks would all be over by the time they caught up.

However, if the posse didn't get that lucky break and stop the gang from reaching the hideout, the smart thing to do would be to wait for Sawyer and his men to arrive before trying to fight their way into the outlaw stronghold.

The problem was, Cole didn't know if Brenda Durand could afford to wait that long . . .

■ ■ ■ ■

Brenda had known fear in her life, but never anything like this. She was cold through and through, the chill of terror. She wasn't sure she would ever be warm again.

Adam Maguire still held her snugly in the saddle in front of him with his left arm looped around her waist. Her skirt was pulled up shamefully high on her legs. She had never ridden astride before today, but the outlaw hadn't given her any choice when he hauled her out of the bank and practically threw her on the back of his horse. Her fear and his rough treatment of her left her too stunned to fight back anymore.

She tried to force her brain to work. When the riders crossed the railroad tracks, she realized they had to be going north. She knew they had galloped out of Wind River to the south, so that meant they had traveled in a big curve, no doubt intended to throw off any pursuit.

Now they were headed for a range of rugged, ugly hills. In the six months she had lived in Wind River, Brenda had never ventured very far out of the settlement itself, so she had no real idea where they were.

As if he knew what she was thinking about, Maguire said, "Pretty soon we'll be where we're going. I reckon you'll be glad to get off this horse."

He seemed to be expecting an answer, and she didn't want to make him angry. She said, "Yes, I . . . I'm not accustomed to riding this much."

"Sorry it's been rough on you. You've got to understand, though, I couldn't leave you behind."

"I don't see why not. You got what you wanted. You cleaned out the bank."

Maguire chuckled. "I didn't expect a pretty little prize like you, though."

"The marshal will come after you. He'll get a posse together and hunt you down."

That brought a full-fledged laugh from Maguire. "I'm not worried about the marshal," he said. "Where we're going, he won't be able to bother us. He won't be able to do anything except go along with what I tell him . . . if he wants to get you back safe and sound, that is."

"Am I going to get back?" Brenda asked. "Safe and sound, I mean."

"I don't plan on hurting you unless I have to." Maguire's voice hardened. "Unless I don't get what I want."

"What is it that . . . that you want?"

"You're a rich girl."

"No, I —"

"Don't bother denying it," he cut in. "You admitted it yourself in the bank. You've got friends and family back there in Wind River, don't you? I'll bet they can come up with a lot more money to pay for you coming back to them."

"You're holding me for ransom?"

"That's the idea."

And it was probably a good one from Maguire's point of view, Brenda had to admit. With all of her holdings, her grandmother could probably raise a considerable amount of cash. But even if the ransom was paid, that was no guarantee she would be released unharmed. After all, the easiest and simplest thing for the outlaws to do once they had the money would be to kill her.

She considered trying to deny that she was really that wealthy, but then she decided it might not be a good idea to convince them of that. Instead she said, "You're right, Maguire. I have plenty of money, a lot more money than you got out of that bank. But you'll never get your hands on any of it if any harm comes to me."

"Now why in the world would I ever want

to hurt anybody as nice and pretty as you?" Maguire asked. Brenda couldn't tell if he was serious or mocking her. He leaned forward and his lips nuzzled the side of her neck, making cold chills go through her again. "Of course, I figure that while you're staying with us, you and I will have the chance to get to know each other better."

"If you get to know me any better than you do right now, you'll regret it," she snapped.

"Oh, I don't reckon I will."

She looked around at the other men, wondering if there was any way she could drive a wedge between them. The man riding at Maguire's side looked even more hard-bitten and dangerous with his thin, drooping mustache and cruel face. Maguire had called him Lije, and he seemed to be the gang's second-in-command. Brenda knew there wouldn't be any help for her there.

The big man in the suit and the derby, though, he had gazed at her with open appreciation. If she got a chance, she might be able to play up to him. It was doubtful that she could ever turn him against the other outlaws, but maybe, under the right circumstances, he would react in her favor.

That would take time to bring about,

though, and she was pretty sure she wouldn't have that much time. As they rode into the hills, steep bluffs rose around them. A narrow opening appeared up ahead, and to Brenda's frightened eyes the dark, ominous gap might as well have been the mouth of Hell.

An overpowering urge to get away seized her. She twisted suddenly and tried to bring her elbow up and back into Maguire's throat. If she could loosen his grip on her, even for a second, she might slip free, leap off the horse, and try to run, even though there was really nowhere for her to go . . .

Maguire moved his head aside, laughed, and used the hand holding the horse's reins to grasp her throat.

"Don't try anything like that again," he warned her. "You don't want to make me mad, Miss Durand."

His grip tightened. Brenda struggled to breathe as the group of riders entered the narrow passage. Her head was tilted back a little, and even in her distress she noticed sunlight reflecting from rifle barrels on the bluffs above them. So the men who had raided Wind River weren't the only members of the gang. Maguire had posted sharpshooters up there to guard the way into the stronghold.

Shadows closed in around them. Maguire let go of her neck. "Now," he said, "are you going to behave?"

"Y-yes," Brenda rasped. "I won't give you . . . any trouble."

"Good. I knew you were a smart girl."

A few minutes later they came to the end of the passage and emerged into the sunlight again. The landscape that spread out before them wasn't exactly pretty, Brenda thought, but it wasn't as bleak and ugly as much of this Wyoming Territory was.

"Welcome to the place that's going to be your home for a while," Maguire said. "Welcome to my valley."

CHAPTER 11

Cole reined Ulysses to a halt when he spotted the hoofprints crossing the railroad tracks in front of him. It was impossible to miss the signs that a dozen or more riders had come through here and headed northwest toward the hills.

The outlaws hadn't even tried to hide their tracks, he thought. That showed how cocky they were, how confident that the law couldn't reach them in their stronghold.

And the tracks proved as well that the posse was too late to cut off the fleeing bandits. Cole's jaw tightened as he gazed toward the hills.

"They're already up there somewhere, aren't they?" Jeremiah asked quietly, although in such a big man, his voice still held a considerable rumble.

"Yeah," Cole said. "It looks like they are."

Nathan Smollet edged his horse up and asked nervously, "Are we going to wait for help, Marshal, or go ahead and try to find them?" The banker looked uncomfortable. Even though the posse hadn't really ridden that far, Smollet wasn't used to spending even this much time in the saddle.

"I don't intend to wait," Cole said. "Every man here, though, is a volunteer. I won't force you to come along if you don't want to."

"It ain't that we don't want to, Marshal," one of the men spoke up. "But we've all heard about how you sent for Kermit Sawyer and those wild cowboys of his, and it seems like we'd stand a better chance goin' up against those outlaws if we had the Diamond S bunch sidin' us."

"No doubt about it," Cole said. "But would we be in time to help Miss Durand?"

Smollet stiffened in the saddle and said, "If we're taking a vote, I say we go on. We can't afford to delay our rescue."

"You sound mighty certain we'll be doin' the rescuin'," another man muttered. "Could be we'll need some rescuin' ourselves."

There had been enough talk, Cole thought. He turned Ulysses's head toward the hills and said, "I'm going. Anybody who wants to come with me, I'll be obliged to you."

Without looking back, he followed the tracks left by the outlaws and rode north-west.

The fact that Jeremiah came up alongside him a moment later was no surprise. Cole had known he could depend on the big man. And Smollet was there, too; despite being a greenhorn, the banker was starting to show a core of toughness. When Cole finally glanced over his shoulder, he saw that all the posse members were following him. No one had turned back to Wind River.

That made him feel a little better, but when he thought about the situation they were still facing, the show of loyalty didn't really help all that much.

The trail led into the hills, twisting and turning among the ridges and bluffs and great humps of rock. They came out onto a narrow bench, and on the far side of it loomed a line of cliff-like bluffs. In the middle of that barrier was a dark gap that marked a passage of some sort.

Cole reined in and held up his hand in a signal for the others to stop. He reached into his saddlebags and pulled out the telescope he always carried there. He'd used the spyglass to help him locate Yankee cavalry patrols during the war. It had saved his life more than once.

He extended the telescope, put it to his eye, and peered through it. The gap in the bluffs came into sharp relief. He couldn't see very far into it, though. Whatever natural forces had carved out that opening had left it zigging and zagging back and forth. Cole could see that boulders cluttered the passage floor, but that was about all.

Something about the opening reminded him of the jaws of a trap, waiting there to snap shut on the posse. But the outlaws and their prisoner were on the other side of it, so they had no choice but to try to make it through there.

"Do you see anything?" Jeremiah asked.

Cole grunted. "Nothing good." He angled the spyglass upward, intending to see if there might be a path they could use to scale those bluffs instead of trying to go through the gap. It didn't look promising. A man might be able to get up those steep slopes to which scrubby pines and a few hardy bushes clung, but horses would never be able to make it up and down.

Cole's survey had just reached the top of the towering bluff when he saw a sudden flash of light, followed by a puff of smoke. As he hurriedly lowered the telescope, he heard a distant boom.

"Get back!" he told the posse. "Get —"

Too late. One of the men let out an explosive "Uh!" and flew backward out of his saddle. Blood spouted from the hole that had appeared abruptly in his chest.

"Back!" Cole yelled again. "Into those trees!"

The possemen jerked their horses around and headed for the shelter of a stand of juniper as fast as they could.

Cole wheeled Ulysses as well, so he didn't see the second muzzle flash, but he heard the dull report as another shot was fired from the top of the bluff. A couple of heartbeats later, dirt geysered into the air as the heavy caliber slug struck the ground next to Nathan Smollet's horse. Smollet's knees banged against the animal's flanks as he tried to get all the speed out of it that he could.

Cole was going to lean down from the saddle and try to grab the wounded man as he went past, but when he saw the man's dull eyes he knew there was no point in making the effort. The man lay on his back, and while the hole in the front of his shirt wasn't all that big, Cole knew the hole in his back where the bullet came out would be large enough to put a fist in. Judging by the location of the entry wound, the slug had blown most of the man's heart out with it.

Instead of pausing, Cole galloped on toward the trees. He reached them without being shot out of the saddle, and he considered himself a little lucky that was the case.

The men had dismounted and taken cover behind the trees. A pale-faced Nathan Smollet said, "Good Lord, Marshal! What happened out there?"

Cole swung down from the saddle and led Ulysses farther back in the trees. Someone, probably Jeremiah, had detailed a couple of men to hold the horses. Cole handed the reins over to one of them, then pulled his Henry rifle from its sheath and went back to where he could keep an eye on the bluffs as he stood behind the trunk of a juniper.

"The outlaws have at least two men up there with Sharps rifles," he answered the bank manager's question. "Big Fifties, from the sound of them."

"But those bluffs are at least half a mile away!"

"And a good hand with a Sharps can make a shot close to a mile," Cole said.

Jeremiah asked, "If they were going to ambush us anyway, why didn't they put more men up there and try to wipe us out?"

Cole's face was bleak as he replied,

"Seems to me what they just did was intended more as a warning."

"A warning?" Smollet repeated. "A man is dead!"

"And you came pretty close to that yourself, Mr. Smollet," Cole said with a humorless smile. "Made us all pay attention real good, didn't they?"

"If they wanted to warn us and not just kill us," Jeremiah said, "there must be something they want from us."

Cole thought about it and nodded. "I reckon you're right." Movement at the base of the bluff caught his attention. His eyes narrowed. He had stuffed his spyglass back in his saddlebags when the shooting started. Now he needed it again. "Everybody find the best cover you can and stay put."

He hurried back to the spot where the men were holding the horses and retrieved the telescope. When he returned to the spot near the edge of the trees and peered through the glass, he wasn't surprised by what he saw. Lije Beaumont sat on horseback at the mouth of the gap, holding a branch with a big piece of white cloth tied to it. The chilly wind that funneled through the passage made the cloth flap lazily.

"One of 'em's waiting with a flag of truce," Cole said as he lowered the telescope. "I guess I'd better go see what he wants."

"Marshal, you can't," Smollet said. "You'll be a perfect target while you're riding across that open ground. They can kill you any time they want."

"That means I have to hope they don't want me dead."

As Cole started back to the horses, Jeremiah moved over to intercept him. Putting a hand on Cole's arm, the blacksmith said, "Are you sure this is the right thing to do, Brother Cole?"

"I've got a hunch that Maguire has a message for us," Cole said. "He's sent his segundo to deliver it. Nobody will try to shoot me until I've heard what Beaumont has to say."

"What about *after* you hear what he has to say?"

Cole had to laugh. "Well, I reckon coming back across that open stretch might be a little harder on the nerves. But I really feel like they want something more than just a kill-or-be-killed showdown."

"I'll be praying that you're right," Jeremiah said solemnly.

"I appreciate that. I'll take all the prayers you've got."

Cole put the telescope away again,

snugged the Henry in the saddle boot, and mounted up. He rode through the trees, pausing at their edge long enough to raise his voice and say, "Remember, if I don't come back, Jeremiah's in charge."

Then he heeled Ulysses into a lope that carried them out into the open. His skin crawled a little. At this range, if a man who was good with a Sharps was drawing a bead on him, he might as well have a big red target painted on his chest.

No shots roared from the bluffs as Cole drew steadily closer. Beaumont stayed where he was in the mouth of the gap, waiting.

That half-mile ride didn't take long, but the seconds seemed to creep past. Finally, Cole was close enough that he and Beaumont could talk without having to shout. He brought the golden sorrel to a stop and rested both hands on the saddle horn.

"All right, I'm here, Beaumont," Cole called. "What do you want?"

Beaumont had a stubby black cigar clenched between his teeth. Smoke drifted up from the glowing coal at the tip of it. Speaking around the cigar, the outlaw said, "Maguire sent me out here to talk to you."

"I figured as much. The two of you are old friends, aren't you?"

Beaumont's eyes narrowed. "How do you know that?" he demanded. "By God, is one of those men we left behind still alive? Did somebody talk? Which one was it? Lanigan? Steeves? Russell? I'll kill the son of a —"

"It doesn't really matter, does it?" Cole broke in to ask. "What's important is that I know the sort of men you are. I know you mean business."

"Damn right we do."

"So what is it you want?"

Beaumont said, "We've got the Durand girl."

"I know that. Is she all right?"

"She ain't been hurt . . . yet. But Maguire knows she's rich. He says that her grandma's got until dawn, the day after tomorrow, to raise fifty thousand dollars. If he doesn't get it . . ." A leer stretched across Beaumont's rawboned face. "Well, I ain't sayin that she'll die right away, but I reckon there's a really good chance she'll wish she was dead."

Almost every fiber of Cole's being wanted to yank out his .44 and blast that leer right off Beaumont's face. He could do it, too, before anyone could stop him. But if he did, he wouldn't be able to make it back to the posse, and he knew he couldn't hope to invade the outlaw stronghold by himself.

More than likely, giving in to the impulse would just get him and Brenda killed sooner rather than later.

"I can't speak for Mrs. Palmer," he said harshly.

"Oh, I reckon she'll do what we want. She loves the girl, don't she?"

That was true. And there was a good chance Margaret would be able to raise that much money, but getting it to Wind River in such a short period of time would be difficult.

"You've got to give us more time than that," Cole said, figuring it wouldn't hurt to try to stall. For one thing, Kermit Sawyer and the Diamond S crew ought to be here before too much longer.

Although for the life of him, he couldn't see right now how the extra guns would help. The gang had picked a good place for the hideout. That valley on the other side of those bluffs seemed to be almost impregnable.

"Forget it," Beaumont snapped in response to the suggestion. "Maguire said dawn, day after tomorrow, and that's what it is. Now, you've got the message, lawdog. Go deliver it."

"If any of you hurt that girl —"

"Don't waste your breath and my time

with threats. There's not a blasted thing you can do, and you know it. We hold all the cards here."

At the moment that was true, Cole thought as he started backing Ulysses away from the gap. But more cards might be dealt before the game was over. He turned the sorrel and rode toward the trees where the posse waited.

The imaginary target on his back seemed even bigger and more tempting than the one he had worn on the way over here.

CHAPTER 12

Lon never looked back as he raced toward Wind River, so he didn't know how close the rest of the boys were behind him. He didn't care, either. All that mattered to him was finding out what happened to Brenda and figuring out some way to help her.

Sure, she was never going to care about him or even pay that much attention to him, but that wasn't important to Lon. He was going to save her, one way or another.

People hurried to get off the boardwalks as he pounded into the settlement, even though he meant them no harm. He supposed they were all spooked by what had happened earlier in the day. He rode straight to the marshal's office. Maybe somebody there could tell him what he needed to know, he thought.

The place was empty, though, except for a prisoner in the cellblock. Lon had never seen the man before, but it made sense the stranger was one of the gang that had raided the town. The man's shirt was off, and he had bandages wrapped tightly around his torso. His eyes widened in fear as Lon rushed into the cellblock.

"Where's the marshal?" Lon demanded. "Has he already gone after the rest of your bunch? You dirty coyote, I oughta —"

Lon put his hand on the butt of his gun.

"Is everybody in this town loco?" the prisoner wailed. "None of this is my fault! I just went along with Maguire's plan!"

"Maguire's the boss of the gang? It was his idea to kidnap Miss Durand?"

"I told the marshal, I don't know anything about the girl —"

A new voice called from the front door of the office, "Lon! Young Rogers! Are you in there?"

Lon recognized Dr. Judson Kent's voice. He started to turn away from the cell where the prisoner was locked up, but then he paused and told the outlaw, "I swear, if anything happens to Miss Durand, you won't get a chance to hang, mister. I'll put a bullet in your head myself!"

Struggling to control his emotions, he stepped into the office and found Dr. Judson Kent standing there looking tired, harassed, and worried.

"I thought I caught a glimpse of you galloping past a few moments ago," Kent said. "Where are Mr. Sawyer and the rest of his men?"

"Behind me somewhere," Lon said. "I came galloping on right away when I heard that Brenda — I mean Miss Durand — had been kidnapped."

"Yes, she was in the bank when the outlaws struck, and evidently their leader decided to take her with them. I'm sorry, Lon. I know you're fond of the young lady."

Lon wondered fleetingly how Kent knew that. Maybe he hadn't been as discreet with his longing looks when Brenda was around as he thought he was.

He shoved that aside and asked, "Has Marshal Tyler already gone after them?"

"Yes, the marshal rode out about an hour ago with a posse. He said for me to tell Mr. Sawyer that the gang's hideout is in an isolated valley in the hills north of the railroad tracks, approximately five miles west of town. He said not to follow the trail that the outlaws left when they rode out, because that was just a ruse to delay pursuit by making everyone think they were headed south. It'll be quicker and more efficient to follow the railroad tracks. I trust that you can pass along this information to your employer?"

"You'll have to tell him yourself when he gets here," Lon snapped as he started toward the door. "I'm not waiting for anybody."

"But how will you find them?" Kent called after him.

Lon paused in the doorway just long enough to look back and say, "Chances are I can just follow the shooting."

An old log cabin sat near the creek that ran through the valley. It looked like it had been abandoned for years. There were no windows, and the door hung crookedly on leather hinges that had rotted from exposure. The roof had a few small holes in it.

"Probably ought to fix that door," Maguire said as he forced Brenda toward the cabin. His fingers were wrapped tightly around her upper arm. He chuckled and went on, "I wasn't counting on having any company. If I'd known somebody like you was going to be staying here, I might have fixed the place up nicer."

Several tents were pitched near the cabin, and a couple of crude lean-tos had been erected in the trees. This was just a temporary camp, not a permanent sanctuary for the gang. They had stayed here long enough for Maguire and Beaumont to scope out the lay of the land in Wind River. Brenda knew from the talk she had overheard among the outlaws that they had planned to come back here and split up the loot from the raid, then scatter for a while to make it more difficult for anyone to trail them. They would get back together later to pull their next job.

Brenda's kidnapping had changed that plan. They would have to stay here until the ransom could be delivered. After that . . .

Brenda didn't want to think too much about what might happen after that.

She hadn't completely given up hope that she might be rescued. She hadn't gotten to know Cole Tyler all that well during her time in Wind River, but she knew the marshal was a stubborn man, and he didn't lack for courage. She was sure he would come after the outlaws.

He wouldn't have Deputy Casebolt to help him, though. The memory of seeing the deputy's blood-soaked form lying on the floor of the bank made a shudder go through Brenda as she stepped into the cabin.

"Hey, now, it's not that bad," Maguire said, misinterpreting what had caused her reaction.

The cabin really was pretty bad, certainly

enough to provoke a shudder from anyone accustomed to more civilized living. Rain had dripped through the holes in the roof and rotted the floor in places. Wild animals had gotten in and made their homes here; the inside of the cabin stunk of their droppings. A thick layer of dust lay over the furnishings, which consisted of a splintery, rough-hewn table, a couple of equally rough chairs that looked like they might collapse if anyone sat on them, and a couple of crates. The only halfway decent thing was the bunk against one wall. A threadbare gray blanket covered its corn-shuck mattress.

"Some old trapper must have built this place, back in what they called the Shining Times," Maguire said. "He probably worked a trap line in that creek. But the beaver eventually ran out and he left. Or maybe the Indians killed him and took his hair. Either way, it was nice of him to leave the place for us."

"You're going to keep me in this rathole?" Brenda asked.

"I've been staying here. It's better than nothing."

She glanced up at the holes in the roof. "Not by much. And I *did* say it was a rathole."

Maguire's face hardened. "Listen, missy,

117

you'd better get it through your head right now that you're not in the Territorial House back in Wind River, and you're sure as hell not in the fancy sort of surroundings you probably came from. You're not in charge here. I am. So you'll do what I tell you and stay where I want you to stay and like it."

Her chin tilted up defiantly as she said, "You can't force a person to like something."

His open hand came up with no warning and cracked across her face. The blow made her stagger back a step and gasp in surprise and pain. She put a hand on the table to steady herself.

"The hell I can't," Maguire grated.

Brenda lifted her other hand to her cheek, which glowed red from the impact of Maguire's slap. "You hit me!" she said.

"And I'll do it again if you keep mouthing off and arguing with me. I'll do worse."

She didn't doubt for a second that he would. But the fierce pride that burned inside her, that had driven her to come west to claim her father's legacy in the first place, wouldn't allow her to back down at first. She continued to glare at the boss outlaw for several long seconds, until Maguire growled and took a menacing step toward her.

Brenda dropped her gaze. She didn't want to, but she knew she didn't have a choice.

"All right," she choked out. "I'll stay here. I won't complain."

"That's right, you won't," he said. "And there'll be a guard outside the door all the time, so don't even think about trying to get away. You'll regret it if you do."

The anger on his face went away, replaced by his usual cocky grin. He moved closer to her and lifted his right hand. She flinched away from it, but all he did this time was brush the back of his hand against her cheek.

"You'll get used to me," he went on. "Who knows, you might even get to where you enjoy spending time with me."

Brenda couldn't force a smile to her lips, even though she tried. Then she thought about how it would feel to watch him kicking out the last seconds of his life at the end of a hang rope. She smiled a little in spite of herself.

"You might be right," she said.

When Cole finished recounting his conversation with Lije Beaumont to the posse, he said to Nathan Smollet, "Do you think Mrs. Palmer can come up with that sort of money? I figure you'd have a better chance of knowing than any of the rest of us."

The banker pursed his lips and frowned in thought. After a moment he said, "I'm not sure, but I believe she could. I'm not privy to all of the lady's financial dealings on her granddaughter's behalf, of course, but I know she's wired a number of deposits back to banks in the east, to accounts in Miss Durand's name. Miss Durand also has interests in businesses elsewhere to go along with everything she owns in Wind River. I'm certain Mrs. Palmer could borrow against them and raise a significant amount of cash, in time." Smollet shook his head. "But not by the day after tomorrow."

"I don't reckon Maguire's really smart enough to know what he's asking," Cole said. "He's cunning, I suppose, or he wouldn't be able to keep that bunch of owl-hoots under control. But he probably thinks rich folks have a ton of money just lying around their houses."

Jeremiah asked, "Why would Miss Durand keep some of her money in other banks when she owns the one in Wind River, Brother Smollet?"

"Because when you keep all your money in one place, it's easier for something bad to happen to all of it," Smollet replied with a faint smile. "Like having a gang of outlaws come in and steal it."

"Oh." Jeremiah nodded. "I reckon that makes sense. But the Lord's blessed me. I'll never have enough money that I have to worry about anything like that."

"I suppose that's one way of looking at it," Cole said. "In the meantime, I need a volunteer to ride back to Wind River and deliver Maguire's demand to Mrs. Palmer. She probably ought to start working on getting the money together, even if she can't do it in the time that Maguire's giving her."

One of the possemen spoke up, saying, "I can do it, Marshal."

He had been looking nervously at the body of the man who had been shot out of the saddle earlier. Cole had stopped and retrieved the body on his way back to the trees, deciding that if the sharpshooters on top of the bluffs hadn't killed him by then, they weren't likely to. The dead man was now stretched out on the ground under the trees. Jeremiah had covered him with a blanket and knelt next to him to offer up a prayer for his soul.

The man who had volunteered to take the message back to town probably wasn't the only one who wanted to cut and run. Cole could tell that several of the others were regretting their decision to come along. He felt a surge of annoyance. Once you'd said that you were going to do something, you damned well ought to stick with it, he thought.

But not everybody felt that way, so he said, "All right, you go ahead and do that, Harry. You can probably find Mrs. Palmer at the Territorial House. If not, I'm sure Dr. Kent will know where she is. And any more of you fellas who want to head back to Wind River are free to go, too."

"But you need us to help you with the outlaws, Brother Cole," Jeremiah protested.

"Nothing's going to happen right away. Sawyer and the rest of those Texans ought to be here soon."

Nathan Smollet said, "We can fight just as well as a bunch of Texans."

Well, that was nowhere near true, Cole thought, but he didn't see any point in hurting the banker's feelings by saying it. "You're welcome to stay, too, and I'll be obliged to those who do. Just letting you know that it's not necessary."

Several of the men shuffled their feet. Cole knew he was losing them, and sure enough they mumbled excuses and then went to get their horses. In the end, four men rode off toward the settlement, leaving Cole with Jeremiah, Smollet, and three other men.

Not enough to fight off that gang of outlaws, but luckily — if you could call anything about this unholy business lucky — the outlaws weren't going anywhere right now.

"So now we wait?" Smollet asked.

"Now we wait," Cole said.

Jeremiah asked, "What do you think are the chances of a couple of men being able to sneak into that hideout once it gets dark tonight?"

"I've been thinking about that," Cole answered honestly. "I reckon it's possible, although it would be a long shot. But the chances of freeing Miss Durand and getting everyone back out alive . . . well, shots don't get any longer than that."

CHAPTER 13

With the wind blowing out of the north, it was chilly under the shade of the juniper trees, but a while later Cole noticed that beads of sweat had broken out on Nathan Smollet's face. The banker used a handkerchief to wipe away the sweat. He fumbled some when he tried to stuff the handkerchief back in his pocket.

Frowning, Cole started to ask Smollet what was wrong. But before he could get the question out, Smollet's eyes rolled up in their sockets and his knees started to unhinge. He would have fallen if Cole hadn't been close enough to spring forward and grab him.

Jeremiah and the other men hurried over as Cole lowered Smollet to the ground. "What happened?" the blacksmith asked.

"Looks like he passed out," Cole said. "There's a canteen on Ulysses's saddle. One of you fetch it for me."

When Cole had the canteen he held Smollet's head up and trickled some water into the man's mouth. Smollet choked a little, but most of the water went down his throat. His eyelids fluttered a few times and then opened.

"Wha . . . what happened to me?" he asked.

"You passed out, Mr. Smollet," Jeremiah said as he leaned over the banker. "You don't remember?"

"I . . . I remember feeling very . . . light-headed all of a sudden. And then . . . nothing until I woke up just now."

"Jeremiah, give me a hand with him," Cole said. "Let's get him sitting up." When they had propped Smollet against a tree, Cole went on, "I'm not too surprised. From what the folks in the bank said, you took quite a wallop from that outlaw, and Doc Kent warned me it might have done some damage."

"My brain is perfectly fine," Smollet said stiffly.

"Maybe so, but you'd better not take any more chances. I think you should head back to town, too." Cole looked at the other possemen. "One of you gents needs to go with him to make sure he gets there all right."

"Blast it, no!" Smollet said. "This . . . this

posse has already dwindled to almost nothing. If you lose two more men —"

"Sawyer's on his way," Cole said, hoping that was actually true. So far he hadn't seen anything of the Texans, and he thought they ought to have shown up by now. "Once that wild bunch gets here, we'll be more than a match for those outlaws. Besides, I've got a hunch an army couldn't get into that valley without losing a lot of men. It's going to take something else besides sheer force to save Miss Durand."

Smollet closed his eyes for a second as he paled. Cole figured he was feeling another wave of dizziness. Smollet didn't pass out this time, though. A moment later when he had recovered some, he said, "I suppose you're right. I should have known I wouldn't be of any use. I'm just not a fighting man."

"I wouldn't be so sure about that," Cole told him. "But it doesn't look like this is gonna be your fight." He looked at the others. "Let's see if we can get him on a horse."

Cole let the men figure out who was going back to Wind River with Smollet. When that was settled, they helped the banker climb into the saddle. Smollet seemed a little steadier now, but Cole knew that probably wouldn't last. Smollet needed rest and possibly even more medical attention from

Judson Kent.

When the two riders were gone, Jeremiah said quietly, "I'm glad you didn't ask me to take Brother Smollet back to town, Marshal."

"I'm not a total fool, Jeremiah," Cole said with a smile. "It's only a matter of time until we have a battle of some sort on our hands again, and I want you here beside me when that happens."

The drumming of rapid hoofbeats caught their attention then. The members of the posse who were left turned to look toward the sound. A rider came into view around a bend in the twisting trail that led up to their camp in the juniper trees and galloped toward them.

"Can you tell who that is?" Jeremiah asked

Something about the rider was familiar, but Cole couldn't identify him just yet. As fast as the horse was going, though, it didn't take long for the man to get close enough for Cole to recognize him.

"It's that Rogers boy from the Diamond S," Cole said. Lon Rogers seemed to be alone, though. Cole wondered where the rest of Sawyer's crew was.

A moment later he realized something else, and Jeremiah was aware of it, too.

"I don't think he's going to stop!" the blacksmith exclaimed.

The part of Lon's brain that could still think sensibly knew that he was on the verge of riding his horse to death, but he couldn't stop, couldn't even slow down. Brenda Durand was somewhere ahead of him and in danger. He had to get to her as fast as he could.

He had barely halted when he ran into the former members of the posse who were on their way back to Wind River, stopping just long enough to get directions to the valley where the outlaws had their hideout. Then he had galloped on and didn't pause when he encountered the banker, Mr. Smollet, and another man. He swept past them without a wave, a nod, or even a glance.

Now a stand of juniper trees loomed at the top of the slope in front of him, and beyond that would be a level bench with a line of bluffs on the far side. Beyond the bluffs was the valley where Brenda's kidnappers had gone.

The same part of his brain that knew he was pushing his horse too hard screamed a warning at him. If he charged across that open flat, obviously intent on reaching the outlaw stronghold, the sharpshooters on the bluffs would cut him down. Dead, he couldn't do Brenda a bit of good. It made sense to slow down and assess the situation.

But the part of him that was filled with love for Brenda and fear for her safety, her very life, didn't listen. That pounding pulsebeat of terror and anger inside his chest drowned out everything else and drove him on.

As he reached the trees, though, he had no choice but to haul back on the reins suddenly. A couple of men had leaped out in front of him, waving their arms for him to stop. For a split-second Lon thought they might be two of the outlaws. That thought sent his hand streaking for the gun on his hip. He stopped his draw, though, when he recognized Marshal Cole Tyler and Jeremiah Newton, Wind River's blacksmith and preacher.

The horse careened to a halt, stumbling a little from exhaustion. Lon glared at Cole and Jeremiah and snapped, "Get out of my way, Marshal."

"You just hold on a minute, Lon," Cole said. "You may not know this, but if you try to ride hell for leather across that bench, you're liable to get shot."

Lon forced himself to control his anger and impatience, or at least try to. He said,

"I know about the outlaws on top of the bluffs. I ran into some of the posse a ways back, and they told me. I don't care. I have to help Miss Durand."

"Getting your head blown off won't help her," Cole said, unknowingly echoing what Lon had thought a short time earlier. "Anyway, I'm not sure your horse can run that far. Poor varmint looks like he's about to collapse."

Lon felt bad about that, too. He loved horses and hated to see them abused. Brenda's safety was more important than any horse, though.

"Listen to the marshal, Brother Lon," Jeremiah urged. "He wants to help Miss Durand just as much as you do."

Lon doubted that — the marshal was courting Rose Foster, everybody knew that — but he was sure Cole wanted to bring the outlaws to justice. With a sigh, Lon nodded. He dismounted and patted his horse's sweat-flecked shoulder.

"Sorry, fella," he muttered. "I appreciate how fast you got me up here."

Cole said, "I reckon if you talked to those men who were on their way back to town, you know the situation."

Lon nodded. "The outlaws have Brenda — I mean Miss Durand — at their hideout

130

in the valley on the other side of those bluffs. They're demanding a big ransom for her."

"That's about the size of it," Cole agreed.

"There's no guarantee that they'll let her go if the ransom is paid, though, is there?"

Cole shook his head. "I hate to say it, but no, there's not. I figure there's a better than even chance they'll kill her anyway, even if they get the money. Or they might keep her with them to use as a hostage while they're trying to get away."

"Those bastards," Lon said. "No-good bastards." He shook his head. "Sorry for the language, Mr. Newton."

"That's all right, Brother Lon," Jeremiah told him. "I completely understand the sentiment."

"What are you planning to do, Marshal?"

Cole answered that question with one of his own. "How far behind you are Kermit Sawyer and the rest of the Diamond S punchers?"

"I don't really know. I left the ranch before they did, as soon as I heard that Miss Durand had been kidnapped. But I think they were about ready to ride out, too, so they should be here before too much longer."

Cole glanced at the sky. "Before nightfall?"

"Unless something happened to them,

yeah, sure."

"All right," Cole said with a nod. "I've got a hunch you're not going to like this, Lon, but for now the plan is to wait."

"You can't do that!" Lon couldn't keep the words from bursting out of him. "You can't just leave Miss Durand over there. She . . . she must be really scared, and maybe she's hurt —"

"Maguire won't hurt her. Right now she's worth too much to him as long as she's safe and sound."

"Maguire?"

"He's the leader of the gang," Cole said. "Adam Maguire. I don't know much about him. He was in town a few days ago, probably getting the lay of the land and planning the raid. He's smart enough to know he'll stand a better chance of collecting that ransom if he takes good care of Miss Durand."

"Unless he's already killed her and he's lying to you about her being all right," Lon said bitterly. "You wouldn't have any way of knowing if that was true, would you?"

Cole glanced over at Jeremiah. He looked like he didn't want to answer Lon's question, but after a couple of seconds he shook his head and said, "No, you're right about that, Lon. I sure wouldn't."

Maguire posted a man outside the cabin door to keep an eye on Brenda Durand and then walked over to the campfire one of the gang had built. They had boiled up some coffee. Maguire poured himself a cup of it and stood there sipping it as he waited for Lije Beaumont to return.

He didn't have to wait long. His keen eyesight spotted Beaumont as the man rode out of the gap. The branch to which the flag of truce was tied rested across the saddle in front of him. Maguire could see the flash of white as the piece of fabric jerked and flapped in the chilly wind.

It took Beaumont about ten minutes to ride across the valley to the outlaw camp. When he got there he dismounted and handed his horse's reins to one of the other men.

"Who did you talk to, Lije?" Maguire asked.

"That damn lawman. Tyler."

"What did he say?"

Beaumont grunted. "What could he say? He was gonna send somebody back to Wind River to let the girl's grandmother know what she's got to do."

"Did he think she would pay?"

"He didn't say she wouldn't," Beaumont said. "He claimed she would need more time to round up that much money, though."

"The more time we give them, the more likely they are to try some sort of trick," Maguire said. "If they're feeling enough pressure, they'll get it done. If they don't . . ." He shrugged. "That would be a real shame for us. It'd be an even bigger one for Miss Durand."

Beaumont gave him a shrewd, speculative look. "Would you really do it?" he asked. "Would you kill her if the grandma don't pay up?"

Maguire smiled. "Think back to the war, Sergeant. Did you ever know me to promise to do something and then back out on it?"

"No, sir, Lieutenant, I never did," Beaumont replied with an ugly chuckle and a shake of his head. "You always done exactly what you said you'd do."

"And nothing has changed, except that we're fighting for ourselves now, not for some damn cause."

Beaumont spat and said, "Once the shootin' starts, nobody's fightin' for a cause anymore. They just fight to stay alive."

That was true, Maguire thought. In the

end, a man's survival was the only cause that really counted.

He turned and started toward the cabin. Beaumont stopped him by asking, "You plannin' on havin' some sport with the gal?"

Maguire heard the hoarse undercurrent of lust in his old friend's voice. Beaumont wanted Brenda Durand, too. In the long run, Maguire didn't really care about that, but he didn't want any other issues to complicate matters now. Getting their hands on that ransom was more important than anything else.

"Not now," Maguire said sharply. "Nobody tries anything with her unless I give the word. Be sure the men understand that."

Beaumont shrugged. "They might not like it."

"As long as they do what I say, I don't care if they like it or not."

"They'll go along with your orders, Adam."

Maguire folded his arms across his chest and smirked. "Yes, I've always inspired loyalty among the men under my command."

"And they know that if they cross you, you'll kill 'em."

"That, too," Maguire said.

CHAPTER 14

Lon had reacted to Cole's suggestion that they wait just about as badly as Cole expected. The young cowboy was angry and impatient and consumed with fear for the girl he had a crush on. Lon was ready to storm the outlaws' stronghold right then and there, although Cole could tell he recognized the futility of that.

Finally, Lon calmed down and stopped ranting and raving and flailing his arms in the air as he stomped around.

"Got that out of your system?" Cole asked.

"Yeah, I guess," Lon replied a little sheepishly.

"Then I reckon you're ready to listen to the rest of the plan. We're going to try to get Miss Durand out of there tonight."

Lon stared at him. "How are you gonna do that? I thought you said there's no way to get into that valley."

"There's no way to get a big posse in

136

there. Two or three men might be able to do it, though."

Lon started to get more animated again, but it was from excitement and eagerness now, not frustration. He said, "I'm gonna be one of them, Marshal. Tell me how we're gonna do it."

Before Cole could start explaining, more hoofbeats drew their attention. A lot more. Cole looked down the slope and saw a large group of riders coming toward them, led by a familiar white-haired figure dressed all in black.

"Let's wait until your boss gets here," he said, "so I'll only have to go over it once."

Cole figured Sawyer and the Diamond S cowboys were still a quarter of a mile away. It took several minutes for them to reach the trees where he and the others waited. As they rode up, Sawyer held up a hand in a signal to stop.

"Lon, next time don't go skalleyhootin' off like that," Sawyer said with a frown. "Ain't no tellin' what you might've run into, and I promised your ma when I brought you off to Wyoming that I'd look after you."

"Beggin' your pardon, Mr. Sawyer, but I don't need lookin' after," Lon said with a frown of his own.

Cole could tell that they'd probably had

this argument before, and he had no interest in it. He said, "Thanks for coming, Sawyer. I can sure use your help."

The cattleman grunted and swung down from the saddle. "That young newspaper fella Hatfield said owlhoots hit the bank and some of the other places in town. I had money in that bank, Tyler. The law's supposed to keep things like that from happenin'."

"If outlaws want something bad enough, there's usually no way to stop them," Cole said. "But we sure as hell don't have to let them get away with it. They kidnapped a young woman, too . . . or don't you care about that?"

"I know they carried off the Durand girl. I'm sorry to hear about it. Hope she's all right. I figure we'll get her back, too, along with the money, when we blast those varmints to perdition."

"Blasting anybody isn't going to be easy," Cole said. "They control the only approach to the valley."

Sawyer snorted. "That just means we got 'em bottled up, don't it? They can't get away."

"As long as they've got Miss Durand, that doesn't matter. But I've got an idea how to go about getting her out of there."

"Let's hear it."

Cole began by explaining what he knew about the terrain, which wasn't as much as he wished it was. Despite the valley's relative proximity to Wind River, nothing had happened during Cole's time as marshal to bring him out here to this spot.

"They'll cut down anybody who approaches the gap during daylight hours," he said, "but they won't be able to see nearly as well once the sun goes down."

Lon had been fidgeting while Cole talked. Now the young cowboy said, "Nightfall is still hours away. We can't leave Miss Durand in there for that long."

"She'll be all right," Cole said, hoping that the declaration didn't sound as hollow to everyone else's ears as it did to his own. As Lon had pointed out, he had no way of knowing that, or if Brenda was even still alive. He continued, "Once it's dark, we ought to be able to get some men on top of those bluffs. If they can take care of the riflemen, then the rest of us might be able to get through the gap."

Jeremiah said, "The rest of the outlaws will still put up a fight, though. And when the shooting starts, they might be more likely to go ahead and kill Miss Durand."

"That's why the shooting can't start until

we've found out where she's being held and have somebody there to protect her."

Cole's plan had developed in his head as he was talking, and he realized now that it had several parts, all of which had to work together for them to have any chance of success.

He held up a finger. "We send a couple of men to infiltrate the valley and locate Miss Durand." Another finger. "They're part of a group that scales the bluffs and kills the sharpshooters, quiet-like so the rest of the gang doesn't know about it." He raised a third finger. "When the fellas down in the valley have found Miss Durand, they signal the ones on the bluff, who signal the rest of the posse. They charge the gap while the men on the bluff strike from the high ground at the defenders inside the passage. When the shooting starts, the two hombres in the valley grab Miss Durand and keep her safe until it's all over."

Cole looked around, waiting to hear the reaction from the other men.

"You make it sound like a military mission," Sawyer said.

"That's about what it amounts to. We'll be hitting them in three places at once, and it all has to happen at the same time."

Lon said, "I'm one of the men going into

the valley to find Miss Durand."

Cole shrugged. "I reckon that'll be all right as long as you do what I tell you, because I'll be the other one."

"What about the men who go after the sharpshooters?" Frenchy LeDoux asked.

"I figured you'd be a good man to ramrod that chore," Cole said. "You can pick three or four men to go with you."

"Hold on here," Sawyer growled. "What about me?"

"You'll be in charge of the bunch that hits the gap from the front," Cole told him.

Sawyer nodded as if satisfied with that, but then he pointed a finger at Lon. "I'm not sure you're doin' the right thing by takin' this young colt with you, though. You're talkin' about goin' right into the heart of that bad bunch. You'd do better takin' Frenchy with you. That Cajun's got more bark on him."

"I can handle the job, Mr. Sawyer," Lon said tightly. Clearly, he was angry with his boss, but he was keeping his temper reined in.

Cole shook his head and said, "I'd rather have LeDoux take care of those sharpshooters. As long as they're up there, we don't stand a chance."

"Lon will be all right, boss," Frenchy said.

"He's not the same wrangler and chuck wagon helper that he was when we came up here. He's grown up an awful lot in the past couple of years."

"All right," Sawyer said with grudging acceptance. He glared at Cole. "But don't you get that boy killed. His mama down in Texas would never forgive me."

Cole said, "I'm hoping that the only ones killed tonight are from the bunch that raided Wind River."

But inside him lay the grim certainty that that probably wouldn't be the case.

The afternoon was a long one, made to seem even longer by Lon's impatience and the all-consuming fear he felt for Brenda. Frenchy tried to get him to eat, and finally he gave in to the foreman's urging and gnawed on a strip of jerky and a biscuit from the provisions that the cowboys had brought along. They boiled up a pot of coffee, too, and Lon sipped from a tin cup of the strong, black brew. Despite the worries that plagued him, he had to admit that he felt a little better after he'd had the food and drink.

While Lon was standing under the trees with Sawyer and Frenchy, Cole came over to them and asked the cattleman, "When you passed through town, did you happen to hear anything about how Billy Casebolt is doing?"

"Doc Kent's the one who told us what was going on and sent us on out here," Sawyer replied. "He said you might ask about that deputy of yours. Casebolt was still alive when we were there. The doc said he hadn't come to yet. Gonna be touch and go for a few days, until Kent can tell if the deputy's strong enough to get over bein' shot."

Cole nodded and said, "Thanks for telling me that, Sawyer. I reckon I'll take all the good news I can get, and right now Billy still being alive is good news."

French said, "That old-timer is tough as whang leather, Marshal. He'll pull through."

"I hope you're right." Cole's voice and expression were grim as he added, "Either way, I'll take particular pleasure in settling the score with that fella Maguire, no matter how it plays out."

The sun seemed to crawl toward the western horizon, but finally that blazing orb touched it and began to dip below the dark line of the earth. Shadows slipped over the landscape.

"You've got your men picked out to go with us?" Cole asked Frenchy.

"Yeah," the foreman replied. "You said we

needed to take care of those sharpshooters without makin' a bunch of racket, so I picked men who I know are good with a knife."

Cole smiled. "That's exactly what we need, all right. I figured you'd see it the same way, LeDoux."

"How long do we wait?" Lon asked.

"Until it's good and dark, but no later. They're probably expecting us to try something, but they might not be looking for it until later in the night. We'll try to cross them up by hitting them pretty soon."

"Can't be soon enough to suit me," Lon muttered.

The men who would go after the sharpshooters and infiltrate the valley would have to cross the flat on foot, because the sound of hoofbeats would carry to the men in the gap and on top of the bluffs. They were armed with revolvers and knives and had rigged slings so they could carry rifles on their backs as they climbed, because if things went as planned, the shooting wouldn't come until later. Cole went around and checked with everyone in the party, nodding in satisfaction when he saw that they were ready.

He and Lon wouldn't take rifles along. Chances were, any gun work they did would be at close range. Each of them carried two Colts, one holstered and the other stuck behind the gunbelt. They would be able to do a lot of damage in a hurry if they needed to.

The wind picked up after dark, and the chill that had lurked in it all day fulfilled its promise, and it became downright cold. Lon didn't really feel it, though. The heat of the emotions burning inside him kept him warm through and through.

Cole finished another cup of coffee and cast the dregs aside with a flick of his wrist. He handed the empty cup to one of Sawyer's men and said, "I reckon it's about time to go."

Lon looked up through the trees at the sky. Stars twinkled here and there in the blackness, but some clouds were moving in and the moon wasn't up yet. Even when it rose, it would be only a thin crescent at this time of the month. The night was good and dark, just the way they needed it.

Sawyer came over to Lon and rested a hand on his shoulder. "I wasn't jokin' about your ma," the cattleman said. "She'll have my hide if anything happens to you, son." Sawyer's grip tightened. "It wouldn't do any good to ask you to let somebody else do this, would it?"

"No, sir," Lon said without hesitation. "Not a bit."

"I didn't think so. You're a Texan through and through, which means you're just about the stubbornest critter on the face of the earth. You be careful up there, Lon."

"I'll try," he promised. "But rescuing Miss Durand comes first."

"You know that gal don't give a flip about you, don't you?"

"That doesn't matter," Lon replied with a shake of his head.

"No, I don't suppose it would." Sawyer let go of Lon's shoulder and patted him on the back. There was nothing left to say.

One of the Diamond S hands went to put out the fire, but Cole stopped him. "Leave it burning," the marshal said. "That makes it look more like we're settled down here for the night. The rest of you move around a lot so they can see your shadows. I want those varmints up on the bluff to have something to look at while we're sneaking up on them." He turned to Sawyer. "You remember the signal?"

"Damn right I remember it," Sawyer snapped. "You figure I'm gettin' forgetful in my old age, Tyler?"

"Just making sure," Cole said with a smile.

"When we see three lights on the bluff,

we'll charge that gap like ol' Sam Houston goin' after Santa Anna at San Jacinto."

"Good enough," Cole said. He shook hands with the rancher and motioned for the men who were going with him to follow him.

He left the trees on the side away from the bluffs. Lon was right beside him, with Frenchy and the other men walking behind them. With the slope to conceal them and the darkness all around them, Lon knew that the sharpshooters wouldn't be able to see them leaving.

Cole angled to the right and led the group about a quarter of a mile before he turned back to the bench that fronted the bluffs. "Stay low," he told the other men. "We're far enough away right now that they shouldn't be able to hear us, but move as quiet as you can anyway."

"We've all fought Comanches," Lon said. "Nobody moves any quieter than they do."

"I hope you learned from them, then," Cole said. He loped out onto the flat, angling back toward the spot where the gap cut through the bluffs.

There were sharpshooters on both sides of that gap, so they had already figured that Frenchy's force would have to split up. Two men would climb each bluff, not counting

Cole and Lon. They would try to eliminate any of the outlaws they encountered, but their real goal was to make it over the bluffs into the valley.

Lon knew the seriousness of the task that faced him. He knew there was a very real chance he would be killed tonight. If he survived, likely that would be because he killed some of the outlaws. He was prepared for that eventuality.

He was willing to run the risk either way if it meant freeing Brenda Durand. As he hurried through the darkness, Lon offered up a silent prayer that she was still all right.

CHAPTER 15

Brenda was thankful that none of the men had bothered her during the long afternoon, and she didn't want to feel that way. She didn't want to experience the least little bit of anything that could be mistaken for gratitude to them.

She wanted to burn with hatred and the need for revenge on them. So far, that wasn't too difficult.

Since the door was barely hanging on its rotten hinges and wouldn't keep anybody inside, the outlaws had posted at least one man outside the cabin to guard her at all times. As the daylight faded into dusk and its inevitable slide into evening, the big man in the derby hat took his turn.

Brenda had been waiting for him to show up. During the ride here she had seen him watching her often enough, with interest and undisguised desire in eyes set deep under bristling brows. She heard the rumble of his deep voice as he talked to the man whose place he was taking, and she caught a glimpse of him through the gap where the door hung crookedly, wedged into place.

She had been sitting on the bunk for the past few hours, trying not to think about the fact that Maguire slept there . . . and asking herself whether or not he intended to tonight. When she realized who was standing guard now, she stood up and went over to the door.

"Hello?" she said through the opening.

"You need something?" the guard asked her.

"I . . . I could use some water."

He laughed. "I know Maguire left you two canteens in there. You're trying to trick me, aren't you?"

"No, not at all. I wouldn't do that," Brenda insisted.

"Sure you wouldn't." He laughed. "I reckon you'd do just about anything to get away from us uncivilized brutes and ruffians, wouldn't you?"

She was surprised at the tone of self-deprecating humor in his voice. Something about it told her he had some education. She hadn't expected that in this bunch of wild desperadoes.

"I know what you're thinking," he went

on, and sure enough he did, proving it by continuing, "You probably figured I couldn't muster up anything more than an inarticulate growl, like some sort of Neanderthal."

"I . . . I didn't think anything of the sort," Brenda protested.

"Sure you did. But I'm not offended. It serves my purposes to have people feel that way. Makes 'em more scared of me, you know, since I'm such a big hombre and that's all they expect, anyway." He paused. "Now, did you really want anything?"

"I could use something to eat."

"The boss said he'd have somebody bring you food later."

"Oh. All right." For a moment, Brenda felt defeated. But her pride still wouldn't allow her to give in to despair, so she went on, "What's your name?"

"My name?"

"It's a simple question," she said a bit tartly.

He laughed again and said, "So it is. Cornelius. Cornelius Van Houten, of the upstate New York Van Houtens. Old Hudson River Dutch, you know."

Brenda couldn't stop herself from laughing. "I'm from Baltimore," she told him. "How did two people like us find ourselves in the wilds of Wyoming Territory, Cornelius Van Houten?"

"I don't know, miss. Just lucky, I suppose."

"If you can call it luck . . . Is he going to kill me, Mr. Van Houten? That man Maguire, I mean."

"Not if your grandmother pays the ransom for you, he won't."

"But what if she doesn't? What if she can't?"

Van Houten didn't answer. Brenda heard the scuff of his boots on the ground as he shifted around on the other side of the door. The man's silence and his uneasiness provided all the answer Brenda needed.

"He's not going to let me go even if he gets the ransom, is he?" she asked in a half-whisper.

"I don't know anything about that," Van Houten said. "Maguire doesn't share his intentions with me or anybody else, unless it's Lije Beaumont."

"That's all right," Brenda said. She went back over to the bunk and threw herself down on it. The inside of the cabin grew dark around her. She knew now that her fate was sealed. She was doomed.

Unless someone showed up to help her, and she didn't hold out much hope for that.

■ ■ ■ ■

Cole couldn't remember how many times he had snuck up on enemy camps during the war and then later when he was working for the army out here on the frontier, battling against the Sioux, the Cheyenne, and the Pawnee.

And now he was doing it again, only this time the enemy was Adam Maguire's gang of outlaws. Cole had always had some respect for the Indians. They were fighting for what they considered to be their land and their way of life, but these bandits were just bloodthirsty killers who wanted to get rich without having to work for it.

When Cole and the five men with him reached the base of the bluff, he put a hand on Frenchy LeDoux's arm and leaned close to his ear to say, "I want you and another man to take the bluff on that side of the gap. You'll have to get down on your bellies and crawl across the opening, otherwise any guards inside the passage might see you silhouetted against the fire down there in the trees."

"I don't much like imitatin' a snake," Frenchy said, "but I reckon there's a good reason for it."

"When you get to the top you'll be on your own. You'll have to scout around, find out how many men are up there and where they are."

"I know what to do, Marshal. You just watch out for Lon if you can. That jug-eared, bone-headed varmint is sort of like a little brother to me now."

Lon whispered, "I'm right here, you know. I can hear what you're saying."

Frenchy chuckled. "Reckon I must've forgot."

Cole patted him on the shoulder and said, "Good luck."

"To you, too, Marshal."

The group split up. Frenchy and the man who was going with him dropped to their knees and then their bellies to crawl across the open space in front of the gap between the bluffs.

Cole, Lon, and the other two Diamond S punchers started up the bluff on their side. It was too steep for a man to walk up, but in most places he could climb on all fours, being careful to test each handhold and foothold before resting too much weight on it.

The bluff was a couple of hundred feet tall. In daylight, it wouldn't have taken too long for an active man to climb it. At night, especially a dark night such as this one where they had to feel their way along, it took what seemed to Cole like a long time for him and his companions to make the ascent. Here and there, sheer rock faces jutted out from the slope, which meant the climbers had to find a way around them. That slowed them down even more.

Despite the cold night, sweat slicked Cole's face and trickled along his sides under the buckskin shirt. That was a result of the effort it took to scale the bluff and also the knowledge that he and the others were climbing right into bad odds. Cole had confidence in the men with him, but he also knew they would need a lot of luck to make it through this deadly night.

Finally he pulled himself over the crest and stretched out on top of the bluff. Lon crawled up beside him, followed by the other two punchers.

Cole lay there for a moment, catching his breath, and then lifted his head to listen intently. He had worried they would climb right up into the lap of one of those sharpshooters, but that hadn't happened. The top of the bluff was relatively level and covered with grass. Dark shapes here and there marked the locations of trees, bushes, and boulders.

A muffled sound that Cole recognized as a cough came from somewhere to his right. A moment later, even though he hadn't seen a match flare, he caught a whiff of tobacco smoke. One of the outlaws had just fired up a quirley.

Cole touched one of the punchers on the shoulder and pointed. The man nodded in understanding. He and the other Diamond S hand started crawling toward the sound of the cough.

Crawling on their bellies, Cole and Lon headed for the other side of the bluff. Disposing of the sharpshooters was up to the other men now. The two of them had to get down into the valley as quickly as they could without giving away their presence.

When they were a hundred yards or so from the edge, Cole risked coming up on hands and knees. Lon did likewise. They could move a little faster that way, and they reached the other slope fairly quickly.

Cole had hoped that climbing down on this side would be easier, but that didn't prove to be the case. The slope fell away sharply into a black void.

Farther out, that darkness was relieved in places by the flickering glow of a couple of cooking fires and the steadier illumination of several lanterns. Those lights marked the site of the outlaw camp, Cole knew.

Lon must have figured that out, too, because Cole heard a sharp breath hiss between the young cowboy's clenched teeth. Lon was probably thinking about how Brenda Durand was a prisoner down there, somewhere around those lights, close enough that he might have been able to see her if it was daytime. Cole gripped his shoulder for a second to reassure him, then motioned that they should start climbing down the bluff.

If anything, the slope was steeper on this side and the climb down more harrowing than the climb up. Cole and Lon turned around to face the rocky surface and slowly descended.

Lon's feet slipped once, and he had to make a desperate grab for the roots of a bush that stuck out of the ground. For a second they were all that kept him from a nasty fall until Cole could reach over and take hold of his arm. With that extra support, Lon was able to find footholds again.

"Sorry," he whispered.

"I'm just glad you didn't fall and bust your neck. Come on."

As they worked their way down toward the valley below, Cole listened for telltale sounds of a struggle from above. The last thing he wanted to hear was a shot. That would alert the outlaws that something was going on and make the chances of this rescue mission succeeding a lot worse.

The night was quiet, though, and Cole was thankful for that.

Anybody who was dying up there on the bluff was doing it silently.

At last they reached level ground. Again they paused to rest, but only for a moment. Cole knew that Lon wouldn't stand for any longer delay than that. The youngster was too worried about what might be happening to Brenda.

So was Cole, to tell the truth. He thought the outlaws would keep her safe for the moment, but you never could tell about varmints like that.

They were liable to do anything.

Despite what she had told Cornelius Van Houten earlier about wanting something to eat, Brenda really wasn't hungry. Maguire himself brought her a tin plate of food, though, and she was too afraid of him not to eat it, although she tried not to let him see her fear.

It was crude fare: bacon fried almost to a black husk, beans, and a stale biscuit that had probably been baked several days earlier. As Maguire handed the plate to her, he said, "I know the food's not as fancy as what you're used to and this isn't fine china, but it's the best we've got right now. You want a cup of coffee to go with it?"

"I don't suppose you have any brandy," Brenda said coolly. "Perhaps some sherry?"

Maguire threw back his head and laughed. "Not hardly!"

"I'll take the coffee, then."

Maguire stepped over to the door and told Van Houten, "Corny, go get some Arbuckle's for the lady."

The boss outlaw had brought a lantern with him, which now sat on the table and filled the room with a smoky, inconstant glow. It was better than the darkness, Brenda thought. Earlier she had heard things rustling around in here with her, or at least she thought she did, and the terrors her mind conjured up were probably worse than the reality. She knew that, but she liked being able to see anyway.

When Van Houten came back with a cup of coffee that he handed through the door to Maguire, Brenda caught the big man's eye and said, "Thank you."

Van Houten smiled. "You're welcome, miss."

"You didn't thank me for bringing your

food," Maguire pointed out.

Brenda didn't say anything. She took another bite of bacon, gnawed on it, and washed it down with a sip of the bitter brew in the tin cup Maguire gave her.

Maguire sat down at the table and rested his arms on it. "You know, you could be a little friendlier," he said.

"I find it difficult to be friends with someone who has kidnapped me."

"You could have been treated a lot worse so far, I promise you. You ought to appreciate how we've handled you with kid gloves."

She stared at him in disbelief, so angry that she couldn't say anything for a moment. Then she told him, "When I woke up this morning, I was in my own bed in my suite at the hotel, living a normal life. Since then I've seen men gunned down in front of me, been thrown on a horse and forced to ride for hours, then shoved into this hovel like I was no better than a slave! I've been threatened repeatedly with death — or worse. And you say I should appreciate the way I've been treated?" She laughed coldly. "We obviously have a much different perspective on things, Mr. Maguire."

He stood up and glared at her. "Eat your supper," he snapped. "Out here on the frontier, you never know when a meal might be your last one."

With that he turned and stalked out of the cabin, slapping the door aside so roughly that Brenda thought it might finish the job of falling down. The old leather hinges held, though.

At least he had left the lantern behind. Brenda was grateful for that.

Van Houten looked in through the open door and said, "It's probably not wise to sass him like that."

"I'm not afraid of him," she declared boldly, which was an absolute lie, of course. "Are you?"

"There's a difference between fear and discretion."

Brenda tossed her hair and scoffed. "Is there?"

"I'm not afraid of Maguire," Van Houten insisted.

"I see," she said, but her tone made it clear she wasn't convinced.

"Maybe you will," Van Houten said. He stepped back and shoved the door closed, as much as it would go in its ramshackle condition.

Brenda sighed. She had planted some seeds. Now if Maguire tried to hurt her and Cornelius Van Houten was around, the big man might feel like he had to prove his courage by stepping in and stopping Maguire. That could work to Brenda's advantage.

She finished the food, turned down the wick on the lantern until it cast only a feeble glow, and stretched out on the bunk to rest. She knew she was too scared, angry, and upset to sleep, but the long ride had left her with stiff, aching muscles and an undeniable feeling of weariness.

Despite what she thought, exhaustion proved to be too much for her. Without even being aware of it, she quickly drifted into a deep, dreamless sleep.

CHAPTER 16

Most of the vegetation in the valley was confined to a strip that ran a couple of hundred yards on either side of the creek, so the landscape through which Cole and Lon traveled at first was mostly rocky and barren. It still provided cover, though, in the form of boulders that littered the ground and fissures in the earth.

They had to slide into one of those fissures and hold their breaths at one point as several riders passed close to them. Cole figured the men were on their way to the gap to relieve the outlaws posted there. Either that, or they were going to replace the sharpshooters on top of the bluffs.

When the men had ridden on, Lon said quietly and urgently, "We don't have much time, Marshal. If they find Frenchy and those other fellas up there, they'll start shooting."

"I know," Cole replied. "We're not far

from their camp, though. We'll be there soon."

Indeed, the smell of woodsmoke from the campfires was pretty strong now as the north wind carried it toward them. Cole and Lon resumed their stealthy journey, and a few minutes later they began slipping through the brush that had grown up near the creek.

The sound of voices drifted to Cole's ears. He had hoped that all the outlaws would be asleep except for one or two guards, but that didn't seem to be the case. Crouching low so they wouldn't be spotted, they moved closer until Cole was able to carefully part the branches of a bush and peer through the gap at the camp.

All the fires except one had burned down to embers. Around the one that was still blazing, four men sat playing cards, using a blanket spread on the ground for a table. Loud snores came from the tents and lean-tos, confirming that some of the outlaws had turned in for the night.

Cole looked past the fire and saw the old cabin about fifty yards away. That seemed to be the most likely place for Brenda to be held. A light of some sort burned inside the cabin, casting enough of a glow for Cole to see that the door hung crookedly on its hinges. It probably couldn't be fastened securely, which explained the presence of the guard sitting on a stool just outside the door. The man held a rifle across his knees.

A familiar laugh came from one of the card players. Adam Maguire said, "Looks like this pot is mine."

"You're lucky, Adam," Lije Beaumont said with a surly note in his voice. He sounded like a man who had been losing regularly all evening.

"Luck's got nothing to do with it," Maguire boasted. "They may call poker a game of chance, but it's all skill, amigo, all skill."

"Sure, sure." Beaumont fished a long black cigarillo from his vest pocket and lifted a burning twig from the fire to light it. "If we hadn't been partners for so long, I might be a little offended by the way you've taken so much money from me tonight. Hell, we just stole it today, and you've already got damn near half my share in your pile!"

"That's the way the cards have been running," Maguire said. A steely edge had come into his voice. "You wouldn't be accusing me of anything, would you, Lije?"

"Me? Hell, no," Beaumont replied with a shake of his head. "Anyway, I know the day'll come when the cards favor me more.

165

Everything evens out in the end, don't it, especially when you're partners like us. Share and share alike, right?" Beaumont tipped his head back and blew a cloud of cigar smoke into the air. "Even things like that little gal's favors."

Cole had had a suspicion where the conversation was going. He was ready to clamp his hand around Lon's arm and remind the young cowboy that they couldn't afford to reveal themselves. He felt the trembling in Lon's muscles and knew that Lon wanted to burst out of the brush with guns in both hands and put those pistols to work.

Instead, Lon just took a deep breath and brought himself under control.

Over by the fire, Maguire said, "Don't push it, Lije. You know good and well that if you just stick with me, everything will work out and you'll get everything you want, sooner or later."

"Better not be too much later," Beaumont growled around the cigar.

Maguire's voice was light and cheerful again as he said, "That's enough talk. Somebody deal the cards. Here, Bob, give me that deck. I won the last hand."

Maguire shuffed and resumed dealing as Cole and Lon pulled back silently. When they were far enough away for a whisper to be safe, Cole asked, "Did you get a good look at the layout?"

"Yeah," Lon replied. "Brenda must be in that cabin, otherwise they wouldn't be standin' guard over it."

"That's my thinking, too," Cole said.

"I didn't see any way to get in, though. The place didn't look like it had any windows in it, just the door."

"We can't be sure of that until we take a look at the back, but you're probably right. That's on old trapper's cabin, and those fellas didn't care about windows." Cole paused as he thought for a second. "That doesn't mean the door is the only way in, though."

"How else —"

"Did you notice the roof?"

A puzzled silence came from Lon for a couple of seconds before he said, "Well, not really. I know the cabin has a roof on it —"

"And I saw light coming through it, too," Cole said, "which likely means there are some places where it's rotted out and fallen in. Some of those holes might be big enough for a man to get through."

Lon's tone was excited now as he asked, "Do you think we could get Brenda out that way?"

"Not without making enough noise to alert the guard. But if he was distracted, which he ought to be once the shooting starts, we could jump him from inside the cabin and take him by surprise."

"It sounds like it might work," Lon whispered. "What do we do next?"

"We need to get around behind that cabin."

The two of them spent the next fifteen minutes doing that, moving carefully and using all the cover they could so they wouldn't be seen. When they reached a spot where they could observe the back of the cabin, Cole saw that his hunch was right in both respects. The ramshackle building didn't have any windows, but light from inside seeped through a ragged opening in the roof.

"Why didn't Brenda climb out and try to get away?" Lon asked.

"She probably can't reach that hole from inside. Even if she could, she might not be strong enough to pull herself up through it."

"Probably not," Lon agreed. "We can boost her up, though."

"We shouldn't have to. If we can get rid of that guard, we can go out the door." Cole gestured toward the roof. "Right now we've got to get up there."

They cat-footed to the rear wall of the

cabin. Using hand signals, Cole indicated that he would boost Lon up, and then in turn Lon could help him. Cole bent over and made a stirrup out of his hands.

The rough logs with crude mud chinking in between provided plenty of little gaps for handholds. Lon dug his fingers into the narrow openings, put a booted foot in the makeshift stirrup of Cole's hands, and lifted himself. Cole clenched his jaw to keep from letting out a grunt of effort as he supported the young cowboy's weight.

Lon reached higher with one hand and shifted some of the burden from Cole. He wedged the toe of his other boot into a gap and took even more of the weight on it. When he reached up again he was able to grasp the edge of the roof, since the cabin wasn't particularly tall.

Lon didn't make much noise as he scrambled onto the roof, but it was enough to make Cole wince and hope that no one else heard it, even Brenda. If she had, she might take it for a wild animal or something like that and be afraid enough to raise an alarm. That would ruin everything.

Cole didn't hear anything but continued silence from inside the cabin, though. After a moment, Lon extended a hand down to him.

Cole had to climb a couple of feet before he could reach up and clasp wrists with Lon. After that it took only seconds for him to make it to the roof, too. Both men stretched out on the rough wooden shakes that served as shingles. Cole hoped fervently that no other sections of the roof were on the verge of collapsing. If he or Lon, or both of them, fell through, that could ruin the plan, too.

They climbed high enough on the sloping roof so that Cole could see the bluffs looming black against the stars. Frenchy was supposed to be up there watching for the signal, which he would relay in turn to Kermit Sawyer and launch the attack.

Cole had several matches in his shirt pocket. He took out one of them, snapped it to life with his fingernail, and held it over his head, moving it back and forth in a steady motion. When it burned down, he lit a second match and did the same with it.

If everything went according to plan, that would send Frenchy hurrying to the other side of the bluff to send his own signal.

Lon's breath hissed between his teeth. Cole heard that and looked over to see the young cowboy peering down through the hole in the roof. Cole crawled over to join him.

From where they were, they couldn't see Brenda, but Cole heard deep, steady breathing that told him she was asleep, probably in a bunk against the rear wall. Cole tested the wood around the collapsed place to see if it was strong enough to support a man's weight as he hung from it and dropped through the hole. He thought it was, although it sagged a bit.

As soon as the shooting started, they would make their move. Cole put his mouth against Lon's ear and breathed, "You go through the roof. I'll slide down the front side and drop on top of the guard. Be ready to give me a hand if I need you to."

Lon nodded. Now all they had to do was wait.

Seconds stretched out into long, tense minutes. Cole wondered when the attack would come. What if Frenchy hadn't seen the signal, he asked himself? What if the Diamond S foreman wasn't even still alive? He and Lon could be waiting for a distraction that would never come.

When something happened it wasn't what he was expecting. At the front of the cabin, a man said, "Step aside, Stafford. I'll take over for you."

The guard replied, "I'm supposed to stand guard over the girl for another hour, Lije.

That's what Maguire said, anyway."

"I don't give a damn what Maguire said." Lije Beaumont's voice was thick and slurred. He'd been drinking while he was playing cards, from the sound of it. "I'm goin' in to see that girl. Her and me got to get better acquainted."

"Maguire won't like —"

"By God, didn't I tell you I don't give a damn about Maguire!" Cole heard the unmistakable menacing sound of a gun being cocked. "Now get out of here."

"All right, but I ain't to blame for this," the guard said with a whining note in his voice.

"Just keep your mouth shut and go get some sleep," Beaumont snapped.

Cole could tell how tense Lon had become beside him. Both of them had heard the conversation clearly, and they knew what it meant. Beaumont was drunk enough to defy Maguire's orders that Brenda be left alone.

Just like that, the two men on the roof had run out of time.

CHAPTER 17

Loud, angry voices woke Brenda. A wave of instinctive fear went through her as she sat up on the bunk and pushed her dark hair out of her face. Whatever the men were arguing about out there, she knew somehow that it didn't bode well for her.

That feeling strengthened when someone jerked the door open, dragging one corner of it in the dirt because it hung crookedly. The man called Beaumont loomed in the doorway, the obvious winner in the argument. An ugly grin that was more of a leer spread across his face.

"Well, now," he said in a gloating tone, "look what we got here. It's time you and me get to know each other better, girl."

Brenda cringed back against the wall behind her. "You . . . you shouldn't be in here," she told Beaumont. "Maguire said —"

"Everybody's so damned worried about

what Maguire says!" Beaumont exploded. "Well, I'm not. I do what I please, and if Adam Maguire don't like it, he can just go to hell!"

He moved another step into the cabin, then another and another. His right hand came up and stretched out toward the terrified young woman on the bunk.

A faint, sudden noise made Brenda look up. She saw movement as something dropped through a hole in the roof.

No, not something. Someone. The man landed on Lije Beaumont's back and his weight knocked Beaumont to his knees. Amazed, Brenda realized that the man who had just tackled Beaumont was Lon Rogers, the young cowboy from the Diamond S.

Lon halfway expected Cole to try to stop him again, but it didn't happen this time.

Just as well, because Lon wasn't going to let anything keep him from helping Brenda. He would have fought his way through a pack of wildcats to get to her.

It felt almost like he had tackled a pack of wildcats as he tried to keep the man called Beaumont pinned to the floor. Beaumont twisted around and hammered a fist at him. Lon jerked his head aside so Beaumont's fist landed in a glancing blow, but it was still powerful enough to drive Lon to the side. That gave Beaumont enough room to buck his body off the floor and throw Lon off of him.

Lon rolled over and caught himself as Beaumont clawed out the revolver holstered on his hip. Lon snapped a kick at the outlaw. His bootheel caught Beaumont on the wrist as the man tried to swing the gun around. The weapon flew from his fingers and clattered across the floor.

Lon still didn't hear any shots coming from outside, so he left his own guns where they were and launched himself at Beaumont. The longer it was before the alarm was raised, the better. Beaumont was trying to get up, but Lon rammed into him and drove him over backward. Lon reached for Beaumont's throat and managed to get his fingers clamped around it.

Beaumont hooked a punch into Lon's midsection. It was like the kick of a mule. Lon wanted to let go and curl up around the pain, but he forced himself to hang on and dig in harder with his thumbs as he tried to crush Beaumont's windpipe.

The outlaw clubbed his fists against Lon's ears. He couldn't shrug off these blows. They made him jerk back. His grip on Beaumont's throat slipped. Beaumont shot up a short punch that caught Lon on the jaw and made his vision spin.

For a moment Lon was helpless as Beaumont shoved him aside and surged to his feet. Beaumont was ready to stomp Lon to death and might have done it, too, if not for Brenda, who darted behind him and swung a tin plate in both hands, smashing it into the back of Beaumont's head with a resounding clang.

Probably more surprised by the blow than actually hurt by it, Beaumont stumbled forward. That brought him within reach of Lon, whose head was clearing. Lon threw his arms around Beaumont's knees and heaved. The outlaw went over backward. As he fell, his head struck the old table.

Beaumont landed in a limp, motionless sprawl. Breathless, Lon scrambled to his feet and looked down at the man. Beaumont was still breathing, but hitting his head like that had knocked him cold.

Before Lon had a chance to think about how lucky he had been, Brenda was in his arms, clinging desperately to him and sobbing. Instinctively, Lon embraced her and said, "It's all right, it's all right."

He didn't know if that was true, though, because at that moment gunfire finally erupted in the night.

■ ■ ■ ■

A short time earlier, Frenchy LeDoux had seen the signal from Marshal Tyler down in the valley. Frenchy's upper left arm had his bandanna tied around it to stanch the blood from a deep cut he had suffered while struggling with one of the sharpshooters. The outlaw had managed to take Frenchy's knife away from him and cut him, but that advantage was short-lived. Frenchy had grabbed the man's wrist and twisted it so that the blade plunged into the sharpshooter's stomach.

Similar struggles had taken place along the bluff on both sides of the gap. One of the Diamond S cowboys had died, but not before inflicting a mortal wound on his opponent. Four sharpshooters had been posted up here to guard the approach to the passage, and now all four of them were dead.

And Cole's signal meant that he and Lon had found Brenda Durand.

Time to put the rest of the plan into operation, Frenchy thought as he turned and hurried across the top of the bluff.

When he reached the other edge, he took out a tin of matches and lit three of them, one after the other, waving them over his head so that Kermit Sawyer couldn't miss seeing them. When the last match had burned down, Frenchy dropped it and unslung the rifle from his back.

His friends on the other side of the gap would have been watching for the signal, too. Frenchy knew they would be in position. He reached the rim where he could look down into the pitch-dark passage and dropped to one knee to wait.

The next move was up to Sawyer. He and the rest of the Texans would charge the gap, shooting as they came, to draw the fire of the defenders. Those muzzle flashes would give away the outlaws' positions, so Frenchy and his companions could pick them off from above. That would open the passage so Sawyer and his men could ride into the valley and finish mopping up the gang.

That was the plan, anyway, but when shots suddenly roared in the darkness, they didn't come from the Texans. Frenchy's head jerked to the right as he heard gunfire in the valley itself, which meant that Lon and Cole must have been discovered.

And from the sound of it, they were fighting for their lives.

Cole knew what Lon Rogers was going to do even before the young cowboy did it.

Lon loved Brenda Durand, whether she returned that feeling or not, and if that had been a woman Cole loved down there, about to be assaulted by Lije Beaumont, he would have done the same thing.

So when Lon dropped through the hole in the roof onto Beaumont's back, Cole let him go and knew there was no point in waiting any longer. He scrambled up to the roof peak and half-ran, half-slid down the other side. The guard Beaumont had told to leave had gone only a few feet when the ruckus broke out inside the cabin. The man wheeled around and reached for his gun when he heard the commotion.

Cole sailed into the air from the roof's edge.

He crashed into the outlaw. Both of them went down hard, but Cole was on top, so the other man's body broke his fall to a certain extent. The impact still knocked the breath out of him for a moment.

He recovered before the other man did and slammed a fist into the outlaw's face. Cole tried to get up, but the man shook off the effects of the blow and grabbed the front of his buckskin shirt. He pulled Cole down and butted him in the face.

Half-stunned, Cole felt himself thrown aside. He rolled and came up on one knee.

That was instinctive on his part, but as he shook his head it cleared enough for him to realize his danger. Enough light spilled through the open door of the cabin for Cole to see the guard's gun rising to line up on him.

Stealth wasn't important anymore. Cole dived forward onto his belly and palmed out his own revolver as the outlaw fired. The bullet whipped over Cole's head, hit something, and whined off into the darkness. The next instant, the .44 in Cole's fist roared and bucked.

The bullet struck the man in the body and twisted him around, but he didn't go down. He fired again, the slug kicking up dirt a short distance to Cole's left. Cole thumbed off another round. This time the bullet ripped into the outlaw's throat and drove him over backward as blood sprayed from the wound. Cole knew he wouldn't be getting back up.

But there were plenty of other enemies nearby, and all of them had heard the shots. Men shouted curses and questions and feet pounded the ground as several of the outlaws charged toward the cabin to find out what was going on.

There was one good thing about being surrounded by enemies, Cole thought grimly. You didn't have to worry about who to shoot. He came to his feet and fired twice more as he ran to his left. He wanted to draw the pursuit away from the cabin so Lon would have a chance to defeat Beaumont and get Brenda Durand out of there.

Colt flame bloomed in the darkness as the outlaws returned Cole's fire. None of the bullets came close to him as far as he could tell. The angry shouts, along with the gunfire, told him the outlaws were pursuing him, just like he wanted.

He ran into something in the dark, the impact painfully barking his shins. His momentum carried him forward and made him topple over what turned out to be a fallen tree. That was a lucky break of sorts. He huddled behind the cover of the thick log as he thumbed fresh rounds into his .44, working by feel since he couldn't see much of anything. He didn't have any trouble reloading under these conditions, though. He'd had plenty of experience.

The outlaws were still yelling and shooting. Most of the bullets went wild, but Cole heard one of them thud into the tree trunk and was glad it was there. When his revolver had a full cylinder, he thrust the gun over the log. Muzzle flashes gave him something to aim at. He fired twice and was rewarded by a man's howl of pain.

Then he had to flatten behind the log again as the outlaws returned his fire. Now they knew where he was. Chunks of bark and a hail of splinters flew into the air as their bullets chewed into the tree trunk.

Cole had jumped from the proverbial frying pan into the fire, and now he had to deal with the heat. It might be worth the risk if it allowed Lon and Brenda to get away.

And now that all hell had broken loose, Cole hoped that help would be arriving soon, in the form of Kermit Sawyer and the rest of that wild bunch of Texans from the Diamond S.

CHAPTER 18

In the trees, one of the punchers said excitedly, "There's Frenchy's signal, Mr. Sawyer!"

"I see it," Sawyer growled. Everyone was already mounted, so he didn't have to tell them to get on their horses. Instead he drew one of his pearl-handled Colts and pulled in a breath to call out the order to charge.

Before he could do that, the crackle of gunfire sounded, but it wasn't coming from the gap between the bluffs. From the sound of it, the shooting was farther away than that, inside the valley where the outlaw hideout was located.

"That's not what was supposed to happen!" one of the men exclaimed.

No, it wasn't, Sawyer thought, but he wasn't really surprised, either. Every plan had things that could go wrong with it, and they usually did. Those shots had to mean that Lon and Marshal Tyler were swapping lead with the owlhoots. The odds would be mighty high against them.

Which meant that help needed to get to them as quickly as possible. Sawyer leaned forward in the saddle and called in a loud, clear voice, "Let's ride!"

With the boss of the Diamond S in the lead, the Texans charged out of the trees and onto the flat. Sawyer rode hard, calling on his mount for all the speed it possessed. Although he would never show it, fear gnawed at his guts. He had faced overwhelming odds and deadly danger more times than he could remember in his long, adventurous life, so he was used to fights like this. He wasn't afraid for himself.

It was Lon who occupied his thoughts. He never should have let the boy go with Tyler, he told himself as the cold wind whipped at his face. People seemed to think it was a joke whenever he said something about promising Lon's mother that he'd take care of the youngster, but Sawyer was completely serious about it. That woman meant a lot to him, and so did the boy . . .

Sawyer forced those thoughts out of his head. There was no time for them now. Even though the range was still too great to do any real damage, he pointed his gun at the dark mouth of the gap, let out a yell, and began pulling the trigger as he shouted, "Give 'em hell, boys!"

Up on the bluff, Frenchy was torn. A part of him wanted to get down there into that valley and give Lon and Marshal Tyler a hand if he could. They would be facing long odds.

But his job was up here, and it was an important one. He and the other two men had to pick off the defenders in the gap, or else Sawyer and the rest of the crew would be galloping right into a storm of lead.

Down below, the men hidden in the rocks opened fire at the charging Texans. It took only a few moments for Frenchy to spot all of them by the muzzle flashes of their rifles. Then he let out a rebel yell. That was the signal for the men on the other side of the gap to open fire.

Frenchy pressed the butt of his Winchester against his shoulder and cut loose, spraying lead down into the gap as fast as he could work the repeater's lever. Slugs ricocheted madly from the rocks. Their high-pitched whines blended together in a melody of sorts, a grim tune of leaden death.

It took less than a minute for the defenders who weren't either dead or badly wounded to retreat from that blistering attack, their nerves breaking under the barrage of bullets. As the hammer of Frenchy's rifle clicked empty, he heard men shouting and telling each other to get the hell out of there. Boot leather slapped rapidly against rock as the outlaws fled.

Frenchy stood up and reloaded on the run as he dashed toward the other side of the bluff. He figured he might have a chance to wing a couple of the fleeing owlhoots, although it might be too dark for that. At the very least he could hurry them on their way and make it easier for Sawyer and the others to get through the passage.

As he reached a spot where he could look down into the valley, he saw the flicker of muzzle flashes from the area along the creek where the outlaw camp was located. The little splashes of orange were like fireflies winking in the night, and they might have almost been pretty . . . if Frenchy hadn't known that men were dying down there.

Lon could have stood there and held Brenda all night. She felt that good in his arms. But with guns going off outside the cabin he didn't have that luxury, so he let go of her and turned quickly to the table where the lantern burned.

"No!" Brenda exclaimed, clutching at him.

"It's all right," Lon told her again. He leaned over and blew out the flame in the lantern. That plunged the inside of the cabin into darkness. Brenda wailed in dismay.

Lon took hold of her arm. She tried to pull away from him. He sensed that she was in such a state of panic that she might run right out into the middle of all that gunfire if he gave her the chance. He tightened his grip so she couldn't get away from him.

That move backfired a little on him. She started struggling and flailed blows at him with her other hand. Lon ignored them and got both arms around her again, wrapping her up as best he could as he tried to steer her toward the door.

"Miss Durand, settle down!" he told her. "It's me, Lon Rogers! I won't hurt you. You're safe now."

That last part was a lie — neither of them were safe, not by a long shot, he figured — but he was trying to get through to her and calm her down. As they reached the doorway he tried to peer past her and figure out what was going on outside. Most of the shooting seemed to be coming from his left.

That meant the safest way to go was right. He lunged in that direction and dragged Brenda along with him.

Lon knew Cole had to be in the middle of

that gunfight, and he felt bad about abandoning the marshal instead of staying and trying to help him. But they had ventured into this valley to rescue Brenda, so getting her away from the outlaws had to come first. Lon was confident that Cole would tell him the same thing.

He hustled Brenda through the trees along the creek as more shots rolled and echoed through the darkness. These came from the bluffs to the south, and that told Lon the rest of the plan was underway. Mr. Sawyer and the other men from the Diamond S were trying to battle their way through the passage and into the valley. All Lon had to do was dodge the outlaws and keep Brenda out of their hands until the other members of the gang were wiped out or captured.

She stopped fighting and went limp as sobs wracked her body. That actually made it more difficult for him, because now he had to manage to keep her dead weight moving. Not only that, but her loud crying might attract attention they didn't want. Lon hated to be even the least bit rough with her, but he shook her and said urgently, "Miss Durand! Brenda! Stop it!"

She continued crying. Lon grimaced and shifted one of his hands to clamp it over her mouth. That made her start fighting again.

"If you'll stop crying, I'll let you go," he told her. "But you've got to cooperate with me. Can you do that?"

She surprised him by nodding. Maybe she was calming down and thinking straighter. He took his hand away from her mouth.

She gasped for air a couple of times, then said, "You idiot! I couldn't breathe! You had your hand over my nose, too."

"I did?" Lon hadn't even realized that. "I'm sorry, Miss Durand, I just didn't want those outlaws to hear us —"

"So you thought you'd suffocate me instead?"

So all it took to get through to her was to make her mad enough, Lon thought. He said, "I swear, I didn't know you couldn't get your breath, Miss Durand. Now if you'll come with me, we'll put some more ground between us and those owlhoots."

"Who else is with you?" she asked as they started through the trees. Lon had a hand on her arm again, this time to steady her since they couldn't see where they were going very well.

"Marshal Tyler and the rest of the fellas from the Diamond S," he told her. "As soon as Mr. Sawyer and the boys get through that gap and into the valley, I reckon this fracas will be just about over."

"You all risked your lives to save me?" She sounded like she had a hard time believing that.

"Well, mostly," Lon said. "Also, we want to bring those owlhoots to justice and get back all the money they stole in town. It'd be a big blow to Wind River to lose that much."

"Yes, it would," Brenda agreed, still sniffling a little. "I knew there had to be another reason besides just rescuing me. Nobody around here even likes me."

"Now, that's just not true," Lon insisted. "I would have come after you even if —"

He stopped short, realizing that he was saying more than he meant to say. Even now, he was aware of the gulf between the two of them and didn't want to overstep his bounds.

"What did you start to say?" she asked. "You would have come after me even if they hadn't stolen all that money?"

"If they hadn't taken as much as a penny."

There. It was out in the open. Maybe she would understand now how he felt about her.

"How gallant of you," she said, but he could tell from her tone of voice that she was mocking him.

All right, he thought as he tried not to

sigh. She didn't have to feel the same way toward him that he felt toward her. There was no rule in life that affection had to be returned. That didn't make his emotions any less genuine.

The shooting was still going on around the cabin and over by the bluffs. Lon figured that he and Brenda had come about half a mile. That ought to be far enough away for them to be safe until the fighting was over, he decided.

"We'll stop and wait here," he said. They were in the thick shadows underneath a tree.

"I think we should keep going," she said. "I don't want to be anywhere close to those . . . those bastards!"

Lon was a little shocked to hear such language coming from a woman, but he supposed Brenda had a good excuse. She had been treated roughly and no doubt threatened and terrorized, and if anybody had the right to cuss those outlaws, it was her.

"I never got a chance to ask you if you were all right," he said. "They didn't hurt you, did they?"

"They made me ride a horse for miles and miles. I'll be so sore tomorrow that I may not be able to walk for a week!"

"Oh, you'll get over that quicker than you

think you will," Lon assured her. "Now that you live here in Wyoming, you should get out and ride more often so you'll get used to it. There's nothing like it."

"Why would I want to do a thing like that?"

"Well, there's some mighty spectacular scenery in these parts."

"If you like rocks and dirt and ugly little bushes."

"There's more to it than that," Lon said. "You just need to get up in the high country, like the Diamond S range." He paused and then told himself to take a chance. "I could show you sometime —"

A gun cocked somewhere close by, and Adam Maguire's voice said, "That's touching, cowboy, but I think your courting days are over."

CHAPTER 19

Cole knew there was a good chance some of the outlaws would try to flank him, so he was ready for them when they charged him. The ones who were still in front of the log opened fire again, forcing him to stay down. The gun-thunder also served to drown out any noise the other men made moving through the brush.

Cole had a gun in each hand, though, and had turned around so that his back was against the log and he could look in both directions by turning his head. He figured the flankers would get too eager, and sure enough, a gun suddenly blasted to his right, flame licking from its muzzle.

He was about to swivel in that direction and cut loose with both revolvers, but some instinct made him stop and roll the other way instead. He was banking on the hope that that first shot had been a feint.

Dark figures loomed up, charging him.

Cole beat them to the punch. He fired both guns at the same time, triggering again and again and sending hot lead shrieking through the shadows. Men yelled in pain and gun flame leaped back at him.

He rolled to his left, still letting his instincts guide him, and fired back at the man who had feinted at him a few seconds earlier. The outlaw spilled off his feet and landed with a heavy thud.

The other members of the gang renewed their frontal attack. Cole twisted and came up on his knees. He thrust both revolvers in front of him, thumbing the hammers and tripping the triggers so that steady streams of fire geysered from their barrels. Bullets whipped past him and sang around his head. A great, grim fatalism filled him. He might fall with outlaw lead in him, but he wasn't going to stop shooting until his six-guns ran dry.

That happened pretty quickly as both hammers fell on empty chambers. Cole was about to dive behind the log again when hoofbeats thundered nearby.

"Tyler!" a familiar gravelly voice roared.

"Over here, Sawyer!" Cole shouted back to the cattleman.

"Hit the dirt!"

Cole bellied down on the ground and

pressed himself against the log as fresh waves of gunfire swept through the trees. The Texans were all mounted, so they figured anybody on the ground was a likely target. Guns roared and roared until it sounded like an earthquake, Cole thought.

When the shooting finally stopped, the silence that dropped down over the landscape like a cloak had a strange, eerie sound of its own. After a moment, Kermit Sawyer called again, "Tyler, are you there?"

"Here," Cole replied as he pulled himself up, braced a hand against the log, and climbed to his feet.

"You hit?"

Cole had to take stock of himself before he answered. Amazingly, as many bullets as had been flying around, he didn't seem to be hurt.

"I'm all right," he said. "How about you?"

Sawyer rode up and swung down from his saddle. "We've got some men wounded, but none of 'em too bad, I hope," he said. "Accordin' to Frenchy we lost one man up on the bluffs, though."

"I'm sorry."

"Yeah, me, too. But it's a hard world. Cleanin' up a bunch of polecats like this sometimes comes with a price." Sawyer paused, then asked with a peculiar tightness in his voice, "Where's Lon?"

"The last I saw of him, he was in the cabin where they were holding Miss Durand, fighting that fella Beaumont. I hope they got away, but I don't know for sure."

Sawyer looked around at his men and ordered, "Somebody get a torch burnin', damn it! We got to find that youngster. Some of those desperadoes might still be roamin' around. We don't know for sure that we wiped 'em all out."

The same thought had occurred to Cole. The fighting might be finished right here, but that didn't mean the danger was over, especially elsewhere in the valley.

Brenda gasped and shuddered against Lon. One of his arms tightened around her while his other hand reached for the gun at his hip.

"Don't move, kid," another voice said, this one belonging to Lije Beaumont. "The way my head hurts right now because of you, I'd like nothin' better than to blow your brains out."

Lon was a little surprised that Maguire and Beaumont hadn't already done that, but then he realized why they were holding their fire. He had Brenda with him, and as long as she was so close to him they couldn't risk any shots. They still regarded her as valuable, which meant they hadn't given up on the idea of collecting that ransom for her.

"Get the horses, Lije," Maguire ordered. "I'll keep an eye on our young friends here."

Lon heard Beaumont hurry off in the darkness.

"You better just let us go," Lon said. "My boss and his whole crew are close by, and they'll find us any minute. You'd be smart to light a shuck out of here while you still can."

"Not without the girl," Maguire snapped. "I've gone to too much trouble to let her go now. Her grandmother will still pay handsomely to get her back."

Lon could see the outlaw leader now, standing about ten feet away. A few stray beams of starlight reflected off the barrel of the gun in Maguire's hand. Maguire was too far away for Lon to try to jump him. All that would get him was a bullet.

He shifted a little, though, putting Brenda more behind him. If there was any gunplay, he wanted to shield her body with his own body as much as he could.

Brenda suddenly said, "You know Beaumont went against your orders, don't you?"

"What are you talking about?" Maguire

asked sharply.

"He sent the guard away and came into the cabin. He was going to attack me. He would have done it, too, if Lon hadn't stopped him."

For a second, Maguire didn't say anything. Then he laughed harshly and said, "That's a lie. Lije told me he ran in there to check on you when the shooting started and found the cowboy with you. You got behind him and knocked him out."

"I tried my best to kill him," Brenda said. "I just couldn't hit him hard enough. His skull is too thick. But what I told you is true. Beaumont came after me. You shouldn't trust him."

Lon knew she was trying to drive a wedge between the two outlaws. It couldn't hurt anything. He said, "She's telling you the truth, mister. I was there and saw and heard the whole thing. Beaumont told the guard he didn't give a damn what you wanted."

Hoofbeats thudded on the ground nearby as Beaumont returned with a pair of horses. He got there in time to hear what Lon said and exploded, "What the hell are you lyin' about, kid? I never said any such thing!"

"You've wanted the girl for yourself all along," Maguire said. His voice had a chilly edge to it now, almost as chilly as the wind.

"Don't try to claim you haven't, Lije."

"Well, hell, of course I want her!" Beaumont said. "Any man with eyes in his head would. But that doesn't mean I went against your orders, Lieutenant."

"You always were a hotheaded fool, even during the war. If I hadn't kept a tight rein on you, you would have ruined things for our outfit plenty of times."

"That's not true, blast it! I always followed your orders."

"And that's why we survived," Maguire said. "Maybe you've forgotten that."

From the tone of the argument, Lon was starting to hope that the two outlaws would turn on each other and give him and Brenda a chance to get away. That hope was dashed as Maguire went on, "We can talk about all that later, though. Right now we've got to get that girl on a horse . . ."

Something crashed through the brush nearby, reminding Lon of a grizzly bear tearing through everything in its way. A huge figure loomed up, staggering. The newcomer's deep voice boomed, "I'm shot!"

"Corny!" Maguire exclaimed.

Lon didn't really know who the newcomer was, but evidently Brenda did. She cried, "Help me, Mr. Van Houten! They're going to kill me!"

The man called Van Houten said thickly, "Miss Durand?"

"Sorry, Corny, there's nothing we can do for you," Maguire said. "We've only got two horses. That's just enough for me and Lije, with the girl riding double with me."

"You ought to . . . let her go," Van Houten said, obviously having to force the words out because he was wounded. "She doesn't belong . . . with the likes of us."

"Back off," Beaumont growled. "We're gettin' outta here."

"Please, Mr. Van Houten," Brenda begged. "Your family would want you to stop them."

Van Houten said, "My family . . . has forgotten all about me. I'm . . . dead to them." He grunted in pain as he took a lumbering step forward. "Just like I'm going to be . . . dead to the whole world soon."

"You're right about that," Beaumont said as he lifted his gun. "We don't need you slowin' us down."

"Lije, no!" Maguire said, but Beaumont ignored him and pulled the trigger. The gun roared, and Van Houten's massive body rocked back as the bullet slammed into him.

But that was the wrong thing for Beaumont to have done. Van Houten caught himself and lunged forward, again reminding Lon of a bear. Beaumont fired again, but the shot didn't slow Van Houten's attack. He crashed into Beaumont.

At the same time, Lon tackled Maguire, who had turned away so that his gun wasn't pointing at Lon and Brenda anymore.

Maguire's gun blasted as Lon drove him to the ground, but the bullet didn't hit anything except dirt. Desperation gave Lon strength as he slugged at the outlaw.

Maguire was just as desperate, though, and swung his gun in a slashing blow at Lon's head. The barrel clipped him, stunning him for a second. That was long enough for Maguire to battle free.

But as he surged to his feet, one of the horses, spooked by the shots, rammed a shoulder against him and knocked him down again. At the same time, Brenda grabbed one of Lon's arms and tugged urgently on it.

"Come on!" she cried. "Let's get out of here!"

Beaumont and Van Houten were still wrestling around on the ground, and there was no telling who would win that battle. Either way, the victor might represent a continuing threat. Lon scrambled to his feet and saw that one of the horses was still close by. He lunged and grabbed the trailing reins.

The quickest way for him and Brenda to

get away was for him to mount first. He leaped into the saddle with the lithe agility he had developed from years of working on horseback around cattle and leaned down to extend a hand to Brenda. She clasped wrists with him, and he pulled her onto the horse's back behind him.

"Hang on!" he told her as he drove his heels into the horse's flanks and sent the animal leaping through the darkness. All he could do was hope a low-hanging branch wouldn't sweep them off the horse's back.

Maguire shouted a curse behind them. The outlaw's gun boomed as he fired after them. He wasn't worried about hitting Brenda anymore, Lon realized. Maguire was so consumed with rage he would rather kill her than let the two of them get away.

He turned his head and told Brenda, "Lean forward! Make yourself a smaller target!"

As he angled his body down over the horse's neck, he felt her huddling against his back as she hung on tightly with both arms around his waist. Even under these desperate circumstances, with bullets cutting through the air around them, he was aware of how good it felt to have her so close to him.

It would be all right with him if she never let go.

Lon wasn't sure where they were going — toward the head of the valley, he thought — but with at least one vicious killer and quite possibly two behind them, all they could do was keep moving. Maybe once they got away from Maguire, they could circle back and find Sawyer, Cole, and the rest of the rescue party. Until then . . .

"Hang on," he told Brenda as they raced through the night.

CHAPTER 20

The cabin was empty. Brenda and Lon were gone, but so was Beaumont. Of course, it was possible that the outlaw's bullet-riddled body was lying somewhere nearby, Cole thought, but his gut told him that wasn't the case.

"Spread out," Sawyer told his men as they sat on horseback in front of the old trapper's cabin, several of them holding torches. "Find Lon and that girl. And if you run into any more of those varmints we ain't killed already, you can take care of that little chore, too."

"It sounds like you're telling your men to commit murder, Sawyer," Cole said.

"I'm tellin' 'em to see that justice is done," the cattleman snapped. "We ain't in town now, Tyler. You don't have any jurisdiction out here. Anyway, there's what's legal, and there's what's right, and you know that just as well as I do."

Cole shrugged. "I won't lose any sleep over those outlaws, that's true. I just want to find Lon and Miss Durand."

"So do I. Come on. Frenchy, you ride with us, too."

The three of them left the cabin, Cole riding on a borrowed horse since Ulysses was still tied in the trees on the other side of the bench, and rode northwest toward the head of the valley. That was the direction Cole expected Lon to have taken to get Brenda away from the fighting, since he had drawn the outlaws' fire the other way. The rest of the Diamond S crew spread out across the valley.

They rode without a torch, since such a blazing brand might have drawn the fire of any surviving outlaws. Cole suggested that they follow the creek, thinking that was what Lon might have done.

They had gone about half a mile when the horses suddenly shied at something. All three men drew their guns. Cole spotted some ominous dark shapes on the ground and said grimly, "Looks like a couple of bodies."

"Strike a match, Frenchy," Sawyer ordered. His voice was as bleak as Cole's.

With a slight rasp, a match flared to life in the foreman's left hand. His right still held

205

a Colt revolver. The match's flickering glow revealed the bodies of two men lying side by side, one facedown and the other on his back. Cole felt relief go through him when he realized that neither of the men was Lon Rogers.

Sawyer let out a heavy sigh. Obviously he was relieved, too. "A couple of those outlaws?" he said.

"Yeah," Cole replied. "The one on his back is Lije Beaumont, Maguire's second-in-command. I don't know the other man's name, but I saw him back in Wind River when I was trading shots with the gang. He was definitely one of them, all right."

Frenchy said, "Looks like that hombre's neck is broke."

Cole saw the same thing. Beaumont's head sat at an odd angle on his shoulders, and his throat was mottled with bruises. Cole dismounted and rolled the big man onto his back. He had been shot at least four times.

"Danged if it don't look like they killed each other," Frenchy commented as he shook the match out just before the flame reached his fingers. "Like the big fella had hold of the other one's neck and snapped it even though he'd been ventilated through and through."

"That's the way it looks to me, too," Sawyer said. "Wonder why they turned on each other."

"We might not ever know," Cole said. "And I don't reckon it matters now, anyway."

"No," Sawyer agreed, "all that matters is findin' those two youngsters. Let's keep lookin'."

"Shouldn't we turn back?" Brenda asked as she held on to Lon. "I think we lost him."

"Can't be sure of that," Lon replied. "We need to find some place to hole up for a while. I've still got two guns and quite a few shells. I can hold off Maguire if he comes after us, as long as we've got some good cover."

"But your friends are back there somewhere. They can help us."

"Maguire was between us and them, the last time we saw him," Lon pointed out. "He could be waitin' to bushwhack us if we try to double back."

Brenda sighed and said, "All right. You know a lot more about this sort of thing than I do, I suppose." She laughed hollowly. "I've never been kidnapped by outlaws and then rescued from them. I'll know more about it next time."

"Bite your tongue," Lon said with a chuckle. "Not gonna be a next time."

He hoped that was true. Unfortunately, other dangers might lurk on the frontier. Wyoming Territory was a long way from being civilized.

That was something to worry about another time, he told himself. Right now they just had to be concerned with making it through the night.

He rode until a dark barrier loomed in front of them. As he reined in, Brenda asked, "What's that?"

"I think it's the cliff at the head of the valley. That creek probably comes out of a spring somewhere along its base. Formations like that are pretty common in these parts."

Her voice held a note of worry as she said, "That means we can't go any farther, doesn't it?"

"Yeah, this is the end of the line." Lon slipped from the saddle. "Let me take a look around."

She scrambled down from the horse's back. "You're not going to leave me alone," she said. "You can just forget about that."

"All right. Can you hang on to the reins with your left hand?"

"Yes, I think so."

"Take hold of them, and then reach out with your right hand."

"Why am I doing that?"

Lon could see her only vaguely, but that was enough. He held out his left hand, and when his fingers brushed hers, he clasped them.

"We don't want to get separated."

"Oh, that's true. We don't."

Her hand was cold, but it warmed some as he held it. The temperature probably wouldn't drop below freezing before morning, but it was going to be pretty chilly anyway. He wanted to find a place where they could get out of the weather. It would have been nice if they could have a fire, but he thought that was too much of a risk. The flames might lead Adam Maguire right to them if he was still looking for them.

There hadn't been any shots from down the valley in a long time, but that didn't mean the fight was over. Some of the outlaws besides Maguire might still be alive. It could be morning before the posse finished rooting out all of them. So lying low was his and Brenda's best bet, Lon told himself again, if he could just find a good place for them to do that.

Holding Brenda's hand while she led the horse, Lon explored along the cliff. He was searching for a cave or something like that, some place that would not only provide shelter for them but could also be defended easily. But in the end it was Brenda who found the place, not him.

Her hand tightened on his as she asked, "What's that up there?"

He tipped his head back to look up the cliff. A massive slab of rock lay at its base, slanting up. At the top of it was a patch of deeper darkness. He couldn't tell if it was an actual cave or just a place where the rock jutted out to create an overhang.

But either way, it looked promising to him. He said, "Stay here. I'll have a look."

"No, I told you that you're not leaving me alone. I'm coming with you."

"We don't know what's up there. Might be a bear settling down to hibernate through the winter."

"I'll take my chances," Brenda said.

Lon could tell that arguing with her wasn't going to do any good. He took the reins from her and tied the horse to a stunted tree that appeared to be dead. Then he asked, "Can you make that climb?"

"I can make it," she said with determination in her voice.

They started up the rock side by side. The slope was too steep to walk without putting their hands down to brace themselves. The climb was about forty feet, and as they neared the top, Lon drew his holstered Colt and whispered, "Hold it a minute. Let me take a look. I wasn't joking about the bear. Or there might be a mountain lion denned up in there."

"All right," Brenda said, "but I'll be right behind you."

He fished out a match with his left hand and scratched it to life on the rock, then tossed it into the dark opening. Light spread from the little flame and reflected back from rock walls. It wasn't an actual cave, Lon saw, but rather an overhang like he'd thought it might be.

The important thing was that it was empty.

"Thank God," Brenda said as she looked past him. "Can we stay here? I'm exhausted." She shivered. "And cold. I don't think I've ever been this cold. Can we have a fire?"

Lon was about to tell her that they couldn't when he decided that maybe the risk was worth it after all. It wouldn't do them any good to escape from the outlaws if they froze to death. Besides, he thought, maybe the fire would lead Mr. Sawyer and the others to them, instead of Maguire.

"I'll go get some branches," he told her. "You can stay here. You'll be all right."

"Wait a minute. You've got two guns, don't you?"

"Yeah."

"Leave one of them with me."

Lon frowned. "You really think you can shoot a gun?"

"If I have to, I can."

Somehow he didn't doubt her. It was true that she had given in to her fear several times tonight, but he sensed a core of strength in her, too. He took the gun that was tucked behind his belt and pressed it into her hands.

"You have to pull back the hammer to cock it and then pull the trigger," he told her.

"I know how to shoot a gun."

"Have you ever used one?"

"Well . . . no. And I hope I won't have to tonight."

"Me, too," Lon said. "Make sure you don't shoot me. I'll be back in a hurry."

He slid down the rock and gathered broken branches from the brush. When he had an armful, he climbed back to the depression in the cliff face.

A few minutes later he had a small fire burning near the back of the cave-like area, so the heat would reflect from the rock walls. The smoke rose and flattened against the overhang, then drifted away. The two of them sat next to the fire and extended their hands toward its warmth. Lon was still pretty cold, but gradually he began to get more comfortable.

Brenda took him by surprise by leaning against him. She was trembling despite the fire. Lon didn't think about what he was doing. He just put his arm around her shoulders and drew her closer to him.

"D-Don't think this means anything except that I'm f-freezing," she said.

"No, ma'am," he said.

"You don't happen to have a blanket or anything?"

"No, I checked the saddlebags on that horse. Didn't see anything that would help us."

"I guess we'll just have to k-keep each other warm, then."

"I reckon," Lon said.

"You d-don't have to sound so pleased about it."

"No, ma'am," Lon said again as he leaned back against the rock and she huddled even closer to him. A smile tugged at the corners of his mouth, but he figured that was all right since her head was pillowed against his chest and she couldn't see his face.

Eventually he could tell by her breathing that she had fallen asleep. That was good. She needed the rest. As for him, he intended to stay awake and keep watch all night. After everything they had been through, he wasn't going to let anything happen to her now.

CHAPTER 21

"Well, if that's not the most touching thing I've ever seen."

The mocking drawl jolted Lon out of the sleep he had been so determined wouldn't claim him. Exhaustion and the strain of fighting for his life — and Brenda's life — had proven to be too much for him. He had dozed off sometime during the night. The fire had burned down to embers, and the gray light of dawn silhouetted the figure who stood at the entrance to the hollowed-out space under the overhanging rock.

It was Adam Maguire, and he had a gun in his hand. He was turned to the side enough that Lon could see the weapon pointing at him and Brenda.

He must have started a little when Maguire's voice roused him from sleep, because Brenda was waking up, too, slowly shaking off the weariness that had enveloped her. She lifted her head and muttered,

"Wha . . ."

"Don't move," Lon told her tensely.

He felt her stiffen against him and knew she had seen Maguire. "No," she said in a hollow voice.

"Oh, yes," Maguire said. He came another step toward them. Lon could see the outlaw's face better now. Maguire had the haggard look of a man who hadn't slept. His face was gaunt. His hollow eyes burned with hate. He went on, "You're my ticket out of here, Miss Durand. I couldn't very well leave without you, now could I?"

"You can't get away," Lon said. "The Diamond S crew is all over this valley."

"I know. I've been dodging them all night while I was hunting for the two of you." Maguire's voice was bitter. "You've caused me a lot of trouble, both of you. I reckon it's only fair that you help me get out of it now."

Brenda said, "I won't help you do anything. You can go to hell."

"I think you will," Maguire said. He leveled the gun. "I've got a bead right between that young cowboy's eyes. You can go with me and be my hostage willingly, Miss Durand, or I'll just go ahead and kill him and take you anyway."

"Don't listen to him," Lon said. "He's an

outlaw and a liar. He'll kill me whether you cooperate with him or not."

"I give you my word I won't. I'm more worried about getting out of here alive than I am about any sort of revenge."

Brenda said, "He might be telling the truth."

"No," Lon said. "You can't believe him."

"Let go of me," she said as she started trying to pull away from him. "I'll take that chance if it's the only way to save your life."

Lon tightened his grip on her. "Damn it! You can't —"

She struck her fists against his chest and cried, "You idiot! Can't you see I have to?"

"How about this?" Maguire suggested. "If you make me wait any longer I'll just kill you both."

Lon glanced at the outlaw and saw such feral rage on Maguire's face that he knew the man was capable of carrying out the threat. That distracted him enough that Brenda was able to twist away from him. He reached for her, but she was too quick. She came to her feet and moved toward Maguire. Lon leaped up and started to go after her, but the threat of Maguire's revolver pointing at his face forced him to stop.

"I meant it," the outlaw said. "I won't kill

you, as long as Miss Durand goes with me. The others won't dare try to stop me as long as she's with me."

"Brenda . . ." Lon said miserably.

She paused and looked back over her shoulder at him. "It's for the best this way," she told him. "I'll be all right."

Maguire grinned and said, "Sure you will be, honey. After you've traveled with me for a while, you'll wish you'd met me a long time ago."

Brenda didn't respond to that gibe. Instead she said, "It's really cold this morning, isn't it?" She slipped a hand inside her dress as if to warm her fingers.

When she brought it back out she was gripping the gun Lon had given her the night before. Maguire must have seen the weapon as she raised it in both hands and drew back the hammer, but he reacted slowly, probably from a mixture of exhaustion and sheer surprise. He had just started to yell and jerk his gun toward her when Brenda pulled the trigger.

The shot hammered painfully against Lon's ears in the close confines of the rocky space. He saw Maguire take a step back as blood flew from his upper left arm where Brenda's shot grazed him. A fraction of a second later Maguire's gun boomed, too.

Brenda screamed and fell.

"Noooo!" Lon roared. He didn't even think about reaching for the holstered Colt on his hip. Instead he launched himself forward, heedless of the danger from Maguire's gun, and crashed into the outlaw. Maguire went over backward. Lon's momentum carried him along, too, as both men fell out onto the steeply slanting slope of the rock slab and started to tumble down it.

The fall was a nightmare, a chaotic shifting of earth and sky. Lon saw Maguire's gun hand in front of him and grabbed it, forcing it away as the revolver spouted flame again. Over and over they went. Lon got his other hand on Maguire's gun and ripped it from the outlaw's fingers.

As they came to a stop at the bottom of the rock, Lon hammered the gun butt into Maguire's face. Yelling incoherently, he lifted the gun and brought it down again and again until Maguire's face had been battered into a red pulp that barely resembled anything human. Finally, Lon dropped the gun and slid backward against the rock, away from the dead thing that had been Adam Maguire.

"Lon!"

The cry made his head snap around. He

looked up and saw Brenda staring down at him from the top of the slope. Relief that she was still alive flooded through him, washing away the last of the killing frenzy that had gripped him a moment earlier. He turned and scrambled up the rock.

"He shot you!" he exclaimed as he gathered Brenda into his arms. "I saw him. Maguire shot you!"

"No, he shot at me and scared me and I fell down," she said, clinging to him as fervently as he held on to her. "I was never going with him, Lon. I . . . I just wanted to get close enough to shoot him. And I still missed!"

"No, you winged him," Lon told her. "If you hadn't, I never would've been able to tackle him. You saved us both."

"We saved each other," she whispered.

That sounded pretty good to Lon. He sure wasn't going to argue about it. He was content just to stand there and hold her until he heard the swift rataplan of approaching hoofbeats. A few moments later, Kermit Sawyer, Cole Tyler, Frenchy LeDoux, and several more men galloped up, drawn by the shots.

Sawyer reined in, leaned forward in his saddle, and called, "By God, Lon, you'd better be all right!"

"I am, Mr. Sawyer," Lon replied with a wave. His other arm was still around Brenda. "I reckon we both are."

Billy Casebolt said wistfully, "I sure wish I could've gone along with that posse. You could've used my help, Cole."

"We sure could have," Cole agreed as he sat on a ladder-back chair beside the bed. He leaned forward to pat Casebolt's knee through the blanket that was spread over the deputy's heavily bandaged form. "But I'm just glad you're still alive. You can help me chase down the next bunch of outlaws."

"That's a deal," Casebolt said with an emphatic nod. He was sitting up with a couple of pillows propped behind him in the bed in one of Dr. Judson Kent's rooms.

"The deputy won't be going anywhere for a while," Kent said from the doorway. "He was seriously wounded, and his recuperation will require several months of extensive rest."

"Dang it, what'll the marshal do for a deputy while I'm laid up?" Casebolt wanted to know.

"Yeah, Mr. Mayor," Cole said with a smile. "What'll I do for a deputy?"

Kent chuckled. "The town council has authorized you to hire a replacement deputy until Mr. Casebolt here is back on his feet."

"Does Billy still get paid, too?"

"Of course. His injuries were suffered in the line of duty."

"I'll bet you had some pretty good arguments about that one," Cole said.

Kent shrugged. "I was able to make the rest of the council see the justice of that position. They're not unreasonable men." The doctor paused. "Well, not *all* of them, anyway. And it helped that Miss Durand volunteered to donate some funds to help with the situation."

"She did, did she?"

"It's only appropriate. She was rescued from a very dangerous situation, after all. Not only that, but all the money taken from her bank was recovered. I'd say her generosity was justified." Kent stroked his close-cropped beard and added, "I wouldn't put it past the young woman to expect some sort of favor at a later date in return for her generosity, however. She may be grateful, but she's still a canny businesswoman."

Cole got to his feet and said, "I'll be back by to check on you pretty often, Billy. In the meantime, behave yourself."

Casebolt snorted. "Not much else I can do, all wrapped up like this and stuck in a bed. There's one thing you might could do for me, Cole."

"What's that?"

"Tell Miz Palmer I done took a turn for the worse and can't have no more visitors. I swear, there ain't a day goes by when that woman ain't here wantin' to read to me, or fluff my dang pillows, or . . . or somethin'!"

Cole grinned. "I'd say that's a medical opinion, Billy, and I'm not qualified to make a judgment like that."

"And I believe that having visitors will speed your recovery, as long as they don't tire you too much," Kent said.

"But that's just it," Casebolt said pitifully. "That woman is plumb exhaustin'!"

Cole was still chuckling over his deputy's dilemma when he left the doctor's office. He had a problem of his own, he realized. He needed to hire another deputy, and he didn't have any idea who that might be.

He saw a couple of familiar figures dismounting in front of the Wind River General Store and went over to join them. "How would one of you fellas like to be my new temporary deputy?" he asked.

Frenchy LeDoux shook his head. "I'm a cowboy, Marshal, not a star packer," he said. "Besides, the weight of that hunk of tin might throw off the lines of my vest. How about you, Lon?"

223

"No thanks," Lon said. "I'm not cut out for law work, either."

Cole nodded and said, "That's what I was afraid you'd say, both of you. Well, if you think of anybody who might be interested in the job, you send 'em to see me, all right?"

"Sure thing, Marshal," Frenchy promised.

Cole hooked his thumbs in his gunbelt and walked on along Grenville Avenue. Wind River was nice and quiet again, so he knew there was one thing he could count on.

It wouldn't stay that way.

Inside the store, Lon looked around while Frenchy went to give the list of the things they had come after to Harvey Raymond. Lon was trying to be nonchalant, but his emotions made that difficult. It had been a couple of days since he'd seen Brenda, and he wanted to be sure she was all right. She had been awfully quiet during the ride back to Wind River.

Maybe she didn't want to have anything to do with him anymore. She had seen the way he beat Adam Maguire to death. Maybe she had decided he was just too loco to be around.

He was standing in front of the candy

counter, peering through the glass, when she said behind him, "Don't tell me you have a taste for licorice."

Lon straightened and turned around quickly. He snatched his hat off his head. Brenda wore an expensive gown and was as lovely as ever. She didn't show any signs of the ordeal she had gone through.

That didn't really surprise Lon. He knew how strong she was. It made sense that she would shake off the effects of the experience in no time.

"No, ma'am," he said. "I mean, yes, ma'm. I'm right fond of licorice." He wished that he wasn't so uncomfortable talking to her. He knew he shouldn't have been. They had spent the night huddled in that sort-of cave, keeping each other warm. That should make a difference . . . but he wasn't sure it did.

"Would you say that you . . . love licorice?"

Lon shook his head. "No, ma'am. There's a big difference in, uh, likin' something and loving it."

"So there is," Brenda said.

Well, that made it pretty plain, he thought. She liked him, she felt grateful to him for what he'd done, but she didn't love him. How could he expect her to, he asked himself? Despite everything they had gone

225

through together, really they barely knew each other.

She frowned in thought and went on, "I think I like peppermint better, myself."

"Peppermint's fine, too."

"Perhaps we should get together sometime and compare other things besides our tastes in penny candy."

Lon's spirits lifted suddenly as hope was reborn inside him. "You think so?" he asked. "I'd like that, I sure would."

She glanced over at the counter, and Lon followed the direction of her gaze. Harvey Raymond had gone into the storeroom for something, and Frenchy had wandered back toward the front of the building and had his back to them as he looked at a display of rifles.

Brenda came up on her toes and brushed her lips across Lon's. Even as surprised as he was, he might have tried to put his arms around her, but she was gone before he could. As her light, graceful steps carried her toward the door, she looked back at him and said, "I'm sure I'll be seeing you around, cowboy."

"Yes, ma'am!" Lon said.

■ ■ ■ ■

OUTLAW BLOOD

■ ■ ■ ■

CHAPTER 1

The sound of gunshots and angry shouts drifted through the open door of the Wind River marshal's office. They were all too familiar to the man who bolted up from the chair behind the desk.

Most folks liked civilization and progress and watching towns grow. Cole Tyler was starting to hate those things, especially the last one. The bigger Wind River got, the more trouble cropped up for him to deal with.

Not bothering to grab his hat, which he had dropped on a front corner of the desk when he came in earlier, he rushed to the door and looked out into Grenville Avenue, the main street of the bustling Wyoming settlement. He had been the marshal here for a couple of years, and in that time he had broken up countless ruckuses, so he was cautious but not particularly worried.

He was more annoyed than anything else.

It was a warm afternoon, especially for winter in these parts, which was why the door was open to let in some fresh air. He'd had a good midday meal at Rose Foster's café and enjoyed the company of the beautiful strawberry blond proprietor, as well. Now it would have been nice to put his booted feet up on the desk and while away a pleasant hour or so.

Not a nap, mind you. He was *way* too young to be taking naps in the middle of the day like an old geezer.

But instead, he had to wade into some sort of gun fracas and try not to get himself or anybody else shot.

Several blasts had thundered close together to launch the trouble, then the reports become more sporadic over the next few moments. As Cole reached the doorway, another shot came from his right, followed closely by two more that sounded farther away. A cloud of smoke blossoming from behind a wagon parked on his side of the street drew his attention. He started in that direction.

As Cole trotted closer, he spotted a man crouched beside the driver's box at the front of the wagon, between the vehicle and the slightly raised boardwalk. The man ducked as a return shot from somewhere diagonally across the street chewed splinters from the brake lever that stuck up near his head.

Cole had seen the muzzle flash of that return shot. It came from behind some crates stacked on the high front porch of the Wind River General Store that also served as the mercantile's loading dock. Somebody had forted up there to fight it out with the man taking cover behind the wagon.

Cole knew better than to get between those combatants. He swung down from the boardwalk and paused at the rear corner of the wagon.

"Hey!" he yelled at the man closest to him. "Hold your fire!"

Cole pressed against the wagon's tailgate, using the vehicle as cover himself in case the man was spooked enough to whirl around and throw lead at him. When no shot sounded, he went on, "Stop shooting! This is Marshal Cole Tyler!"

"This ain't my fault, Marshal!" the man responded. From the glimpse Cole had gotten of him, he appeared to be a stranger to Wind River. "I was bushwhacked!"

"Hold your fire anyway! Innocent people are gonna get hurt!"

He moved along the tailgate to the other rear corner of the wagon and risked a glance

231

around it. Cole couldn't get a good look at the man crouched behind the crates, but he saw the barrel of the revolver the man held as it stuck over the top of the makeshift fort.

Cole saw something else that made him stiffen with alarm.

Clancy Madigan was creeping along the opposite boardwalk against the mercantile's front wall. His big right fist clutched the thick, knobby club he was seldom without. Obviously, he was trying to sneak up on the second gunman — the bushwhacker, if the man behind the wagon was to be believed.

Other than the shillelagh, as he called it, Madigan was unarmed. He didn't like carrying a gun and refused to do so in his regular duties as Wind River's deputy marshal.

A club, even a sturdy one wielded by the strong arm of Clancy Madigan, wasn't much of a match for a gun. Madigan had been Cole's deputy only for a relatively short time; Cole didn't want to lose his services so soon.

Besides, they had been friends ever since they had both worked for the Union Pacific several years earlier, Cole as a buffalo hunter providing food for the men building the railroad, Madigan as a track layer. Cole didn't want to see the big Irishman hurt because of Madigan's refusal to pack iron.

Cole waved a hand and tried to catch Madigan's eye, but the deputy had all his attention focused on sneaking up on the gunman and never glanced in Cole's direction.

"Marshal, you'd better do something," said the man who stood beside the driver's box at the front of the covered wagon. "That fella over there is loco! He started shootin' at me for no good reason."

Maybe that was true, maybe it wasn't. Cole didn't know, but he figured he could hash it all out later. Right now the important thing to do was to make sure the men didn't start blazing away at each other again. The people who had been on the street when the fight started had all scurried for cover, but a stray bullet could easily penetrate a window or a wall and strike an unintended target.

"You just keep holding your fire," Cole snapped at the man on his side of the street. He took a deep breath and stepped out into the open, holding his hands away from his body so the hombre on the store's porch could see he wasn't reaching for the Colt .44 on his right hip.

He was about to call out to the man to put his gun away, but as soon as Cole made his move, so did the man who had taken cover behind the wagon.

He burst into a run and bolted toward a horse tied at a hitchrack a few yards away.

Cole saw that from the corner of his eye and realized the man was trying to take advantage of the distraction. He figured the bushwhacker would be looking at Cole.

For a second that might have been true, but then the man behind the crates leaped out, pointed his gun at the fleeing man, and shouted, "Tatum! Stop!"

That gave Clancy Madigan an opening. The Irishman lunged forward and swung the shillelagh. The club crashed across the gunman's forearm and sent the revolver flying. The man yelled in pain and anger. His right arm, numb from the blow, flopped at his side as he spun toward Madigan.

Cole could see now that the man wore two guns, the one on the left butt-forward in a cross-draw rig. He hauled it out with his left hand, awkwardly enough to confirm that he wasn't a natural two-gun fighter.

But he was fast and accurate enough to get the gun out and aimed at Madigan as he sprang backward, out of reach of the backhanded sweep the deputy made with the club.

Cole's keen eyes took in the danger in a

fraction of a second. Madigan was big and lumbering, nowhere near fast enough to dodge the bullet the man was about to send at him.

No choice, then. And no time to try anything fancy.

In a blur of movement, Cole drew and fired, sending a .44 round smacking into the gunman's upper left chest.

The slug's impact was enough to knock the man against the crates. The gun in his left hand boomed as his finger jerked spasmodically on the trigger. Cole's bullet had knocked him around so that the shot just kicked up dirt in the street, though.

The man leaned against the crates for a second and then started sliding slowly down to the porch planks.

A swift rataplan of hoofbeats made Cole twist his head to the right again as he pulled his gaze away from the man he had just shot.

The other man, the one who had taken cover behind the wagon, had reached his horse. He had leaped into the saddle and now was galloping hell-for-leather along Grenville Avenue, away from the scene of battle.

For a second Cole felt like sending a bullet after him, too. He still didn't know what had happened here, but he had just killed a

235

man — more than likely — and the only person who could explain it was racing away, taking all the answers with him.

Instead of raising his gun and firing, Cole grimaced and took a cartridge from a loop in the shell belt he wore. The fleeing man rode around a corner and disappeared. Cole replaced the round he had just fired and then walked across the street.

Madigan stood over the man who lay on the porch. The deputy had kicked both of the man's guns well out of reach, Cole noted with approval.

"Dead?" he asked as he went up the steps.

"Aye," Madigan said. "Got him right through the ticker, ye did, Cole, m'lad."

Cole didn't holster his gun until then. He frowned down at the dead man's rugged, lantern-jawed face. The man's hat had fallen off, revealing a thatch of straw-colored hair.

"You know him?" Cole asked.

Madigan shook his head. "Never laid eyes on the skalleyhooter before."

A female voice said, "That's because he just rode into town and stopped here to pick up some supplies."

Cole lifted his gaze from the corpse to the young woman who stood in the open double doors with her arms crossed. Not quite twenty, Brenda Durand possessed a sultry beauty and a self-possessed air that made her seem older than her years.

She was also richer than sin, almost, having inherited many of the businesses in town, including this store, from her late father, William Durand, one of the co-founders of Wind River.

"I overheard him saying as much to one of the clerks," Brenda went on. "Then he looked out through the door, said, 'Tatum!', and ran out, drawing his gun. Do you know what this is all about, Marshal Tyler?"

Cole rubbed his chin as his frown deepened. He shook his head.

He hated having to kill a man.

He hated even more having to kill a man without knowing why.

But he didn't have time to ponder it just then because another man was striding across the street toward him, and in a booming voice, this stranger declared, "Hallelujah and praise the Lord! You have delivered us from evil, Marshal!"

CHAPTER 2

This was his day for running into strangers, Cole thought as he went back down the steps to the street, because he had never seen this man before, either.

The man was a medium-sized, gray-haired, clean-shaven gent in a worn black suit, collarless white shirt, and gray, round-crowned hat. Judging by the direction he was coming from, he had been *inside* that wagon while the bullets were flying around. Some of the shots had to have struck the vehicle, but the thick sideboards must have stopped the bullets.

The man stuck out a hand as he came up to Cole. "God surely guided your aim just now, my friend, because you saved us from certain death with your accurate shooting. Such a shame that a man had to die in order to prevent greater slaughter. My name is Woodson, Marshal, Franklin Woodson. You can call me Brother Woodson."

The man had a bigger voice and a more powerful grip than Cole would have expected from someone of his size. "I hope you'll forgive me, Mr. Woodson," he said, "but I already have a brother of my own, although I haven't seen him in a good number of years."

"All men are brothers in the eyes of the Lord, are they not?"

"Uh, I reckon." Cole cocked his head a little to the side. "Did you say 'us' a minute ago when you were talking about me saving you?"

"That's right." Woodson waved a hand toward the wagon. "Me and the rest of my family." He turned his head toward the vehicle and made a summoning gesture.

The first person to emerge from the wagon was a woman in a dark blue dress and sun bonnet. She started to climb down, but a boy followed her and jumped down from the other side of the seat, then hurried around in front of the team of mules to help her. More of a young man, really, Cole noted, since he appeared to be sixteen or seventeen, mostly grown.

One more person got out of the wagon, a girl about the same age as the boy. Cole expected to see a family resemblance between them as they approached, figuring they were brother and sister, maybe even twins.

Instead, the boy was as dark as the girl was fair, and much leaner, to boot. They looked nothing alike. The boy was the odd one out, since the girl definitely took after Franklin Woodson and the woman, who Cole supposed was Woodson's wife.

Woodson confirmed that by saying, "This is my wife, Phillippa, Marshal."

Cole nodded to the woman and started to raise his hand as if to touch the brim of his hat before he remembered he wasn't wearing one.

"Ma'am," he said politely. "I'm pleased to meet you. My name is Cole Tyler. That big fella up on the porch is my deputy, Clancy Madigan, and the young lady there is Miss Durand, who owns the store."

A few strands of graying brown hair strayed from under Mrs. Woodson's bonnet. She might have been an attractive woman at some time; now she was pleasant-looking but definitely careworn. She didn't acknowledge Cole's greeting but instead said in a worried voice, "Franklin, the children shouldn't be exposed to this . . . this terrible display . . ."

"The dead man. Of course. Simon, take your sister back to the wagon."

So maybe the two youngsters *were* brother and sister, despite their lack of resemblance.

The girl, blond, curvy, and round-faced, said, "Good heavens, Father, it's not like we haven't ever seen a dead man before. Mother and I worked in a field hospital during the war, remember?"

"You were doing the Lord's work by helping those poor men, and even so, I never liked the two of you being there," Woodson said. "But this is different. These men here today were different. They did battle like primitive savages. They were probably both outlaws, with some sort of grudge against each other that arose from the sordid lives they led . . ."

"You're at least half right, mister," Madigan said. He had been kneeling beside the dead man, going through his pockets. He held out a piece of paper he had unfolded.

Cole came up the steps to take the paper and study it. The Woodson youngsters hadn't returned to the family's wagon as their father had told them, but Woodson seemed to have forgotten that order. He pressed closer to the store's front porch, as did many of the other bystanders who had begun to gather now that the shooting was over.

The paper Cole held in his hand was a

241

wanted poster from Kansas, declaring that there was an $800 reward for one Harry "Hog" Tatum, wanted on charges of murder, armed robbery, and assault. Above the crudely printed words was an even more rudimentary drawing of a man who might have been the one who'd been hiding behind the wagon, the man who had told Cole he'd been bushwhacked.

Madigan said, "If that spalpeen on the other side of the street was an outlaw, and the fellow in the store recognized him and went gunnin' for him, like Miss Durand just told us . . ."

Cole looked down at the dead man at his feet, the man dead by Cole's own hand, and said, "Then there's a good chance this hombre here was a bounty hunter and not an outlaw at all."

"It doesn't matter in the least," Dr. Judson Kent said as he tipped the bottle and poured whiskey into the last of the four glasses he had set out. "You fired to save Clancy's life, Cole, so there's absolutely no reason for you to feel any guilt in the matter."

"Yeah," Cole said, "all I did was let an outlaw escape and kill the man who was trying to bring him to justice."

"If that bounty hunter was all that concerned with law and order, he wouldn't have tried to shoot me," Clancy said.

Dr. Kent, a tall, bearded Englishman who was also the mayor of Wind River, picked up the tray with the four drinks on it and carried it over to the table in his parlor. Cole was sitting in an armchair, his legs stretched out in front of him, crossed at the ankles. Madigan had picked up a ladder-back chair, turned it around, and straddled it. Sitting in a rocking chair not far from Cole, with a blanket over his legs, was the thin, graying figure of Billy Casebolt, Cole's regular deputy.

Casebolt had been staying here at the doctor's house for the past couple of months while he recuperated from some gunshot wounds he had received while trying to stop a bank robbery. The town council had allowed Cole to hire a replacement deputy, and along about that time, Madigan had drifted into town looking for work. Cole had been happy to pin a badge on the big Irishman's vest. He knew he could count on Madigan.

Kent handed the glasses to the men and settled down in another armchair with his own drink. He asked, "Did you find anything on the dead man to indicate his identity?"

"He had a letter in his pocket addressed to Will Sumner," Cole said. "I reckon we have to assume that was him." The marshal gave a little shake of his head. "I don't recognize the name, though. I wired the authorities in Cheyenne, Laramie, and Rock Springs. If he was actually a bounty hunter, maybe some lawman in one of those places will know him."

Cole sipped the drink in his hand. The afternoon's events had taken a tragic turn, and whiskey wouldn't change that. But it was what he had at the moment.

Madigan took off the derby perched on his rusty hair so he could tip his head far back as he downed all the liquor in his glass in one swallow.

"Ah," he said in satisfaction after licking his lips. "I know ye feel bad about what happened, Cole, but 'tis glad I am you ventilated the fellow before he could kill me."

Casebolt said, "Likely he didn't know who you was, Clancy. He might've figured you were one of this owlhoot Tatum's partners." The grizzled deputy clucked his tongue. "Bad luck all around. But he shouldn't have been so quick to try to shoot."

Cole swallowed the rest of his drink, set

the empty glass on a small table close at hand, and leaned forward to clasp his hands together between his knees.

"You were looking right at him, Clancy. Was he really going to shoot?"

Without hesitation, Madigan answered, "Aye. I saw it in his eyes. I'd kept him from downin' Tatum by whackin' his gun hand, so he was gonna plug me instead. There's nary a doubt of it in me mind."

Cole nodded slowly. There was a chance Madigan was lying to spare his feelings, but he doubted if that were true. They had never been less than honest with each other.

"Question now is, what do I do about Tatum?"

"I don't understand," Kent said with a frown. "I know the man is a wanted criminal, but he didn't break any laws here in Wind River, did he?"

"Not that I know of," Cole admitted.

The doctor spread his hands. "Well, there you have it. If he were to ride back into town, you'd be justified in arresting him and holding him for the authorities in other jurisdictions that have brought charges against him, but otherwise you have no real responsibility in the matter."

"He's an outlaw, and he used me to help him get away," Cole snapped. "I don't like that." He shrugged. "But you're right. There's no telling where he's gone, and even though sometimes I haven't worried all that much about jurisdiction, I've got no call to go chasing all over the country after him."

"Precisely. So, for all intents and purposes, this unfortunate incident is over."

Cole wished he could believe that. A feeling gnawed at his gut, though, telling him it wasn't true.

Hog Tatum rode along a narrow gulch in the foothills north of Wind River. The brush was so thick that his progress was slow, but that wasn't a bad thing. The harder it was for anybody to get up in here, the less likely it was the camp would be discovered.

A man stepped out from behind a boulder, causing Tatum to rein in sharply. The man held a Winchester at a slant across his chest, but he lowered the rifle and grinned as he recognized Tatum.

"Howdy, Hog," he said. "I should've known it was you, the amount of racket you were makin' as you came up the gulch."

"I'd like to see you or anybody else ride through this brush without makin' a racket," Tatum said as he glared at the sentry.

"You find out what Blade wanted to know?"

Tatum ignored the question and nudged his horse into motion again. The sentry had to step back to avoid being ridden down. He cast an angry look at Tatum's retreating back, but he didn't do anything else.

The only man he wanted to cross less than Hog Tatum was their mutual boss, Blade Kendrick.

Tatum followed the twisting, difficult path another quarter of a mile until the gulch made a sharp turn to the left. Around that corner, it widened out into a pocket about fifty yards wide where trees grew around a spring and there was enough grass for the dozen horses picketed there. A campfire burned not far from the pool formed by the spring. Bedrolls were spread on the ground under the trees.

A few of the men were asleep. Others played cards, cleaned their guns, or mended their harnesses. One stood alone near the head of the gulch, which ended in a rock wall with a precarious trail climbing it. Mountain goats had carved out that trail. A man could follow it, but probably not a horse. No one would even try that except in a dire emergency.

A member of the gang came up to Tatum as he dismounted. "I'll take care of your horse, Hog," the outlaw offered. He was a young man, maybe not even out of his teens. Tatum nodded curtly and handed him the reins, then walked toward the man standing alone.

Blade Kendrick had a cigar clenched between his teeth. He was seldom without one. Smoke curled around his dark, heavy-featured face. He was half turned away and acted like he didn't see Tatum approaching him, but Tatum knew that wasn't true. Kendrick never missed anything.

Finally, Kendrick turned toward the newcomer and said without any sort of greeting, "Well? Was he there in the town?"

Not allowing the nervousness he felt to show in his face or voice, Tatum said, "I never even got the chance to look or ask around, Blade. I hadn't been in Wind River fifteen minutes when that damn bounty hunter, Will Sumner, spotted me and threw down on me. You remember him. He killed Joe Bob Tucker down in Indian Territory last year."

Kendrick grunted. "Sumner. You kill him?"

Tatum couldn't help but grin. "I didn't have to. The local badge-toter took care of that for me. He thought I was just some innocent fella who'd been bushwhacked for some reason."

248

That irony didn't seem to amuse Kendrick. He asked, "What did you do?"

"Well, since I'd already drawn the lawman's attention by gettin' shot at, I jumped on my horse and lit a shuck out of town. I didn't want *him* getting a good look at me and recognizing me from some reward dodger, too."

"So you didn't do your job."

The flat tone of Kendrick's voice made Tatum stiffen in a mixture of anger and apprehension. He didn't think the boss was being fair to him, but at the same time he worried about what Kendrick might do next. The man was given to explosive fits of anger, and when he lashed out, he didn't much care who was in the way.

"It was a bad break, Blade. I'm sorry it turned out that way, but it wasn't really my fault. You can send somebody else into town to have a look around. What about the kid, Grady?"

Tatum saw Kendrick's jaw tighten as the boss outlaw's teeth clamped harder on the cigar. He might have made a mistake there, Tatum thought, so he added hurriedly, "Or maybe Wolters. He'd be good for the job."

With a visible effort, Kendrick forced himself to relax. He took the cigar out of his mouth. "Wolters," he agreed. "But if that doesn't work, we'll all go into town. Every trail, everything we've found so far, has led us here. I'll find who I'm looking for, and by God, they'll give him to me or I'll burn Wind River to the ground!"

CHAPTER 3

The unseasonably warm weather didn't last long. Cole hadn't expected it to, so he wasn't surprised when a cold wind swept down from the mountains a couple of days after the gun battle that had resulted in the bounty hunter's death.

The wind brought with it thick gray clouds but no snow. As Cole walked along Grenville Avenue, he turned up the collar of his sheepskin jacket and tugged his hat down tighter on his long brown hair.

It was late afternoon, and because of the overcast, darkness would be falling soon. Yellow lamplight glowed warmly in the windows of the marshal's office as he approached the stone building.

When he had first taken the marshal's job, the office had shared space with the Wind River Land Development Company, owned by William Durand and Andrew McKay, the co-founders of the town.

251

Durand and McKay were both dead now, as was McKay's wife, Simone, and the land development company had its office in the bank. That was fine with Cole. As far as he was concerned, the fewer reminders of everything that had happened during the turbulent early days of the settlement, the better.

Cole opened the door and stepped into the warmth of his office. Clancy Madigan sat behind the desk, and as Cole closed the door, he saw that the lawman had a visitor.

"Hello, Jeremiah," he said as he took off his hat and hung it on a nail beside the door. "Are you here on business, or just spreading the good word? Although, come to think of it, I reckon that *is* your business, isn't it? At least, one of them."

Jeremiah Newton stood up from the chair where he'd been sitting in front of the desk. He was a massive man, with muscular arms and shoulders that bulged the material of his shirt and coat. That burly frame was a result of Jeremiah's work as a blacksmith, one of the jobs Cole had mentioned.

Jeremiah's other job — the one he considered his true profession — was as pastor of Wind River's first and so far only church. He had gone to a great deal of effort and trouble to get the church built over sometimes violent opposition from the more immoral elements in town.

"I'm here to lodge a complaint, Marshal," Jeremiah said, which took Cole by surprise since the easygoing blacksmith got along well with just about everybody in town, as far as he knew.

Jeremiah's broad, ruddy face had a worried frown on it. That told Cole the matter was serious. Jeremiah was nearly always smiling.

Cole took off his jacket and hung it up, then went to the stove to pour himself a cup of coffee. He asked, "Did you do some blacksmith work for somebody and now they don't want to pay you?" That was the only thing he could think of that might bring Jeremiah to the law.

"No, this is church business." Jeremiah grew more agitated and said, "That fella who calls himself Brother Woodson, he says he's going to start his own church here in Wind River!"

Cole cocked an eyebrow, then had to take a sip of the strong black coffee to keep from laughing in response to Jeremiah's impassioned outburst. It didn't help that Clancy Madigan seemed to be amused, too.

When Cole trusted himself to speak again, he said, "Well, that's all right, isn't it? A

253

town can have more than one church. To tell you the truth, I'm a mite surprised there's not more than one already."

"But he's one of those hard-shell Baptists. For all I know, he's going to be handling snakes and things like that!"

Cole drank some more coffee and then said, "I don't really hold with handling snakes, but if that's what somebody wants to do, I don't suppose there's any law against it. As long as he doesn't hurt anybody else besides himself while he's doing it. Do you know for a fact that's what he's planning?"

Jeremiah blew out a breath and shook his head. "No, I reckon not," he admitted with obvious reluctance. "All I know for sure is that he rented an empty storefront from Miss Durand and painted a sign he put up on it that says *First Baptist Church of Wind River.*"

Jeremiah's church wasn't part of any particular denomination, but as Cole had said, he figured sooner or later they would have all sorts of houses of worship here in Wind River — Baptist, Methodist, Episcopalian, what have you. A Catholic mission, for sure. It was only a matter of time, part of that march of civilization and progress that Cole sometimes wished would slow down.

He set his coffee cup on the desk and said, "Jeremiah, I'm sorry, but there's not a thing in the world illegal about what Woodson's doing. When it comes to churches especially, the law's got to leave 'em alone, within reason."

"Aye," Clancy said, "there be nothin' wrong with a little soul-savin' competition, eh, Brother Newton?"

Jeremiah's face flushed even more than usual. "Woodson didn't go through everything I went through in order to start his church. He can't just waltz in here and . . ."

"Yeah, I'm afraid he can," Cole broke in. "I'm sorry, Jeremiah, but there's nothing I can do." He paused and thought for a moment. "This is Saturday. When does Woodson intend to start having services?"

"Tomorrow. That's what the sign he put in the window of the place said."

"Maybe nobody will show up, and he'll see that the, uh, spiritual well-being of Wind River is already in good hands."

Jeremiah just shook his head ponderously and turned to lumber toward the door. He paused with it open and looked back over his shoulder.

"No good's going to come of this, Cole.

Mark my words."

With that, he went out and closed the door behind him.

When the blacksmith was gone, Madigan chuckled and said, "Did ye ever see the like? I've heard of range wars, but never . . ."

"Pew wars?" Cole suggested when his deputy couldn't come up with anything.

"Aye! Pew wars! Before 'tis over, Brother Newton and Brother Woodson will be singin' hymns and quotin' scripture and slingin' the fire and brimstone at each other, and any innocent bystanders best run for cover!"

Cole smiled, but uneasiness stirred inside him. Strangers had brought trouble to Wind River in the past. He hoped the arrival of the Woodson family didn't herald another occurrence of that.

Despite the chilly winds outside, it was warm inside the storefront because of the fire that burned in the cast-iron stove in the corner. Along with heat from the stove, the sound of two hammers driving nails filled the room.

Simon Woodson paused in his carpentry work and sleeved a few drops of sweat off his forehead. A few feet away, Franklin Woodson stopped hammering, too, but only long enough to snap, "No lagging, son. We have to finish these pews by tomorrow. Besides, you know what the Good Book says about the Devil and idle hands."

"Yeah, Pa," Simon muttered. He knew he sounded disrespectful. Woodson pursed his lips, and Simon figured he would pay for that disrespect later.

Not now, though. There was too much work to be done to worry about him not honoring his father and his mother.

The two of them had spent the day so far nailing together plain wooden benches with short backs on them. As pews went, they were far from fancy or even comfortable. But Brother Franklin Woodson didn't care a whit for fancy and not much more for comfort. All that really mattered was his preaching.

Woodson intended to have twenty of these pews ready for the services tomorrow morning, and he and Simon were already more than halfway to that goal. Whether anyone would show up to fill those seats was anybody's guess, Simon thought.

Well . . . anybody's guess, except his father's. Woodson wasn't guessing. He was absolutely sure there would be people here for the service. His confidence in himself and his beliefs wouldn't allow him to expect anything else.

After the two of them had worked for a while longer, Woodson said, "We're going to need another keg of nails. Go back to the camp and fetch one, Simon."

"Yes, Pa," Simon said in a more deferential tone this time. He set the hammer aside, picked up his jacket, and left the storefront.

He was going to have to start thinking of it as the church, he told himself as he shrugged into the jacket and walked toward the edge of town where they had parked the wagon and pitched their tent.

The money Franklin Woodson had saved during their time at the last place they lived had gone for the rent on the storefront and lumber for the pews. They already had several kegs of nails in the wagon, ready to be used, along with a couple of cans of paint and other building supplies.

This church in Wind River would not be the first one Woodson had started from nothing, although he had also been called to preach at several existing congregations during the past dozen years since Simon had come to be part of the family. If they stayed in Wind River long enough, they would rent or even build a small house, but getting the church started came first.

Until then, they would live in the wagon

and in the tent. Its canvas sides popped a little in the wind as Simon approached.

He glanced at the tent but went to the wagon and lowered the tailgate so he could reach inside and pull out one of the kegs of nails stored under the bunk where his mother and father slept.

Through the narrow opening in the canvas flaps at the front of the tent, a voice called, "Is that you, Simon?"

The young man stiffened. "Pa just sent me to fetch some more nails, Deborah."

"Come in here a minute, would you?"

"I've got to get back. You know how Pa is. Time's a-wastin'. We've still got pews to build before tomorrow morning."

"Oh, for goodness' sake. I just want to ask you a question. It won't take but a second."

Simon sighed. His sister was nothing if not persistent. He knew he ought to pick up the keg he had just set on the lowered tailgate and head back to the storefront — the church, he reminded himself. But something turned his steps toward the tent instead.

He pushed through the opening. Because of the gloomy day, it would have been dark inside the tent if not for the lantern that burned on a small table between the cots. Deborah stood in front of the lantern as she turned toward Simon and lifted the dresses she held, one in each hand.

"Which do you think I should wear tomorrow?" she asked.

Simon didn't know and didn't care. Dresses all looked alike to him. Besides, he couldn't tear his eyes away from the shape of her body in the thin shift that was all she wore right now. With the light behind her like that, it was almost like she didn't have anything on.

He swallowed hard and forced himself to look down at the ground between them. "Either one," he said. "It doesn't matter."

"Why, Simon, you're not embarrassed, are you?"

He didn't answer. Instead he snapped, "Where's Ma?"

"She went to the store. Said she would be gone for a while." She shook the dresses she held up and down, and even though he wasn't looking directly at her, he could tell that the movement did interesting things with what was under that shift. "Now come on, tell me which one you like the best."

"The, uh . . . the green one, I guess."

"You think so? I like it, too. But I want to make a good impression, what with it being Pa's first service here in Wind River and all. Do you think anybody will show up? Usually there are at least a few people who come out of curiosity, if nothing else."

"Yeah. I got to get back . . ."

"You don't have to run off, you know." Deborah sounded a little irritated now. "You act like you don't even want to talk to your own sister."

"You're not . . ."

He choked off what he was about to say. It wouldn't serve any purpose. They weren't brother and sister, not by blood, even though he had taken the Woodson name and Franklin and Phillippa Woodson always treated him as if he were theirs by birth.

Deborah treated him that way, too, but only sometimes. Other times, like now, she took great delight in teasing and tormenting him, and not in a sisterly way at all.

He started to turn away, but she stopped him by saying, "Why don't you like me, Simon?"

"I like you just fine," he said, still looking at the ground. "You're my sister and I love you. But you shouldn't act like . . . well, it's not decent and all . . ."

"You mean like that day a couple of years ago? You didn't seem to mind all that much."

Simon didn't have to ask her what she meant. The memory was still vivid. Burned into his brain, in fact.

They had been living in Colorado at the time, about a year after the end of the war. Franklin Woodson had been preaching in an established church at the time, and the congregation had furnished a small house for the pastor and his family. That was one of the few places where Simon had had a room of his own.

But that hadn't kept Deborah out of it, and he would never forget waking up early one morning, with sunlight streaming through the window, to find her standing there beside his bed, smiling down at him without a stitch on. He'd looked, of course; he couldn't help it. And she had just kept on smiling, fully aware of the power she possessed, until finally she turned and sauntered away, picking up the robe she had dropped on a chair and pulling it on as she left the room.

When Simon had first come to live with the Woodsons, Deborah had given him trouble because she was a bratty child. What she had done as she grew older was worse. So far, Simon had resisted the temptations she had thrown in his path, but he didn't know how long he could hold out.

But he wouldn't give in today, he told himself sternly. He turned and pushed out of the tent, ignoring the plaintive "Simon!" that Deborah sent after him. He grabbed the keg of nails from the tailgate and headed for the storefront church.

He still had hammering to do. Lots and lots of hammering.

CHAPTER 4

Sunday morning dawned very cold but mostly clear, with only a few white clouds floating in the arching blue sky. The mountains in the distance looked close enough to reach out and touch, Cole Tyler thought as he walked along the street with his breath pluming in front of him.

He had never been much of a churchgoer, at least once he got old enough that his mother couldn't force him to attend services anymore. He thought of himself as a spiritual man — sort of — but he preferred to do his worshipping, if you could call it that, out in nature where he could be closer to whatever force was responsible for the universe.

However, from time to time he went to Jeremiah's church, out of friendship as much as anything else.

This morning he was headed for Brother

Franklin Woodson's new church, out of curiosity.

The night before had been a busy one, as Saturday nights usually were. Quite a few cowboys from the Diamond S, Latch Hook, and the other spreads in the area had come into town to drink and carouse. The ranch crews were smaller at this season of the year than they would be once it came time for spring roundup and the drives to the railroad, but there were still enough punchers around to make things hectic . . . especially when there was some bad blood between two of the spreads, in this case the Diamond S and Latch Hook. Cole and Madigan had had to break up several saloon fights.

Nobody had been hurt badly enough to require a visit to Dr. Judson Kent's office, so that counted as a successful Saturday night as far as Cole was concerned. The cowboys who were still in town were sleeping it off this morning, so only the more respectable citizens were out and about, most of them walking toward the church at the edge of the settlement. Cole nodded to the men he met and pinched the brim of his hat to the ladies.

As he came closer to the storefront that was now the First Baptist Church of Wind River, he saw Franklin Woodson standing at the door, hatless, a Bible in his hand. He had a silk tie knotted in a bow at his throat today, and all the trail dust had been brushed from his black suit.

"Good morning, Marshal," Woodson greeted Cole. "The Lord has given us a beautiful day, hasn't He?"

"A mite chilly, but otherwise I can't argue about that," Cole said. As Woodson opened the door for him, he tried to look past the preacher into the church. "Got any customers this morning?"

"People in need of spiritual guidance aren't exactly what I'd call customers. I'm not selling anything, Marshal. I offer it freely."

"I thought I might take in your sermon, if that's all right."

Woodson stepped back a little and waved with the hand holding the Bible. "Come in, and welcome," he said.

Cole took off his hat as he stepped into the room. Woodson had set it up with two rows of ten pews, separated by an aisle. At the front was a pulpit, flanked by a chair on each side.

Most of the pews were empty. Maybe a dozen people were here, in a room that would have seated a hundred or more. Cole had no idea if that was a good turnout for a

266

first service, but it didn't seem too impressive to him. If Woodson was disappointed, though, he didn't show it.

Cole recognized all but a couple of the people in attendance. Two men he didn't know were seated on different pews. That wasn't unusual. He tried to keep track of everybody who came into town on the train or rode in, but that was difficult. He couldn't be everywhere at once, couldn't see everything.

He sat down at the far end of a pew from one of the men he didn't know, a mild-looking gent in range clothes who had thinning dark hair, several days' worth of beard stubble, and a battered old hat sitting on the bench beside him. Might be a grub-line rider who hadn't yet found a spot to hunker down for the winter. He wasn't wearing a gun and didn't look like a troublemaker, and that was all Cole really cared about.

Woodson's wife and children were nowhere in sight, which surprised Cole a little, but they might be in the back room, he decided. A few minutes later, that guess proved to be right as the woman and two youngsters emerged from a door in the wall behind the pulpit. Woodson closed the door, so he wouldn't be letting the warm air out anymore, and joined the other members of his family at the front of the room. Mrs. Woodson sat down in the chair to the left of the pulpit, while Woodson took the one on the right. Their son and daughter sat down on the front pew to the left, a few rows in front of Cole. They were all dressed nicely this morning, although the clothes clearly weren't new.

Woodson sat quietly for a few moments with his head down, as if he were gathering his thoughts, then lifted his head and stood up to move to the pulpit. He placed his Bible on it and then gripped the sides of the stand.

"Good morning," he said. "Welcome to the Lord's house on this beautiful morning, for the first service of the First Baptist Church of Wind River. My name is Franklin Woodson, and I have been called to be the pastor of this church. My wife and my children," he nodded to them, "and I all join together to tell you how pleased we are that all of you are here this morning. Now, let us pray."

He cleared his throat and bowed his head. Cole bowed his head, too, but he left his eyes slitted open, just out of habit.

"Dear Lord," Woodson began.

That was as far as he got before the doors at the back of the room slammed open and a harsh voice demanded, "Is this where the preachin's supposed to be?"

Cole saw Woodson stiffen as if a ramrod had been shoved down his back. His hands tightened on the side of the pulpit and made the knuckles stand out whitely. For a second, a surprising amount of anger burned in the man's eyes.

But then he controlled himself and said, "Come in, my friends, come in. All are welcome in the house of the Lord."

The disturbance had brought Cole to his feet. He half-turned to see three men swaggering into the room. Their thick canvas trousers, buffalo coats, and heavy work boots marked them as freighters. Although the railroad had extended through southern Wyoming, there were plenty of smaller settlements to the north where the steel rails hadn't reached yet, and several freight lines served their needs.

Bullwhackers were just about as troublesome as cowboys whenever they found themselves in town long enough to get a snootful of liquor. From the bleary-eyed looks of these bearded ruffians, Cole figured they had been doing plenty of drinking the night before. If he got close enough to them, he could probably smell the Who-Hit-John on them. He wasn't sure why they were up and about or even awake this early, but he had no doubt they had causing trouble in mind.

"What kind o' sky pilot are you?" asked one of the freighters as they stomped up the aisle between the rows of pews.

"I'm a Baptist minister," Woodson answered.

"No, no, I mean, are you the kind who likes to tell folks they're goin' straight to hell if they don't act as prissy and lily-livered as you do?"

Again Cole saw that spark of anger in Woodson's eyes. He thought he ought to step in here before things got out of hand, so he moved toward the freighters and began, "You boys hold on . . ."

Woodson surprised him by stepping out from behind the pulpit and saying, "That's all right, Marshal. I'm perfectly willing to address this gentleman's question. Perhaps if he likes my answer, we can continue with our service."

Another of the freighters squinted at Cole and said defiantly, "Lawdog, eh? You ain't got no call to arrest us, Marshal. Talkin' to a preacher ain't against the law."

"Disturbing a church service is," Cole insisted.

"We ain't disturbin' nothin'! He said he

was willin' to talk to us, didn't he?"

"Indeed I am," Woodson put in as he came toward Cole and the three burly strangers.

"Franklin, be careful," his wife urged as she clutched her fingers together in her lap.

Woodson didn't seem to hear her. He planted himself in front of the freighters and said, "You wanted to know if I was going to condemn you to hell, didn't you? Well, the answer to that is simple. I can't condemn anyone to hell. That's in the hands of God. Not only that, but the Bible says to let him who is without sin cast the first stone." Woodson spread his hands and smiled. "I am far from without sin, gentlemen, so I cast no stones."

"You?" one of the freighters said. "You claimin' you're a sinner?"

"Like everyone else here."

The three men thought that was funny. Two of them laughed while the third said, "Unless you spent last night in a bawdy house soakin' up booze and playin' slap-and-tickle with some soiled doves, you ain't sinned near as bad as us, preacher!"

"Oh?" Woodson smiled, but his eyes were as cold as the wind whipping over the Wyoming plains. "How about being responsible for the deaths of more than eight hundred men?"

That question, asked in a clear, powerful voice, shut the freighters up in a hurry. Maybe even sobered them up a little, too. It certainly made the rest of the folks in the church take notice. Cole reacted the same way, wondering what in blazes Woodson was talking about.

After a moment, one of the freighters blew out a scoffing breath and said, "You never done nothin' like that."

"As a matter of fact, I did," Woodson said calmly. "I underestimated the size of the enemy's force and sent the men under my command into a battle they couldn't survive, let alone win, at a place called Pittsburg Landing, in Tennessee. There was a church meeting house nearby known as Shiloh. You've probably heard of it."

A frown creased the forehead of the man who had scoffed. "You was in the war?"

"I was."

"Which side?"

"Does that matter?" Woodson shook his head. "A man slaughtered in battle is just as dead no matter which color uniform he wears. I learned that lesson quite well that day . . . which is why I walked away from command. I had been arrogant and callous and proud, and it cost the lives of many,

many men. I asked the Lord for forgiveness, resigned my commission, and became a chaplain. My wife followed my path and worked as a nurse. Even my children helped where and when they could, although I hated to expose them to the horrors of war any more than was necessary."

Silence fell over the room. The small number of people who had shown up for the service had listened to Woodson's story with rapt attention, probably more so than they would have to a regular sermon.

Cole let that silence stretch out for a moment, then said, "You fellas got your answer. Are you ready to move on now, or would you rather sit down and listen to whatever else Brother Woodson has to say?"

Judging by the solemn looks on their faces, they might have done just that . . . if another big man in a buffalo coat hadn't barged into the church then; yelled, "Harley, you son of a bitch!"; and charged toward the trio of freighters, swinging his hamlike fists in wild, powerhouse punches.

CHAPTER 5

"Stop!" Woodson cried as he threw himself into the attacker's path. "Please, no fight . . ."

Cole made a grab for the preacher's arm to try to pull him out of harm's way, but Woodson was too quick. He lunged forward, right into one of those wildly swinging fists.

The blow smacked into Woodson's jaw with a meaty thud and flung him backward with his arms flailing.

One of the other freighters instinctively caught him. "Damn you, Turk!" the man yelled. "You just walloped a preacher!"

"I don't care!" Turk bellowed back. "You three varmints snuck outta the whorehouse and left me with the bill for all four of us, and I'm gonna take it outta your hides!"

That explained why the freighters were awake this early. They had spent the night in one of Wind River's two houses of ill repute, which were grudgingly tolerated by the town's more respectable citizens because they furnished another outlet for the cowboys, railroaders, and freighters upon whom so much of the settlement's business depended.

Turk's three friends would have considered it a good joke to slip out of the house while he was still asleep, so he would have to settle up with the madam for the night's festivities. But Turk hadn't taken it well, as he demonstrated by charging again at them.

As big as those three were, Turk was even bigger. He slammed a punch into one man's jaw and sent him sprawling back over a pew. The man who had caught Woodson flung the still-stunned preacher aside so he could defend himself. Woodson's son, Simon, was close by, though, and was able to grab his father before Woodson fell to the floor.

Cole started to wade in and try to bring the freighters under control even if he had to wallop them over the heads with his Colt. But if he attempted that, he knew there was a good chance they might all turn on him and stomp him into the floor.

If they wanted to whale away on each other for a while and wear themselves out first, that might be best, he decided. As long as they didn't bust things up too bad while they were doing it . . .

During his days as a hunter, Cole had seen buffalo bulls battling for supremacy in the herd on several occasions. With their size and the shaggy coats they wore, the freighters reminded him of those beasts and their epic struggles as they slammed punches at each other. Those fights were always one on one, however, while the massive Turk had two opponents. The first man Turk had hit was still lying on the floor, evidently out cold next to the pew he had overturned by falling against it.

Mrs. Woodson was on her feet. As she gazed at the men in horror, she cried, "Stop them! For heaven's sake, stop them!"

The Woodson girl was watching the brawl, too, but she didn't seem particularly upset by it, Cole noted from her intent expression. She was breathing hard, too. She couldn't look away from the spectacle of these big men slugging away at each other.

The struggle surged back and forth. The freighters rammed into several of the pews as they fought, but they didn't turn over any more of the benches. The other people who had come to attend the service here this morning had stood up and moved back to the other side of the room, where they watched with great interest, too. Life in a frontier settlement was often uneventful and boring. Anything that broke the monotony was welcome, even a bloody fight in a house of worship.

If Turk's two opponents had been able to knock him out, that probably would have ended the fracas. Turk proved to be surprisingly resilient, though. He absorbed what seemed to Cole like a tremendous amount of punishment without appearing to feel it, and he dished out plenty of his own to the two men battling him.

Woodson regained his senses at last. His son still had hold of him, but he pulled loose and stumbled toward the freighters, saying, "Please, in the name of all that's holy, please stop profaning this house of . . ."

Cole grabbed his arm and pulled him back as he saw another wild punch streaking toward Woodson's face. Woodson fell against him and clutched his buckskin shirt.

"Marshal, you have to stop them," he said. "We can't let them destroy all my hard work."

As far as Cole could see, other than building the pews, Woodson hadn't worked all that hard so far. But he understood why the man didn't want Turk, Harley, and the other two to bust the place up. He turned to the bystanders on the other side of the room and said, "One of you men run down to my office and tell my deputy I need his help. Tell him to bring a shotgun."

Cole didn't intend for there to be any shooting, but often just the sight of a Greener's twin muzzles staring at a man, looking like a pair of cannon, was plenty to settle down the most rambunctious hombre. Not only that, Clancy Madigan was big and strong enough to hold his own if it came to a tussle with the freighters.

One of the townsmen ran out of the church, leaving the doors open behind him.

"I . . . I can't stand by and watch them do this," Woodson said.

Cole tightened his grip on the man's arm. "Just stay back, preacher. That's the best thing you can do right now. Those fellas are too loco to listen to reason. They're gonna have to pound it out of each other."

Woodson continued to fret, and so did his wife. Mrs. Woodson let out an anguished little cry when the brawlers lurched against the pulpit and knocked it over, then sent the nearby chairs flying. Turk snatched up one of the chairs, holding it by the back as he raised it above his head.

"No!" Woodson cried.

Turk ignored that plea. He brought the chair crashing down on one of his opponents. The chair broke into several pieces as the impact drove the victim to his knees. Turk backhanded him with the piece of chair he still held. The man slid on his back until he bumped up against the first man Turk had knocked down.

That left the odds even for the first time in this clash.

Turk brandished the broken piece of furniture as he advanced toward his remaining opponent. Facing Turk on his own, the man suddenly seemed to lose all desire to fight.

He backed off and held up both hands, palms out. "Turk, take it easy. Blast it, we'll make good on what you had to pay. It was just a joke!"

Turk slashed the piece of wood back and forth and said, " 'T'weren't funny! It was humiliatin', havin' the madam chew me out like she did. That's why I got to wallop you, Harley."

"But you already knocked out Akins and Kellogg! Ain't that enough? Anyway, it was, uh, their idea."

Turk smacked the broken piece of chair into the palm of his other hand and shook his head. "I don't believe that. Them two ain't got the brains to come up with somethin' like that. But you do, Harley. You always was a mean-spirited sort."

Cole knew that if Turk hit the other man with that makeshift club, it might stove his head in and kill him. He had been willing to let the fight run its course, but he wasn't going to stand by and watch murder being committed.

He stepped forward and said in a loud, clear voice, "That's enough, Turk."

Turk glanced back over his shoulder and let out a contemptuous snort. "This ain't none o' your business, lawman. It's just betwixt this varmint and me."

"You go to killing a man in the town limits of Wind River and it dang sure *is* my business," Cole insisted. He rested his hand on the butt of his Colt. "I'm the marshal here, and it's my job to keep the peace."

Turk sneered and asked, "You gonna shoot me and get blood all over the floor of this nice new church?"

"At least this brute realizes he's no longer in a house of ill repute," Woodson said.

Talk like that wasn't helping matters, Cole thought.

Nor was the fact that Harley had taken advantage of Turk being distracted to grab up one of the broken chair legs. Cole caught a glimpse of him stepping up and swinging it at Turk's head. With Turk's big, bulky body in the way, he couldn't risk a shot.

But Simon Woodson was close enough to grab Harley's arm. He clung to it and his weight was enough to make the blow smack across Turk's shoulder instead of catching him in the head.

Harley cursed and threw a punch with his other hand. It landed just above Simon's left ear and knocked him loose, sent him staggering back. Simon lost his balance and fell to one knee.

"Son!" Franklin Woodson cried. But instead of going to Simon's aid, he went after Harley, wading in with a flurry of short but powerful punches that appeared to take the freighter by surprise as they drove him backward.

Cole was certainly surprised by the ferocity of the preacher's attack. Looked like Woodson didn't believe in turning the other cheek when his son was hurt.

Harley was still a lot bigger than Woodson, though. He stopped giving ground, set himself, and hit Woodson in the face again. The blow rocked Woodson's head back and stopped him in his tracks.

While Harley was busy with that, Turk dropped the piece of broken chair and wound up for a haymaker that he delivered with perfect timing to Harley's jaw. Harley's feet left the floor and he crashed down on his back with such force that Cole felt the boards shiver under his feet.

Turk was the only one of the freighters left upright. As he turned toward Cole, evidently caught up in battle lust and eager to continue the fight, Clancy Madigan hurried into the storefront with the man Cole had sent to fetch him close behind. The double-barreled shotgun Madigan held appeared almost small in the Irishman's big hands as he pointed it at Turk.

"Want me to feed this fella a load o' buckshot, Cole?" Madigan asked.

Turk stopped and held up both hands. A grin appeared on his bearded face.

"I ain't a big enough fool to go up against a scattergun, Marshal," he said. "Besides, I already handed them three so-called friends o' mine their needin's. You gonna take us all to jail now?"

"Yeah, I sort of had that in mind," Cole answered dryly.

"That tussle was almost as much fun as the night that started all this." Turk chuckled. "I reckon it was worth it."

"Worth it?" Mrs. Woodson repeated. "You . . . you horrible animal! My husband and my son are hurt . . ."

"I'm fine, Phillippa," Woodson said as he lifted a hand to his chin and worked his jaw back and forth. "A bit bruised and sore, but I can still talk well enough to preach the gospel, and that's all that really matters." He turned to Simon, who had gotten back to his feet, and put a hand on his shoulder. "What about you, son?"

"I'm all right," Simon replied. Gingerly, he rubbed the side of his head where Harley had punched him. "Like you said, Pa, just a little sore."

The two Woodson females gathered around Simon to start fussing over him, while Woodson said to Cole, "There's the matter of damages."

"Yeah, they broke a chair, all right," Cole agreed. "How much do you think it'll cost to replace it?"

Woodson thought about the question and shrugged. "Three dollars ought to cover it."

"I'll collect it from 'em and see that you get it. In the meantime . . ." Cole gestured toward the overturned pew and pulpit and told Turk, "Pick those up and put 'em back like they belong. Then you can get to work hauling your pards to jail, since you're the one who made them groggy as drunk mules."

Mrs. Woodson turned from her son long enough to say, "You should lock them up for a year, Marshal!"

"That'll be up to the judge," Cole said, "but that seems like a pretty heavy sentence for a fight, ma'am."

"Don't worry, Phillippa," Woodson told her. "Man's law, imperfect though it is in comparison to the Lord's, will deal with these men."

Once Turk had set up the pew and the pulpit, Madigan took charge of shepherding the prisoners to jail. The other three freighters were starting to come around, so Turk didn't have to carry them after all, even though they were pretty unsteady on their feet.

"Sorry your first service was ruined, preacher," Cole said to Woodson.

"Ruined?" Woodson repeated as he brushed off his Bible. It had fallen on the floor when the pulpit was knocked over. "Not at all, Marshal." He raised his voice as he looked at the townspeople in attendance. "If you'll all take your seats again, we'll finish that prayer and then sing a hymn."

Blade Kendrick and Hog Tatum were sitting on rocks near the campfire when Frank Wolters rode in later that afternoon. The dark-haired, deceptively mild-looking outlaw swung down from the saddle and turned his mount over to Grady, the youngster whose job it was to take care of the horses.

Unable to contain his impatience, Kendrick stood up and said to Wolters, "Was he there?"

Wolters nodded as he pulled off the gloves he wore. "He's there. Just like you described him, Blade. I'm a little surprised you were able to do that, as much time has passed since you saw him last."

"Some things a man never forgets," Kendrick said. "He just knows. What we heard about the church, that was right?"

Wolters nodded again. A faint smile tugged at his mouth. "I attended the service this morning. Sat on the same pew as Hog's friend, the marshal, in fact."

"I never said he was my friend," Hog spoke up with a scowl. "He got that bounty hunter off my back, but it was a pure accident, I reckon."

Kendrick made a curt gesture and said, "Never mind about that. Tell me what else happened."

"How do you know anything else happened?" Wolters asked.

"Because I can see you're busting to talk about it. Spill, Frank, before I lose my patience."

Wolters had been about to get himself a cup of coffee, but hearing the dangerous tone in Kendrick's voice, he didn't bother with that. Instead he explained about the four freighters and the fight between them. When he said, "The boy got in the middle of it there for a minute . . . ," Kendrick's hand shot out and gripped his arm hard enough that he winced.

"Was he hurt?" the outlaw asked.

Wolters shook his head and sighed in relief when Kendrick let go of him. "He took a little punch but afterwards looked like he was fine, even though his ma and sister were taking on like he was the bravest thing ever."

A new voice said, "That woman's not his ma, and he doesn't have a sister! Ain't that right, Pa?"

The three men turned to look at Grady, the young wrangler, and after a moment, Blade Kendrick said, "That's right, boy. Simon's *your* brother, and it's not going to be long before he's back with his real family where he belongs."

CHAPTER 6

Missouri, 1858 — Twelve Years Earlier
Five-year-old Simon Kendrick heard the door of the family's cabin crash open and flinched as he lay on the straw-stuffed mattress in the loft. Beside him, his brother, Grady, fourteen months younger, continued slumbering soundly. Nothing woke Grady once he had gone to sleep. The boys' ma said sometimes that the angel Gabriel could blow his trumpet right in Grady's ear and the boy wouldn't stir.

Simon, though, often lay awake at night until he'd heard his father come in and determined what sort of mood he was in. Blade Kendrick wasn't much of a drinking man, but he was foul-tempered and didn't need to be drunk in order to be mean. Based on whatever whims were swimming around in his brain, he might fall into bed and start snoring almost right away, or he might argue with Simon's mother over something — or nothing — and wind up treating her badly.

Of course, it was his right to do so, since he was her husband. The law said so. But that didn't mean Simon had to like it. He might be only five years old, but he knew already that some things were right and some were just . . . wrong.

One of these nights, he thought as the door slammed, one of these nights he would do something about it. Maybe tonight.

The soft tones of his mother's voice floated up to the loft. Simon couldn't make out the words. Depending on how his father answered, he might be able to relax, roll over, and go to sleep.

Instead, Blade Kendrick's voice was loud and angry as he said, "What the hell business of yours is it where I've been, woman? You reckon you can start demanding that a man spill his guts as soon as he walks in the door?"

The woman's response was still quiet and placating. All Simon understood was her saying, "Please, Blade . . ."

She stopped short, followed by a soft cry and a sound Simon recognized as furniture scraping sharply on the puncheon floor. His father seldom struck his mother, but he sometimes pushed her roughly away from him when she tried to get close to him and calm him down. Simon figured that was what happened just now. His father had pushed her, and she had caught herself on one of the chairs next to the rough-hewn table.

Maybe that would be the end of it. Maybe she would retreat to the bed in the corner, behind the blanket she had hung up to take the place of a wall that wasn't there. Then he would sit down and brood deep into the night before finally going to bed himself.

Maybe that was the way things would have happened if a fist hadn't pounded on the door just then.

Even up in the loft, Simon was able to hear the high-pitched but harsh voice that called, "Open up in there, Kendrick! This is Tom Bayless!"

Simon knew the name. Tom Bayless was the constable of the little town where the Kendrick family lived. For the life of him, Simon couldn't think of any reason why the man would be banging on the door after nightfall like this.

With his curiosity too strong to resist, Simon scooted over to the edge of the loft so he could look down in the cabin's main — indeed, only — room.

Simon's mother stood beside the table.

His father was over by the fireplace. Both of them had turned their heads toward the door. In a half-whisper Simon wouldn't have been able to hear if he had remained in his blankets, his mother asked, "Blade, what have you done?"

"Not a damned thing," he said.

The constable's fist hit the door again. "Kendrick!"

Simon's father slashed a hand toward the table. "Sit down. Keep your mouth shut."

He went to the door, pulled the latch string, and jerked it open just as Tom Bayless was about to hammer on it again.

"What's the idea, Bayless? My kids are asleep, blast it. You can't come around raising such a commotion . . ."

"Reckon I can do what I want, Kendrick. I'm the law in these parts." Bayless was a tall, heavyset man with a pleasantly big-nosed face and curly dark hair under his pushed-back straw hat. He looked more like a farmer — which he also was — than a lawman.

He had a shotgun tucked under his arm, though, and Simon felt a shiver of apprehension as he stared at the menace of the weapon's twin barrels.

"Somebody busted into Mr. Carter's house tonight," Bayless went on. "Two men.

The housemaid got a glimpse of 'em, but not enough of a look to tell who they were."

"What business is that of mine? If you've got robbers to catch, that's your job."

Bayless squinted and cocked his head to the side. "How'd you know they stole anything? All I said was some fellas broke in."

"Why else would they do that?"

With his free hand, the constable rubbed his chin. "As a matter of fact, they got into Mr. Carter's strongbox and made off with a hundred dollars. Busted it wide open, looked like with a shovel. That's what woke up the housemaid."

Simon's father shook his head and said, "It must not have been much of a strongbox if somebody could crack it open that easy. I still don't know why you're telling me about this."

"Where you been this evenin', Kendrick?"

His eyes opened wider. "Oh, so that's it. You're accusing me of being a thief."

"I just asked you a question," Bayless insisted. "You've done work for Lonzo Carter. You went out there and shoed some horses for him just two days ago. He took his strongbox out to pay you, so you knew where he kept it."

"Housemaid tell you that, too, did she?"

"That's right."

"I've shoed horses and done odd jobs for plenty of folks around here. You gonna come pounding on my door every time something happens on one of their places?"

"I just might," Bayless said. "I've had my eye on you and that pard of yours, Dave Childers, for quite a while. I ain't been able to find Dave yet to ask him any questions, but I knowed you might be here."

Simon's father turned his head to look at Simon's mother. She had sunk down wearily into the chair she had been holding on to earlier.

"Damn right I'm here. I've *been* here since before sundown. Isn't that right, Harriet?"

Simon knew good and well that his father hadn't been home since that morning until just a short time earlier. His mother had to know that, too.

But she just lifted her eyes from the floor and nodded slowly.

"That's right, Mr. Bayless," she said. "Blade came in from working late this afternoon and hasn't stepped foot outside since."

Bayless frowned. "You sure about that, ma'am?"

"I think I know where my husband's been."

"I guess you would at that," Bayless said, but he didn't sound happy about it, or like he really believed it, either. "We'll see what Childers has to say about it, once I catch up to him."

"You do that," Simon's father said, smiling now. "I haven't seen ol' Dave all day, so I can't speak to what he's been up to."

Bayless grunted and said, "Yeah." He raised his pudgy hand in a half-hearted gesture toward his hat and added, "Ma'am," as he backed out of the cabin.

Simon's father closed the door hard behind him, then stood there breathing heavily. Simon knew the signs. His father was trying to control the rage inside him that was never buried very far down.

It was the wrong thing for Simon's mother to do just then when she said, "Blade, what have you done now?"

Simon caught his breath in horror as his father whirled around and charged across the room toward the table. His mother threw up her hands to try to protect herself, but Simon's father bulled into her, knocking over the chair and sending her to the floor. He dropped on top of her and grabbed hold of her throat.

Simon could feel his heart hammering in his chest. He wanted to scramble down the ladder from the loft and run over to help his mother, but he knew he couldn't do anything to stop his father. He wasn't old enough or big enough or brave enough . . .

"What is it?" Grady asked sleepily from beside Simon. He hadn't even heard his brother crawling over to him. He wasn't even sure why Grady was awake; the commotion surely hadn't roused him.

But whatever the reason, Grady was awake, and as he pushed his head up alongside Simon's shoulder and looked down at what was happening in the cabin, he started to scream. The shrieks filled up the small space under the roof and tore at Simon's ears. He clapped his hands over his ears, closed his eyes, and shouted, "Stop it, stop it, stop it!"

He wasn't sure how long that went on. He wasn't even sure if he was telling Grady or his father to stop what he was doing. But when Simon opened his eyes again, he recoiled from his father's face, which was flushed brick-red with anger. He had climbed the ladder and was perched with his shoulders just above the level of the loft.

"Shut up!" Blade Kendrick bellowed. "Both of you little brats shut up!"

He reached for Simon, but terror made the little boy's muscles work. He grabbed his brother and scooted backward as fast as he could, dragging Grady with him. Their father swiped a hand at them but missed.

Kendrick didn't climb the rest of the way into the loft to go after the boys. With his mouth twisted in a snarl, he glared at them for a moment, then said, "Quit that caterwauling, or I'll whip the hide off you!"

With that, he went back down the ladder.

Simon had backed all the way to the spot where the roof came down and he couldn't go any farther. He sat there holding the trembling Grady and staring at the spot where their father had disappeared, hoping that he wouldn't come back again. Simon wanted to crawl forward and make sure their father wasn't hurting their mother again, but he couldn't summon up the courage.

Even at five years old, he hated himself for that failure.

There wasn't any more yelling or banging around down below, however, so Simon allowed himself to hope that his father had gone to bed to sleep off his rage.

Grady huddled against his older brother. Simon had his arm around the younger boy's shoulders and held him tightly. After a while, Grady stopped trembling, and not long after that, his deep, regular breathing told Simon that his little brother had gone back to sleep. Simon was thankful for that. He hooked the mattress with his foot, dragged it closer, and carefully leaned Grady over onto it. He picked up Grady's legs and swung them onto the mattress.

A light still burned below. Someone blew it out, and peace and quiet descended over the cabin.

For now. Simon knew it was only a matter of time until something else happened to set his father off.

He stretched out beside Grady and tried to get to sleep, too, but he hadn't dozed off when he heard the faint sounds of someone moving around in the cabin. Then he felt a slight vibration and knew someone was climbing the ladder.

For a moment, terror filled Simon's heart. Was his father climbing up to the loft to kill him and Grady? To Simon's eyes, Blade Kendrick was huge and immensely power-ful. He could take both boys by the neck and choke them to death without any trouble, like a dog killing a rat. Would he do that, so that they would never annoy him again?

Then a dark shape appeared at the top of

the ladder, and Simon's mother whispered, "Simon? Are you awake?"

Simon almost cried from the relief he felt when he recognized her voice. "I'm here, Ma," he said. "I'm here."

She climbed all the way into the loft. "Is your brother asleep?"

"He was awake earlier, when Pa . . . when . . . but he's asleep now."

She picked up Grady and held him against her with his head resting on her shoulder. He didn't awaken. He was a fairly hefty four-year-old, so there was strain in her voice as she said, "I'll carry him down the ladder. You get some of your clothes and some of his and put them in that sack I gave you."

She had given him a burlap sack several days earlier and told him to put it away in the loft. He hadn't been able to figure out at the time why she would have done such a thing, and even now he didn't grasp that she'd had some use for it in mind all along. He just did what she told him.

Then, with a glimmering of the insight that can come even to the very young, he asked, "Are we leaving, Ma?"

"We are," she breathed. "Oh, yes, we surely are."

Slowly, she climbed down the ladder,

bracing herself against it so she could manage with one hand while the other arm held Grady. Simon could tell she was trying to be very quiet, so he did the same. He heard soft snoring from behind the hanging blanket on the other side of the room and knew his father was asleep over there.

At that moment, more than anything else in the world, Simon wanted his father to stay asleep.

His mother was already at the door with Grady by the time Simon reached the bottom of the ladder. When she opened it, enough light from the moon and stars came in for him to see that she was fully clothed in one of her old dresses. He and Grady just wore nightshirts. But that would do for now. They could get dressed later, in some of the clothes Simon had stuffed in the bag.

Simon started toward the door. The thick puncheons in the floor made no sound under his bare feet. But in the dim light, he bumped against one of the chairs by the table and it scraped faintly as it moved an inch or so.

Momentarily frozen with terror, Simon stood there listening to the snoring on the other side of the curtain.

It broke off. Blade Kendrick made a snuffling sound. Simon's heart pounded so hard in his chest he thought it would burst right out of his body.

Then the snoring resumed. Simon looked at the door and saw his mother beckoning to him with her free hand. He resumed his slow, careful way toward her.

She moved aside, put a hand on his shoulder, and guided him outside the cabin. Then she pulled the door closed behind her. The leather hinges creaked a little. There was no way to find out if her husband's slumber had been disturbed without going back inside, and she wasn't going to do that.

Instead she took Simon's hand that wasn't holding the bag of clothes and led him quickly away from the place. It was the only home he remembered in his young life, but he didn't feel bad about leaving it. Not with his father there.

"Ma," he asked when they had put some distance behind them, walking along the trail that led to the settlement, "where are we going?"

"Not here anymore."

That didn't really answer his question, but Simon understood what she meant.

They reached the settlement a while later. Simon's mother paused in front of the church and then looked at the small house beside it. She had brought the boys to services here several times. Simon didn't like church much because it meant sitting still, and he got restless pretty quickly. So did Grady. But he kind of enjoyed listening to the singing. He was too young to know the words to any of the songs, but they sounded nice.

"Simon, get dressed," his mother told him. "Hurry."

He pulled on a regular shirt and a pair of trousers over his nightshirt, then asked, "Are we going to see the preacher, Ma?"

"You are," she told him. "Take the rest of the clothes out of your bag. I want you to go stand up there on the porch and wait for a while. Then knock on the door, and when Brother Woodson answers it, you tell him I said that he needs to do what we talked about a few days ago. You'll stay with the Woodson family until I come back and get you. Do you understand, Simon?"

He felt his eyes grow wet with tears. "I don't want to stay with them," he said. "I want to stay with you."

"You can't right now, but you'll be all right. They'll take good care of you, I promise. And Brother Woodson and his wife have a little girl about your age, so you'll have somebody to play with."

"What about Grady?" Simon asked as he

fought back sniffles. "Is he staying here with me?"

"No, he's coming with me," Simon's mother answered. "But we'll just be apart for a little while, Simon. I promise. Then we'll all be together again, and we won't have anything more to worry about."

"Are . . . are you sure?"

"I told you, didn't I? I wouldn't lie to you."

That was true. Simon's mother never lied to him. He still didn't like the idea of staying with somebody else instead of with her, but if that was what she wanted . . .

"All right, Ma."

She knelt, still holding Grady, and suddenly caught Simon in a hug that startled him with its fierceness. "Oh, my God," she said in a voice as hoarse and husky as if she had the grippe. "Oh, Simon. My boy. My darling. If there was any other way . . ."

He felt tears on her face, too, and returned the hug as hard as he could to try to make her feel better. "It'll be all right, Ma," he said.

She let go of him, put her hand on his head for a second, then told him, "Go on up there. Stay on the porch. How high can you count?"

They had been working on counting. He said proudly, "All the way to ten."

"Well, then, you count all the way to ten, and then do it some more times. Keep doing it for a while. Then you can knock on the door, and remember to tell Brother Woodson what I told you."

"I will, Ma," he promised.

Then, choking back a sob, she was gone, half-running into the night with Grady in her arms. She took the bag of Grady's clothes with her.

With a wadded-up bundle of his clothes in his arms, Simon walked up onto the porch of the preacher's house and started counting. He didn't know how many times he had counted to ten — it seemed like a lot — when he finally knocked on the door. He wasn't very big, and he had to knock quite a few times before somebody opened it at last and looked down at him. The man held a candle, and in its flickering light, Simon recognized the preacher.

"I'm Simon Kendrick," he said. "My ma told me to tell you . . ."

"I know," the preacher said. "Thank God she finally decided to leave that brute. Come in, child, come in. We'll see that you're well taken care of, and we won't let anyone know you're here until your mother is able to come back for you."

"You mean . . . you'll be hiding me . . .

like playing a game?"

The preacher smiled, but that didn't do much to change the stern look on his face. "Yes," he said. "Like a game. Until your mother comes back."

But she never did.

CHAPTER 7

Kansas, six months later

"I might've known I'd find you working in a whorehouse," Blade Kendrick said to the woman for whom he'd been searching these past months.

He had come up behind his wife as she cut through the alley toward the back of the house where she had been working. It was twilight, but the streets of Topeka were still busy. Busy enough for the sounds of wagons and horses and people to cover up anything that happened back in here in the shadows.

Harriet jerked her head around toward him and gasped, then tried to run. She was too slow. His left arm went around her waist and pulled her back against him. He clapped his right hand over her mouth as she started to struggle. His grip was brutally tight as he muffled any outcry she might try to make.

He put his mouth next to her ear and rasped, "Where are my sons, you bitch?"

She made incoherent noises. She wouldn't be able to say anything he could understand as long as he had his hand over her mouth. He forced her deeper into the alley.

"If I let you talk, you're gonna answer my questions," he told her. "If you try to yell for help, I'll just go ahead and break your neck. It won't be any great loss to the world. What's one more soiled dove . . . or less?"

She stopped fighting. It was as if all the strength ran out of her like water. She sagged against him, limp and unresisting.

Kendrick took his hand away from her lips. Air rasped between them as she caught her breath. Then she said, "I'm not a whore."

"You think I'm a fool?" Kendrick snapped. "I asked around about that place after I saw you coming and going from there."

"I don't do . . . that," Harriet said. "I cook and clean and do laundry, and that's *all.*"

Kendrick stood there silently for a second, then gave her a little push away from him. He caught hold of her shoulders and turned her to face him.

"Yeah, I guess it'd be hard to find even a grub-line rider desperate enough to fork over hard-earned money for a worn-out harridan like you. I don't give a damn either way about that. I just want my sons back."

Enough light filtered into the alley from the main street for him to see the defiant tilt to her chin as she said, "Those boys are somewhere you'll never find them, Blade. They deserve better than a thief and a . . . a murderer for a father."

"Those are mighty bold words."

"They're true. I know good and well you broke into Lonzo Carter's house and stole that money from his strongbox, just like I know about those other robberies you were behind. You bragged to me about them, remember? You said only a fool would work hard for things that he could just take."

"You called me a murderer," Kendrick said in a low, dangerous voice.

"I heard about what happened to Dave Childers," Harriet said. "The next day after I left, he was found in that shack of his with his throat cut. You killed him, Blade, so Tom Bayless couldn't pressure him into admitting that the two of you were behind all the robberies around there."

Kendrick's lips pulled back from his teeth. "If I was that worried about somebody talking to the law, wouldn't I have killed *you*?"

"I lied for you more than once. You knew I wouldn't betray you."

Kendrick's open hand flashed up and cracked across her face, knocking her head

306

to the side. She stumbled and would have fallen if not for his other hand's cruel, claw-like grip on her shoulder.

"Wouldn't betray me?" he repeated. "What do you call stealing my children from me?"

"I didn't steal them," Harriet said, her voice thick now because her lips were already swelling up from the blow. "I rescued them. Saved them from you. Sooner or later you would have hurt them, Blade. You know that. I might have been able to live with knowing what you'd do to me, but I . . . I couldn't leave them there."

He shook her so violently her head rocked back and forth and her teeth clicked together. "Tell me where they are!"

"Go to hell," she managed to say.

He hit her again. This time her knees buckled and he thought he had knocked her out. That was all right. He could take his time, wait for her to regain consciousness, and then ask her again where the boys were.

She had tricked him, though. As she leaned closer to him, her knee came up and rammed into his groin. Pain burst through him. He groaned and bent over as his hands slipped off her shoulders. Instinct made him start to clutch at himself.

She turned and ran.

Cursing bitterly under his breath, Kendrick forced himself upright and went after her. She had a head start, but his legs were longer and she was stumbling in the darkness. He reached out, got hold of the back of her dress, and tried to haul her to a stop. Fabric ripped and came free in his hand. Harriet kept going.

Kendrick left his feet in a flying tackle that caught her around the knees. She cried out as she fell, and then he heard a sudden dull, mushy thud, as if someone had dropped a melon on the ground and it had broken open.

Kendrick had hit the ground hard when he brought her down, and that, along with the pain still flooding out from his groin where she had kneed him, made it almost impossible for him to catch his breath. He lay there on the hard ground for a long moment, gasping, until he got enough air and strength in him to move again.

He pushed himself onto hands and knees and crawled up beside her motionless form. Grabbing her shoulders again, he rolled her onto her back.

Her face was a dark smear from the blood that coated it. Blood that welled from a gaping wound in her forehead. Kendrick shook her, but she was limp, her head flopping from side to side.

He felt around in the darkness until his hand encountered an old crate of some sort that somebody had left lying in the alley. The corner of it was wet and sticky. Kendrick made a face in the darkness as he rubbed his fingers together.

Harriet's head had landed on that corner when she fell, he realized. She'd busted her skull wide open and was dead. To make sure of that, he rested his hand on her chest. No heartbeat, no rising and falling as she breathed. She was dead, all right.

And she had taken the knowledge of where Simon and Grady were to hell with her, he thought.

The camp was a couple of miles west of Topeka in a grove of cottonwoods, a hundred yards off the main road. The fire had burned down to embers that weren't visible for very far, even in the thick darkness. Kendrick knew where to find it, though. He had picked out the spot.

He slowed his horse to a walk as he approached the trees. A moment later, a wary voice called from the shadows underneath them, "Who's there? Better sing out, mister."

"It's me, Frank," Kendrick replied.

Frank Wolters, who was standing guard, stepped out into the open holding a single-shot rifle. Kendrick and Wolters had been riding together for two months, along with Abner Hammond and Cy McKee. During that time they had robbed three stores, held up seven stagecoaches, and bushwhacked two lone travelers who looked prosperous. Turned out one of the well-dressed men had only twenty cents in his pocket, but the other had had almost three hundred dollars in his wallet and a mighty nice pocket watch.

Any man who dressed fancy and pretended to be well-to-do deserved whatever happened to him, Kendrick had declared over the corpse of the fellow who'd had twenty cents.

Wolters held the rifle in one hand and slanted the barrel back over his right shoulder. He asked, "Did you find what you were looking for, Blade?"

Kendrick didn't answer immediately. It wasn't that he didn't want to admit his wife had died at his hands, although by accident. He had killed before, coldly and deliberately, starting with Dave Childers. Harriet had been right about that. Dave had been a friend and partner in crime, but he was also a threat to Kendrick, so he had to go.

He didn't want to tell Wolters that Harriet

was dead and had taken the secret of the boys' whereabouts with her, because then Wolters and the other men might decide that Kendrick's search for his sons was pointless and refuse to indulge him in it. Kendrick would ride by himself if he had to, of course, but having partners made it easier pulling jobs to finance his quest.

"Didn't have any luck," Kendrick said. "We're going to have to keep looking."

Wolters just shrugged and said, "Too bad. I know how determined you are. A man shouldn't have his own flesh and blood taken away from him like that." He let out a short, humorless laugh. "But what do I know? I never had any kids, leastways none that I ever knew about. Never even had any friends except fellas I met along the dark trails, like you, Blade."

"That's better than nothing," Kendrick said. "Any coffee left?"

"Don't know. You'll have to check the pot."

Kendrick nodded and heeled his horse into motion again. He rode among the trees to the small clearing where the others were camped. Hammond and McKee were rolled up in their blankets. They stirred, roused by the sound of Kendrick's horse, but then muttered and went back to sleep when they saw who the newcomer was.

The smart thing to do, Kendrick mused as he hunkered on his heels by the fire and sipped the cold, bitter coffee he poured for himself, would be to move on and put Topeka behind him as a dead end — literally — in his search.

The next evening, he walked into the house where Harriet had worked, got himself a drink, and stood around in the parlor making small talk with the madam and a couple of the painted young women in skimpy outfits who worked there. Some men were like that, Kendrick knew. They had to work themselves up to it before they could take one of the girls upstairs.

Something had occurred to him, and that was why he was here this evening, smart thing to do or not. He didn't have any trouble getting the madam to talk about what had happened the previous night. All he had to do was say that he'd heard there had been some trouble involving one of the girls.

"Oh, no, not one of my young ladies," the heavily rouged madam responded without hesitation. "A woman who worked for me — an older woman, you understand, who helped out around the house — she fell and

312

hit her head and died from it. A terrible tragedy, of course, but nothing for you to be concerned about, sir."

Kendrick frowned. "She wasn't attacked? I thought I heard somebody say that."

"Oh, no," the woman said as she shook her head emphatically. "It was just an unfortunate accident."

Kendrick nodded slowly. He could see how Harriet's death might look like that to someone. She could have tripped and fallen in the dark, hit her head, and then rolled onto her back to die. If that was what the local law believed, it meant nobody would be looking for Harriet's killer. He was safe here after all and could continue trying to find his sons.

"That must have been terrible for her friends," he said. "I suppose she had friends?"

"Harriet, you mean? Friends?" The madam shook her head. "Honestly, I couldn't say one way or the other. She never mentioned any friends, and no one came to visit her here except that preacher."

"Preacher?" Kendrick said. "In a whore-house?"

She had surprised the question out of him. His reaction made the madam frown in disapproval. She probably didn't like him referring to the place with such a blunt term. Not that Kendrick really cared what she thought.

"He wasn't a customer," the madam said icily. "He seemed to know Harriet from before. He didn't like her working here, but she told him she had to make a living somehow. He didn't stay long, when he saw she wasn't going to budge."

Harriet was a stubborn one, all right, Kendrick thought. And something else was percolating around in his brain, a memory that made his heart kick up to a faster rate. She remembered Harriet going to church back where they had lived in Missouri, and she had dragged the boys along with her, of course. A damn waste of time as far as Kendrick was concerned.

But a sky pilot was just the sort of man Harriet might believe would take the boys in and care for them, raise them until she could provide for them again. Kendrick tried to remember what had happened to that preacher, but he couldn't force the memory out of his brain, at least not for sure. He thought he might recall that the man and his family had left that settlement not long after Harriet disappeared . . .

"Come to think of it," the madam went on, evidently over her moment of irritation, "a woman came here once looking for Harriet, too. I didn't know her, but I got the feeling somehow that she was after money. You get a sense of that after a while in this business. All kinds of people show up looking for a payoff, especially the ones who wear badges." She rolled her eyes toward the ceiling. "I've got one up there now, indulging himself in a little side benefit, if you know what I mean."

Kendrick didn't care about that. He said, "This other woman, do you remember her name or anything about her?"

"Say, you've got a lot of questions, don't you, mister? Why'd you come here tonight, to talk or to . . ."

"I'm sorry," Kendrick said. "I guess I *am* just a mite nervous." Humbling himself like that annoyed him, but he wanted to soothe the madam's suspicions.

"Well, I can't tell you anything about that other woman anyway, except I think she said something about a wagon train. Maybe she was going west with one, I don't remember."

That complicated things. Kendrick could imagine Harriet leaving both Simon and Grady with the preacher, but if she had done that, then who was this wagon train woman?

Was it possible that Harriet had split up the boys?

⌐ That seemed unlikely at first, but the more Kendrick thought about it, the more he realized it was a possibility. Harriet might have thought that leaving them with two different families would make it more difficult for him to track them down. The woman who had come here to the whorehouse could have been demanding more money from Harriet before she headed west with one of the boys . . .

"Mister, you just stand around and talk," said one of the soiled doves who had been standing around trying to look seductive while Kendrick talked to the madam. "Are you gonna take one of us upstairs or not?"

A burst of anger erupted inside Kendrick, but he brought it under control. To excuse his actions, he pulled a watch from his pocket and looked at it, then said, "Damn, I lost track of the time. I'll have to come back later." He started to turn away.

"Hold it right there, mister."

The harsh, twangy voice came from the door between the parlor and the foyer. A man in a brown tweed suit stood at the bottom of the stairs, holding a brown hat in his left hand. Under the lapel of his coat, a badge was visible, pinned to his vest.

316

Kendrick hadn't broken any laws in To-peka, at least as far as anyone knew. He wasn't worried about the authorities. He asked, "What is it, Marshal?"

"It's sheriff," the man rasped. "Where'd you get that watch?"

Kendrick drew in a sharp breath and looked down at the watch in his hand. It was the one he had taken off the dead man he and his partners had ambushed. A large, fancy letter *D* was engraved on the case.

"That's Mitchell Davenport's watch," the sheriff went on. "I was with him when his wife gave it to him for his birthday. Mitch was killed a few days ago out on the trail, and I want to know how come you got his watch."

There were any number of ways Kendrick might have been able to lie his way out of this predicament. He could claim he bought the watch from a stranger. Or found the damn thing. Let the law prove otherwise.

But he was already mad because of the damned whore pouting and whining at him, and now as the red fury exploded through his brain, he stopped thinking and just grabbed for his gun instead. The sheriff wasn't packing iron . . .

Except he was. The lawman's hand came out from under his coat with a revolver plucked swiftly from a cross-draw rig, and as scantily clad young women screamed and dived for cover, Kendrick's gun and the one the sheriff held roared at the same instant. Kendrick felt a hammerblow on the side of his head, and everything went dark, with no time for him to even wonder if this was what Harriet had experienced as she died.

CHAPTER 8

Leavenworth, Kansas, 1868

The gate clanged shut behind Blade Kendrick. The last time he had heard that sound, he'd been going into the territorial prison, not out. Into ten years of hell.

He knew it could have been a lot worse. If the law had been able to prove that he had killed Mitchell Davenport, he would've wound up dancing on air at the end of a rope.

The only real evidence they had, though, was the fancy watch and the fact that Kendrick had gone for his gun when the sheriff confronted him. The clever lawyer Kendrick had hired with the last of his money had claimed in court that Kendrick had bought the watch — as Kendrick should have done all along — and the prosecuting attorney couldn't prove otherwise.

The lawyer had also tried to convince the jury that Kendrick had panicked because he didn't want being arrested in a whorehouse to ruin his reputation, and that was the reason he had slapped leather. That story didn't persuade the twelve jurors. They had found him guilty of attempted murder, and the judge had sentenced him to ten years in prison.

More than likely, everybody in the courtroom believed that he had killed Davenport, too, even though it couldn't be proven. Under the circumstances, they might not be able to hang him, but they could damn sure send him away for a decade behind bars. It was less than he deserved but better than nothing.

He had the scar on the side of his head where the sheriff's bullet had creased him, the white streak in the dark hair above his right ear, to show for the dustup in the whorehouse, too. It had been enough to knock Kendrick out cold and cause his shot to smack harmlessly into a parlor wall covered with flowery wallpaper.

"Come back to see us, Kendrick." The voice of the guard on the other side of the gate shook Kendrick out of his reverie. "We'll be waiting for you."

Kendrick looked back over his shoulder and said, "Go to hell. No, wait, you're already there, aren't you?"

"But I can leave any time I want. Once you're locked up again for whatever you do next, you won't be able to." The uniformed man leered at Kendrick through the small, barred window in the gate. "Or maybe next time they'll just put you down, like the mad dog you are."

With an effort, Kendrick controlled his temper and forced his legs to work, carrying him away from there. He walked into the nearby town of Leavenworth, conscious of the wary gazes on him. Even if the people who lived there wouldn't be suspicious of him to start with because of the direction he came from, they could tell right away from the cheap suit he wore that he'd just been released from prison.

He had a five dollar gold piece in his pocket, also from the prison. That wouldn't get him very far, but he had heard that a man who owned a livery stable in town sometimes gave jobs to former prisoners. Felt like he was doing a good thing by helping them get on their feet again. Kendrick had no trouble finding the place.

Ed Downey looked him up and down, then asked, "What is it you want, now that you're out, Kendrick?"

"Just to be with my family again," Kendrick replied. That was true. The boys were all he had left in the world. Simon would be fifteen, Grady a year younger. Chances were, they had forgotten all about him. But once he found them, they would remember. Everything would be all right once the three of them were together again.

"I'm willing to take a chance on a man who cares about his family," Downey said. "I'll give you a job. Fifty cents a day and a place to sleep in the loft, for as long as you do the work and want to stay."

Kendrick made himself nod, smile, and say, "I appreciate that, Mr. Downey."

He worked in the stable for three days, slept in the loft for three nights. By the morning of the fourth day, he had figured out where Downey kept the money in the office. He stepped up behind the man while Downey was in one of the stalls, running a comb over the horse kept there. Downey glanced over his shoulder, then said, "What do you . . ."

Kendrick rammed the pitchfork he held into the man's back, aiming good so that one of the tines had to penetrate Downey's heart. Downey gasped, dropped the comb, and when Kendrick ripped the pitchfork out, he fell at the horse's hooves, spooking the animal and making it skittish.

Kendrick had thought about killing

322

Downey by hitting him over the head and then trying to make it look like a horse had trampled him, but that seemed like too much work. He stabbed the man twice more while Downey lay on the ground, just to make sure he was dead, and then tossed the bloody fork on a pile of hay and went to get a saddle.

Five minutes later, he rode out the stable's rear door, not hurrying because he didn't want to attract attention, and loped away from the settlement. He had put several miles behind him when he looked back and saw dust rising in the distance. That had to be a posse coming after him, but with the lead he had, they would never catch him.

They didn't.

He had missed the war completely while he was behind bars, but he had heard plenty about all the blood spilled between the various factions along the Kansas–Missouri border. In the years since Appomattox, the area had settled down a little, but outlaw gangs, including the Reno brothers and the James–Younger bunch, had replaced the wartime guerrillas and it could still be a pretty wild place. Blade Kendrick fit right in.

The first thing he'd done after going on

the dodge again was cast around for news of his old partners, Wolters, Hammond, and McKee. He had never mentioned them to the law when he was arrested. A man didn't betray the fellows who rode with him.

He found Frank Wolters in a saloon in Abilene. Wolters had told somebody back up the trail that he was heading for there, and that news had finally gotten to Kendrick. Wolters looked surprised to see him.

"I didn't know you were out, Blade," he said as he motioned toward one of the empty chairs at the table. Wolters had a glass and a bottle and a half-finished solitaire hand in front of him.

"It's only been a few weeks," Kendrick said as he took a seat. He caught the bartender's eye and pointed to Wolters's empty glass. "You hear anything from Cy and Abner these days?"

Wolters frowned down at the table and didn't say anything while one of the serving girls brought over an empty glass for Kendrick. Then he splashed whiskey in both glasses and pushed Kendrick's over to him.

"They're both dead," Wolters said. "We held up a little crossroads store outside of Salina a while back, and when we came out there was a fella waiting with a shotgun. I reckon he'd ridden up while we were inside, saw what was going on, and waited out there for us. Probably figured he'd capture us and turn us in to a deputy U.S. marshal for the reward. But Hammond shot him and he shot Hammond. Both barrels right in the gut. Blew a hole big enough to put a fist through, all the way to his backbone. Shot-gunner didn't live to see it, though. Abner'd already plunked a slug right in his ticker."

"What happened to Cy?" Kendrick asked. "He go down with a gun in his hand, too?"

A sad smile curved Wolters's lips. "No, he got kicked in the head by a mule, the dumb son of a bitch. Dropped him like a rock." Wolters lifted his glass. "To absent friends."

"Absent friends," Kendrick repeated. They both tossed back the drinks. Then Kendrick went on, "I'm surprised you fellas stayed together for so long, to tell you the truth. Usually somebody gets killed sooner, or just rides away."

"They were good boys to ride the trails with," Wolters said wistfully. "We did all right."

"You heard what happened to me?"

Wolters shrugged. "Sure."

"It never occurred to any of you to try to do something for me?"

"Do what?" Wolters demanded bluntly. "Ride in and try to snatch you out of that courtroom? Or bust you out of prison? We'd have wound up either shot to pieces or on the gallows, and you know it, Blade."

"I did ten years. Never once did I put any of the blame on you fellas or even let on to the law that you existed."

"Appreciate that. But if you figure on collecting for that favor, you're too late. Hammond and McKee are dead, and I'm flat broke."

"You can still pay me back."

"How?"

"Ride with me again," Kendrick said. "Help me find my sons."

Wolters stared across the table at him. "You're still looking for them? Hell, it's been more than ten years! They were little kids, Blade, and now they're half-growed men. They probably don't even remember you."

For a second, that old familiar fury threatened to drop a red haze over Kendrick's vision. The only thing stopping it was that the same thought had occurred to him more than once. He couldn't very well lash out at Wolters for putting into words the ugly possibility that already lurked in his brain.

"They haven't forgotten me," he said, his voice rough with emotion. "No son could ever forget his father. I'll find 'em. I've got a couple of leads to follow."

"You'll need money," Wolters said with a shrewd expression on his normally dour face. "How do you plan to get it?"

"There are ways," Kendrick said. "Ways that would be easier with two men instead of one."

"Easier still with three or four."

"If they're good men." Kendrick jerked his head in a nod. "You know any?"

"I might know a few," Wolters said.

By the time six months had gone by, Hog Tatum was riding with the bunch, as well as Jack Crosby, Slick Ryan, Johnny Medford, and Hoyt Yates. Hard men, dependable when the shooting started. Blade Kendrick was the unquestioned leader, and Tatum, through sheer ferocity, rose to the position of second-in-command. The men speculated among themselves that someday those two would clash over who was the boss, and they were pretty evenly divided on which man they thought would emerge triumphant.

They were careful, though, not to let Kendrick or Tatum hear them talking about that.

They didn't bother holding up stores. The payoff wasn't good enough anymore. And they seldom stopped stagecoaches. Instead, they went after banks and trains, and nearly always, the gang galloped off with a nice amount of loot. They had picked up a few nicks and scrapes shooting it out with posses and townspeople, but none of the bunch had been killed yet. They knew that run of luck couldn't go on forever, but they would ride it out as long as they could.

Even while that was going on, Kendrick never gave up the search for his children. Unable to make any progress himself, he used some of his share of the loot from the robberies to hire detectives, who went to Topeka and all the way back to Missouri to try to pick up the trail of whoever had Simon and Grady. Tatum thought it was hilarious that Kendrick was employing detectives, the same sort of men hired by the banks and railroads to track down outlaws like the Kendrick gang.

Kendrick would resort to whatever means were necessary, though.

The detective who went back to Missouri sent Kendrick a report about the preacher who had departed from the small town shortly after Harriet had run off with the boys. The man's name was Woodson. He had a wife and daughter and never seemed to stay in one place for very long, always moving on to another church where he felt called to spread the Gospel.

Kendrick wired back instructions for the man to stay on the trail.

The other detective turned up somebody in Topeka who remembered the wagon train that had set out for Colorado that year. That lead was more vague, since there were a number of families with children in the group, and it would be difficult to determine where they had all wound up.

However, that was the trail that bore fruit first. One of the families had started a horse ranch in eastern Colorado, not far over the Kansas line. They had a son in his middle teens, and his name was Grady.

Kendrick's hand clenched involuntarily on the telegram he had received from the detective bearing that news. He had ridden into a tiny settlement, not much more than a railroad stop, a saloon, and a general store, where the detective had instructions to contact him. Wolters and Yates were with him, and when Wolters saw Kendrick's reaction, he said, "What is it, Blade?"

"My youngest boy," Kendrick breathed. "He's in Colorado."

"You know that for a fact?"

"No . . . but I will soon. It's got to be true!"

They rounded up the rest of the gang and rode west.

CHAPTER 9

Three days later, Miles Clayton, his wife, Sophie, and their children, Noah, Thomas, Ingrid, and Grady, were just sitting down to supper when they heard the unexpected clatter of hoofbeats outside the sod house.

Clayton had already put his napkin in his lap. He picked it up and tossed it on the table as he got to his feet. He started toward the door.

"Careful, Pa," Noah said. "Might be Indians."

They had never had any real trouble with the Pawnee or Arapaho since settling here nearly a decade earlier. They lost a few horses now and then, but the Indians never ran off the whole herd, so Clayton considered the occasional loss a small price to pay for being left alone otherwise.

Still, it never hurt to be careful, so he took down his Henry rifle from the pegs where it hung on the wall and worked the lever to put a cartridge into the chamber.

"Miles . . ." his wife said worriedly.

"Just go on and eat supper," Clayton said. "I'll see who's come calling."

He pulled the latch string and pushed the door outward with his foot. The sun had set, but an arch of red and gold light with a few streamers of white clouds running through it still filled the western horizon.

That light played over the hard, beard-stubbled faces of the seven men who had reined their horses to a stop in front of the cabin. One of them edged his mount forward a couple of steps and said, "Miles Clayton?"

"That's right," the horse rancher replied. He didn't like the looks of these men, and a cold knot of fear formed at the pit of his stomach. Not fear for himself, but for his family.

The spokesman for the group smiled, but it wasn't a very convincing expression. Still, his voice sounded friendly enough as he said, "We've probably interrupted your supper. My apologies for that."

"Just sat down to eat," Clayton said. "I'd sure like to invite you to join us, but there's not really enough and my wife would tan my hide if I did."

Most of that statement was a lie. Sophie

had made a big pot of stew, and there would have been enough to go around. But Clayton didn't want these men in his home. No way in hell did he want that.

"We're not looking to impose, although we wouldn't mind watering our horses before we ride on."

Clayton nodded, gesturing with the Henry. "Got a good well right over there. You're welcome to help yourselves."

"Obliged." The man shifted slightly in the saddle. "I'll get right down to it. I hear you have a boy living with you named Grady."

That statement took Clayton completely by surprise. These strangers looked like outlaws, and if they had come to steal his herd, he might have expected that. Or if they believed he had money hidden on the place and had come to rob him of that. But why would they be interested in Grady?

Unless . . .

"I have a son named Grady," Clayton said.

The leader slowly shook his head. "Except he's not your son by blood, is he? He's just a boy you took in to raise, more than ten years ago when you headed west from Topeka with a wagon train."

"How did you . . ." Clayton bit off the question that had been startled out of him, but it was too late. He saw the way the

333

man's eyes lit up in his heavy-featured face. The truth was out, and it couldn't be called back.

"Grady!" the stranger called. "Grady, come on out here!"

Anger welled up inside Clayton. His hands tightened on the rifle. "Damn it, mister, you got no right . . ."

The other six riders tensed. Clayton saw the way their hands drifted closer to the guns they all wore. He licked his lips and knew that if he made a move with the Henry, he wouldn't get more than one shot off. After that, he'd be blown full of bullet holes and his family would be at the mercy of these men.

"Pa?" Grady said behind him. "Pa, what . . ."

Clayton glanced over his shoulder and saw Grady in the doorway with Sophie holding on to his arm, urging him, "Come back inside."

Grady ignored her, as, honestly, he usually did whenever they told him to do something. They had tried, Lord knew they had tried, but the boy had never fit in. He had a rebellious streak in him that just couldn't be tamed.

Grady's mother had given money to Sophie to partially pay for his keep and the trouble of taking him in. Clayton hadn't wanted to take it; that just didn't seem right to him. But his wife, always more practical, had insisted, and later on, considering the trial Grady had turned out to be, Clayton was glad of it.

But despite the clashes, they all considered the boy to be part of the family now. Clayton said sternly, "Grady, go inside."

The stranger on horseback said, "Grady, boy, I'm your father. You remember me, don't you? By God, I remember you. I'd know you anywhere, son."

Grady just shook his head in confusion and said, "What's going on here?"

The stranger swung down from his saddle. Clayton started to angle the Henry toward him, but he froze as a couple of the men put their hands on their guns. Emotion roiled inside the rancher. He couldn't stand up to seven hardcases, but if he didn't, he would be letting his family down.

"Your name is Grady Kendrick," the stranger went on. "I'm your father, Blade Kendrick. You've got to remember, son."

He seemed desperate to have that affirmation from the boy. A hard, powerful man he might be, but he was helpless in the face of whatever he was feeling at this moment.

Grady shook off Sophie's hand and said,

"I . . . I don't remember. The earliest thing I remember is being in a wagon, with my ma and pa . . ."

"They're not your ma and pa," Kendrick snapped. He drew in a deep breath, visibly controlled the anger he felt, and went on, "Look, Clayton, I'm obliged to you and your wife for taking care of my boy for so long, but I've come to take him back. He's my flesh and blood, and he needs to be with me."

"No!" Sophie cried. "He's our boy. You can't take him."

Clayton took a deep breath. He had to try to reason with this man.

"Look, Mr. Kendrick. You got to understand how we feel. Grady's been with us for so long . . ."

"So it's true," Grady said. "I'm really not your son."

Clayton wished the truth had never had to come out, but now that it had, he thought maybe it would be better to be honest with the boy.

"Your ma . . . your real ma . . . said there was some sort of trouble and that she needed somebody to look after you for a while, until she could come back to get you. You seemed like a good boy, so we agreed to do it." Best not to say anything about the money changing hands, he decided. "Only she never met up with us like she was supposed to. We figured something must have . . . well, that something must have happened to her, and she wasn't coming for you, so from then on you were just part of our family, son. You still are."

Grady shook his head. "No," he said in a flat voice. "I've always known there was something different about me. You never treated me the same as Noah and Tom and Ingrid."

"Grady, that's not true!" Sophie said. But Clayton knew that it was. There had always been subtle differences, not only in the way Grady acted but in the way the rest of the family acted around him as well.

Grady looked at the man called Kendrick and asked, "Where's my real ma? Why didn't she ever come back for me?"

"I'm sorry to have to tell you this," Kendrick said, "but your ma is dead. Has been for a long time."

Grady's lips thinned and he nodded. "Figured as much," he said, but he didn't show any other reaction.

"She wasn't right in the head. She ran away with you and your brother to try to hurt me."

"I have a brother?"

"Yeah. His name is Simon. He's a year older than you. You don't remember him?"

Grady shook his head. "This is the first I ever knew of him. Where is he?"

"I don't know," Kendrick said. "I'm looking for him, too. It's taken me this long to find either of you. But I won't stop looking, son. Now that I've found you, I'm more determined than ever to find Simon, so all three of us can be together again."

Sophie came to Clayton and clutched his arm. "Miles, *do* something!" she begged. "He's going to take Grady away from us."

"Maybe he's got a right to," Clayton said gruffly. Sophie was the one who had done most of the talking to the woman back in Topeka, but he had seen her enough to know that she'd had something of a wild-eyed look about her. After all, she had run away from her husband and taken her son — no, *two* sons, according to Kendrick — with her. What sane woman would do that?

"No, no, no . . ." Sophie moaned.

Grady looked at Clayton. "Pa . . . I mean, Mr. Clayton . . . what do you think I should do?"

Clayton's heart had twisted at the way Grady had just called him *Mr. Clayton.* But there was no getting around what had happened. The family had sat down to dinner, and before they could even get started the whole world had changed around them. It was a hell of a thing.

"I reckon you've got to do whatever you think is right," he said. "There'll always be a place here for you, you know that."

Grady swallowed hard. "You don't want me to stay?"

"I didn't say that. But you're getting pretty near to being a man. You got to make up your own mind about things."

"I . . . I don't know . . ." Grady looked down at the ground, then up at Kendrick. "You're really my father?"

"I am," the man said. "I swear it."

"And you really want me to come with you?"

"More than anything."

"Then I guess . . ." Sophie let out a wail as Grady paused. The boy looked torn, but he went on, "I guess I ought to go, then."

"Get your things," Kendrick said. "You have a horse?"

"He does," Clayton said. "A good one."

Grady looked over at him. "Pa . . . Mr. Clayton . . ."

Clayton leaned the rifle against the cabin's sod wall and put his arms around the boy. He hugged Grady close, thumping him on the back.

"You come back to see us," he said in a voice thick with emotion.

The next few minutes were a blur. Grady gathered his personal belongings from the house — there weren't that many — and saddled the big steeldust gelding Clayton had given him a couple of years earlier. Sophie sobbed against Clayton's chest as he held her. The other children awkwardly said goodbye to Grady. He had been their brother, of sorts, for a decade, but they were all older than he was and had known the truth all along of how he had come to be with them. That had created a reserve keeping them from ever fully accepting him, Clayton supposed as he watched Grady uncomfortably shake hands with Noah and Thomas and then clumsily embrace Ingrid.

Then Grady climbed into the saddle and rode off with Kendrick and the other men. Sophie said, "They're outlaws, Miles! You can tell that by looking at them! What sort of life have you condemned that boy to?"

"We don't know that," Clayton said. "There are plenty of rough men out here on the frontier who aren't outlaws."

Deep inside, though, he had a hunch his wife was right. In the face of the facts, he hadn't known what else to do except let Grady go, but he prayed that he hadn't, indeed, condemned the boy to a life of lawlessness.

Either way, though, he wasn't sure Sophie would ever forgive him for what had happened here in the twilight.

The men rode for several miles as darkness gathered before Kendrick called a halt beside a tiny creek and told the others to make camp.

"You don't know how happy it makes me to have you with me again, son," he told Grady.

"I never saw you before today, Mr. Kendrick . . . Pa." Grady shook his head. "That just sounds strange. Feels that way, too."

"I know. I reckon it'll take some time for us to get used to each other. But it'll happen. I'm gonna make sure of that." Kendrick paused. "I reckon you'll miss those other folks."

"The Claytons? Yeah, I . . . I thought I was one of 'em. But at least now I know why it never really felt right."

Kendrick clapped him on the shoulder and said, "Well, now you've got a whole new life, and it's going to be a good one. Why don't you tend to your horse? You missed out on supper back there, but we'll eat here in a little while. Maybe not as fancy, but it'll be good grub."

Grady nodded, summoned up a smile, and moved off toward the horses. Kendrick drifted along the creek bank, apparently aimlessly, but he caught Tatum's attention and motioned for the man to follow him.

When they were out of easy earshot of the camp, Kendrick said to his second in command, "Hog, after the boy's asleep, I want you to take three or four of the boys and ride back to that horse ranch."

"What've you got in mind, Blade?"

"From what I saw of it, Clayton's got a pretty good horse herd. You could get a nice price for them if you drove them over to Pueblo. The rest of us could wait for you there."

"I don't reckon that rancher would take kindly to us drivin' off his horses," Tatum said.

"I don't expect so. But he won't be able to do anything about it after you kill him."

"And the others?"

"Kill them all," Kendrick said. "You can have some fun with the woman and the girl first, if you want, but they all need to be dead when you ride away from there, and burn out the inside of that cabin, too."

A grin split Tatum's ugly face. "Want to make sure the boy ain't got nothin' to go back to, eh?"

"That'll never happen. Grady's back where he belongs." Kendrick drew in a breath. "Now I just have to find Simon."

CHAPTER 10

Wind River

The fight with the freighters had left Simon Woodson a little sore and stiff, but he was young and resilient and by Sunday night had all but forgotten about the eruption of violence in the converted storefront that morning.

Except for the way his father had torn into those men when he saw Simon knocked down. That was a side of Brother Franklin Woodson that Simon hadn't seen before.

Over the years, his father had had to deal with opposition to some of the churches he started up. Often, the saloon owners and the madams and the dance hall owners didn't want some sky pilot coming in and telling folks that they would go to hell if they patronized those establishments, so they would threaten trouble. Usually that was all it would amount to, just threats, but Simon's pa would stand up for himself when he was forced to.

He had never been a real fighting man, though. He had defended himself and his churches with words. He had never launched himself into physical combat with such ferocity. That he had done so in defense of Simon made the youngster feel good.

At the same time, he didn't want anybody getting hurt on his account. It was a good thing Marshal Tyler had been there, and that big redheaded deputy had shown up with a shotgun to make sure things didn't go any further.

Simon was thinking about that as he drifted off to sleep in the tent. Deborah was a few feet away, curled up in her blankets. Earlier, she had suggested that on such a cold night, it would help keep them warm if they both wrapped up together, but Simon had shaken his head in stubborn refusal of that suggestion. He didn't believe for a second that staying warm was all Deborah had in mind. She wanted to torment him more.

When he woke up, sometime in the night, he was shivering despite the blankets pulled tightly around him. Maybe he had been too quick to turn down Deborah's offer. It wouldn't do him any good to be strong in the face of temptation if he froze to death in the process.

Even worse, it was a full bladder that had awakened him. He was going to have to crawl out of the blankets and leave the tent. That was a mighty unappealing prospect, but he didn't have any choice.

Being quiet about it so he wouldn't wake Deborah, he got up and stepped out into the night. At least the wind had died down. The sky was crystal clear, with millions of stars visible above him, and the air was cold enough to bite a man's nose as he inhaled. Simon's breath fogged thickly in front of his face as he walked into the trees a few yards from the wagon and the tent.

He took care of his business, not wasting any time because of the cold, and turned to head back to the tent. As he did, a soft footstep sounded behind him. For a second, Simon had the wild thought that Deborah had followed him out here, but an arm looped around his neck and a hand clapped over his mouth as he was drawn backward, forcefully but not too roughly.

His first thought was to believe that the freighters had come back to revenge themselves on his family by giving him a beating. But then a harsh voice whispered in his ear,

"Take it easy, kid. Nobody's gonna hurt you."

Simon smelled whiskey on the man's breath, but he didn't seem drunk. He was strong, that was for sure. Simon didn't think there was much chance of him breaking free of the man's grip. He wasn't going to get loose unless that was what the man wanted.

"You're comin' with me."

The man dragged Simon through the trees. Simon twisted and struggled for a moment, but it didn't do any good. They went a good hundred yards before the man stopped.

"I'm gonna let go of you," the man said, "but don't you yell. It'll just cause trouble if you do. Trouble for you, and for that preacher and his family."

Something about what his captor said made Simon stiffen. The way the man had phrased it, he sounded like he *knew* Simon wasn't the flesh and blood son of Franklin and Phillippa Woodson. How was that possible? Nobody knew that except the Woodsons and Deborah and . . .

And his mother, Simon thought. Did this man know his mother? Was it possible that after all this time, she had finally come for him?

Simon heard horses shifting around and

blowing a little. Whoever the man was, he hadn't come alone. There was only one way to find out what was going on here.

Simon nodded.

"What? You mean you understand? You ain't gonna raise a ruckus?"

Again, Simon nodded. He gasped a little in the cold air as the man's hand went away from his mouth and nose.

"I'm gonna let you loose now. Don't you run."

A new voice said, "He won't run, Hog. He's a smart boy. Always was."

Something about that man's voice was familiar. Simon couldn't place it at first, and then when the memories began to well up and fear blossomed inside him, he turned, drawn by a horrible fascination.

A dark, broad-shouldered, bulky shape moved toward him. Cold starlight cast a silvery sheen over the heavy features.

"Simon," the man said. "Son."

Over the years, Simon's memories of his real father had faded. He had never completely forgotten the man's face, though, or the way he sounded. There was no doubt in his mind that Blade Kendrick was the person who stood before him now.

Nor had he forgotten the way his mother had lived in fear of this man. Kendrick's actual deeds had faded in Simon's memory; he had been only five years old, after all, when his mother had taken him and Grady and left the family home in the middle of the night.

"It's me, boy," Kendrick went on. "Your father."

"I know who you are," Simon said. His voice was as cold and unfriendly as the night.

"But you're not glad to see me, is that it?" Kendrick laughed. "Your mind's still poisoned against me after all these years? Your ma did a good job of filling your head with lies."

"They weren't lies," Simon insisted as he glanced around. He saw several other indistinct figures standing around in the darkness, including the big, hulking shape of the man who had grabbed him. Given the circumstances, it might not be smart to antagonize his captors, but he couldn't stop the words from coming out. "I remember all the terrible things you did."

Kendrick's voice had a mocking tone to it as he said, "Is that so? Tell me about them, then. Remind me of all those terrible things I did."

Simon struggled to dredge some details out of his memory. Surely he ought to be able to remember *something* other than the way his mother had felt about this man. He remembered the terror he himself had felt, and there had to be good reasons for that . . .

"You were cruel. You were mean to Ma . . ."

"You remember me ever laying a hand on her?" Kendrick broke in. "Remember seeing such a thing with your own eyes?"

Simon didn't, but as he stammered and hesitated, he considered lying. What good would that do, though, he asked himself?

"She was afraid of you," he said instead. "Why would she have been so terrified of you if she didn't have good reason?"

"You'd have to ask her about that," Kendrick said, then as if to prove that he could indeed be cruel, he added, "And you can't do that because she's dead."

"You killed her!" The exclamation was started out of Simon's mouth.

Kendrick shook his head. "She would've had it coming if I had. You can't expect to steal a man's sons away from him and not pay for it. But I reckon fate took care of that, because she died in an accident in Topeka. Where she was working in a whorehouse."

In spite of the fact that he was surrounded

by men who evidently were his father's friends, those harsh words made Simon lose control of the emotions raging inside him. He lunged at Kendrick as he yelled, "That's a lie! You're a damned liar!"

Kendrick slipped aside, easily avoiding the charge, and grabbed Simon. He twisted the youngster around and clamped a forearm across his throat from behind. Simon tried to writhe free, but he had no more chance of doing so than he'd had a few minutes earlier when the other man grabbed him. Kendrick's arm tightened dangerously.

"Don't make me hurt you, boy," he said in Simon's ear. "I didn't look for you all these years and finally find you just to have to choke you to death. You keep yelling, though, and it'll attract attention we don't want."

Simon stopped fighting. He went limp in Kendrick's grasp as despair flooded through him. He wouldn't put it past his father to lie about his mother being dead, but the man's words had had the ring of truth to them. Even the part about her working in a whorehouse.

"That's more like it," Kendrick said. "You're gonna see that I'm right, Simon. Now, there's somebody else here you need to meet." He swung Simon around so that he faced the other men, then loosened his grip. "Grady, step up here."

Grady! Simon had never forgotten his brother, but he had come to accept the bitter realization that he would never see Grady again. He had no doubt that his mother had believed she was doing the right thing by splitting the boys up. That would have made it more difficult for her husband to find them, and Simon knew she planned to reunite them in the future.

But her death had changed that plan, and when Simon was old enough to understand more, he had realized that he had no idea where Grady was, no way of tracking him down. It would be just pure luck if the brothers ever encountered one another again.

Luck . . . or fate in the form of Blade Kendrick.

A slender figure, a little below medium height, moved closer in the shadows. Kendrick let go of Simon and gave him a little push that sent him stumbling toward the person approaching him. Simon caught his balance and said in a strained voice, "Grady? Is that really you?"

"Simon? Pa tells me you're my brother."

He doesn't remember me, Simon thought wildly. That shouldn't come as a complete surprise, he told himself. Grady had been four when they were separated. Some people remembered things from their lives before that age; some didn't. Simon's own memories from before the night their mother had fled from the cabin with them were murky.

Grady would be sixteen now. Nearly a man, like Simon. But also like Simon, still a boy, and he sounded suspicious.

"I *am* your brother," he said. "I remember you, Grady, even if you don't remember me. We lived in a cabin in Missouri. We slept in the loft." Simon's voice caught a little. "We were best friends."

"And now you're together again," Kendrick said. "All three of us are together. A family. You have a horse, Simon?"

Simon was still so stunned by this unexpected reunion that it took him a second to realize Kendrick had asked him a question. He gave a little shake of his head and said, "What?"

"A horse," Kendrick repeated. "Do you have a horse?"

"A saddle mount? No. We have the mules that pull our wagon, that's all."

"No matter. You and Grady can ride double until we can lay our hands on one for you."

Something about the way Kendrick said

that made Simon frown. "You mean buy one?" he asked.

That brought a laugh from the big man who had first grabbed him. "Buy one!" the man repeated. "That's rich, ain't it, Blade?"

"Shut up," Kendrick snapped, but it was too late. The damage had been done. Simon understood now.

"You mean to steal a horse for me," he said. "You're outlaws."

"Don't sound so high and mighty about it," Grady said. "We do what we have to to get by, ain't that right, Pa?"

"Never mind about that. Go on back there to that camp on the edge of town, Simon, and get anything you want to take with you. Be quiet about it, though. Don't wake any of those people up."

"Those people are my family." Simon said it without thinking.

Kendrick's hands shot out and closed around his arms, gripping him so tightly that Simon drew in a sharp breath.

"That's a lie! We're your family, Grady and me. That preacher, he just helped your ma steal you from me. He's a bigger thief than me or any of these fellas will ever be!"

Simon tried to pull away but couldn't. "You're wrong," he cried. "They've been good to me. They raised me. I don't want

354

to leave them!"

"You're my boy, damn it! You'll do what I tell you, and I say you're coming with us!"

All the old fears had faded in the dozen years Simon had been apart from his father. But as he caught the note of fury in Kendrick's voice, those fears roared back to life and set his heart to thundering in his chest. That reaction fueled unexpected strength.

He jerked his right arm free from Kendrick's grip, balled that hand into a fist, and smashed it into his father's face.

CHAPTER 11

This time Blade Kendrick was so surprised that he wasn't able to avoid Simon's attack. The punch landed squarely on his cheekbone, under the left eye, and rocked his head back. His grip on Simon's left arm loosened enough for the youngster to pull completely free. Simon turned and ran, panic making him forget about Grady and everything else except getting away from his father.

The other outlaws seemed shocked, too, and didn't react right away. For a split second, Simon believed he might have a chance to get away from them.

Then the big man who had grabbed him, the one Kendrick called Hog, stretched out a long arm and snagged his coat collar. Simon came to a halt as if he had run into a wall. With seemingly no effort at all, Hog flung him backwards to the ground. Simon landed hard enough that it knocked the breath out of him and left him stunned.

He struggled to get up anyway, some instinct for self-preservation fueling his action, but somebody planted a boot in his chest and forced him back down. It came as a shock to Simon when Grady spoke above him.

"You hit Pa!" Grady said. His foot pressed hard, pinning Simon to the ground. "What the hell is wrong with you?"

"Let him up." That was Blade Kendrick's voice.

"But Pa, he's loco . . ."

"No, he's not. He's just scared and confused. It's gonna take him a while to get used to the way things are now. I figured it might be that way. Now let him up."

With obvious reluctance, Grady removed his foot from his brother's chest and stepped back. Kendrick reached down and extended a hand to Simon.

The outlaws were standing all around him. Simon knew now that he couldn't get away. After a moment's hesitation, he clasped Kendrick's wrist and let his father pull him to his feet.

"I told you I don't want to hurt you," Kendrick said, "but I'm not going to let you go back to that mealy-mouthed preacher."

"You don't even know him," Simon said.

"He's not mealy-mouthed. He's a good man."

"A good man wouldn't have helped a crazy woman steal two little boys away from their father." Kendrick made a curt gesture. "But that's all in the past now. If there's nothing you want back there, we'll just ride on now. You don't have to go back at all."

Maybe that would be best, Simon thought. That would keep these men away from his family. Kendrick hadn't said anything about hurting them if Simon didn't cooperate, but he had a hunch that might be next.

At the same time, just leaving like that, disappearing into the night, seemed terribly cruel. His mother and father — he couldn't think of the Woodsons in any other way after all this time — and Deborah would always wonder what had happened to him. They might think he had run away, or they might believe he was dead. Either way, they would grieve.

But if Kendrick would allow him to go back to the camp to gather up a few things, maybe he could snatch an opportunity to write them a note. He could scribble something on the flyleaf of his Bible, he realized. He wouldn't tell them where he was going or with whom, but he could reassure them he was all right and ask them not to worry about him . . .

"Well," Kendrick said, "what's it going to be?"

"I'll do what you want. I'll go with you. But I . . . I'd like to go back to my tent for a minute. You said that would be all right."

"Yeah. But don't go thinking it'll give you a chance to raise an alarm. You're not going by yourself. You never were." Kendrick turned his head to look at the others. "Grady, you'll go with your brother. And you, too, Hog. The rest of us are pulling out, but you know where we'll be. We'll leave a couple of horses for you." Kendrick put a hand on Simon's shoulder again. "Listen to me, boy. You cause any trouble, raise any sort of ruckus, and Hog's going to kill that preacher. You understand me?"

There it was, the threat that Simon expected sooner or later. But despite expecting it, hearing the words filled him with horror. He knew Blade Kendrick meant every word of it.

"I won't cause any trouble," he promised.

"See that you don't." Kendrick jerked his head. "Get moving. I want to put some miles behind us by morning."

Hog said, "You want me to grab a horse for the kid while we're at it, Blade?"

"If there's a good opportunity to do that,

sure. But don't take any chances. We can always get one later."

Hog motioned to Simon and Grady. "You two pups come with me."

The big outlaw made the brothers go first. With Hog right behind him and Grady beside him, Simon knew there would be no chance for him to get away.

When his instinctive fear of his father subsided a little, he wasn't sure he *wanted* to get away. For the first time in a dozen years, he was with his brother again. He remembered how much he had missed Grady for a long time after they were separated. The pain of that loss had dulled some over the years, but it had never gone away completely.

Grady believed what their father said about their mother, but only because he had been too young back then to remember any of it now. If Simon stayed with him, maybe eventually he could get Grady to see the truth, to understand that both of them would be better off as far from Blade Kendrick as possible. Simon was sure that sooner or later they would have a chance to get away from the gang of outlaws.

"Hold on," Hog said as they reached the edge of the trees. He stepped up beside Simon and looked at the wagon and the tent. After a moment he grunted in apparent satisfaction. "No lights. Ever'body's asleep. You be careful, kid, and make sure they stay that way. If I have to quiet anybody down, it'll be permanent-like."

The deadly menace in Hog's voice made a chill go through Simon. This was a man who would kill without compunction or hesitation, he thought. Hog probably had plenty of blood on his hands already, so a little more wouldn't make any difference.

"I'm just going to slip into the tent for a minute. I won't be gone long, and I'll be as quiet as possible."

"Wait a minute." Hog's whisper stopped him. "Is there anybody else in there?"

"Just my sister," Simon said, then immediately wished he could call the words back.

"That good-lookin' blond girl?" Hog said.

"We have a sister, too?" Grady asked.

"No, she . . . she's the Woodsons' daughter, but we were raised like brother and sister."

A throaty chuckle came from Hog. "But you ain't blood kin, boy, and if I was sharin' a tent with a gal like that, I'd sure be thinkin' about that little fact. I bet you thought about it a lot."

The intense cold seemed to make the flush

that came into Simon's face burn even hotter. He didn't want to talk about Deborah with this outlaw. He wished he had never mentioned her.

"I'm gonna stay here," Hog went on. "Grady, you go with your brother and keep an eye on him. You know how much your pa trusts you, so if Simon tries anything he hadn't ought to, you stop him, hear?"

"He's not going to try anything," Grady said. "Not if he knows what's good for him."

Grady sounded wary, as if he still weren't sure about this whole business of having a brother. Simon supposed he couldn't blame him for that. Brother or not, he was a stranger to Grady.

Would Grady try to prevent him from leaving a note? Maybe it would be best to be honest with him. As they walked quietly through the frigid night toward the tent, Simon pitched his voice low enough that Hog wouldn't overhear and said, "When we get in there, I want to write a note in my Bible and leave it for my pa."

Grady was instantly suspicious. "So you can tell him where we're going?"

"I don't *know* where we're going," Simon pointed out. "I don't have any idea where Pa plans to head next. Anyway, I'm not going to say anything about that. I just want to tell my folks that I'm all right, that I had to leave and they shouldn't worry about me."

"You think they'll believe that?"

"They won't have any reason not to."

Simon wondered suddenly if his mother was going to cry when she found out he was gone. She might. Even Deborah might shed a few tears.

Brother Franklin Woodson, though, would be as stoic as ever. If he said anything, it would be that it was God's will Simon was gone. That was the way he reacted to everything, good or bad.

"Simon," Grady whispered as they neared the tent.

"Yeah?"

"Do you really remember me? Truly?"

Even though Grady had put a foot on his chest earlier, at that moment Simon wanted to give his brother a hug. Grady might take that the wrong way, so Simon settled for saying, "Of course I do. If you had been a year or two older the last time we were together, you'd remember me, too."

Grady drew in a breath. "These folks you've been living with . . . they've treated you good?"

"Really good. They're fine folks." Even Deborah, in spite of her teasing ways, he thought.

"Well, maybe so. And I'm glad they didn't do you any harm. But they shouldn't have helped Ma steal you away from Pa."

It was going to take time to make Grady understand, Simon told himself. He just had to be patient.

"You don't have to come in with me," he whispered as he paused at the tent's entrance. "I promise I won't try anything."

"Better not. You don't want Hog havin' to take a hand in this."

That was certainly true. Simon didn't want that at all.

Noiselessly, he pulled the tent flap back. It was pitch dark inside, but as Simon stood there in the opening, enough moonlight penetrated around his body for him to be able to make out a few things. He saw the motionless, blanket-wrapped form of Deborah lying a few feet away. In the stillness of the night, he heard her breathing.

Over on the other side of the tent was a small crate he used as a table of sorts. On it were the Bible, his watch, a jackknife, a stub of candle, some sulphur matches — Brother Woodson wouldn't tolerate anybody calling them lucifers around him, since that was another name for the Devil — and a pencil. Simon wanted the watch and the knife.

Brother Woodson had given him both of those things.

Simon turned to Grady and breathed, "Hold the flap open, will you, so I can see what I'm doing."

"Hurry," Grady whispered back, but he took hold of the canvas as Simon asked and held it so that moonlight continued to spill into the tent.

It wouldn't be easy, writing a note by such dim illumination, but Simon knew he'd just have to do the best he could. He went down on his hands and knees and crawled over his scattered blankets to the crate.

He got the watch and the knife and slipped them into different trousers pockets so they wouldn't bump together and make any noise. He fumbled around in the shadows until he found the pencil, then took the Bible and opened it to the first page.

Was it a sin to write in a holy book like this? The thought gave Simon pause for a second. People wrote in Bibles, of course: names and dates, births, marriages, deaths. Brother Woodson sometimes made notes in his while he was preparing his sermons. Holy or not, the Bible was the tool of his trade, and Franklin Woodson was nothing if not a diligent worker.

On his knees, Simon turned a little so he

could see the page better and held the pencil poised above it as he tried to think of what he wanted to say and how to say it. Did he call the people who had raised him Pa and Ma, or Brother and Mrs. Woodson? That seemed awfully cold-blooded. Finally he settled on a third alternative.

Folks, I'm sorry but I have to leave. This is not your fault, and I bear you no ill will. Please know that I will always be grateful to you for everything you have done for me over these past years. I have tried to be a good and faithful son to you, but now I must go. I am fine and in no danger, so please don't worry about me.

That last was a bit of a lie. He was in danger, all right, and he probably would be as long as he traveled with Blade Kendrick. But right now he had no other option, not if he wanted to keep his parents and Deborah safe. He didn't like the leer that had been in Hog's voice when he talked about Deborah. If Simon didn't cooperate with what his real father wanted, there was no telling what the outlaws might do.

Simon drew in a deep breath. He hoped his writing was legible enough for Brother Woodson to make it out. It wasn't easy, writing in near darkness like this. But all that was left to do was sign his name.

He was about to do that, concentrating on the task at hand, when he heard a sudden scratching noise and light suddenly flared up inside the tent. Deborah had a crate on her side of the tent with a candle and matches, too, and she had just struck one of them, filling the air with a faint scent of brimstone and a garish light that struck at Simon's eyes and made him wince.

"Simon," she said, "what in the world are you doing?"

CHAPTER 12

Simon was too surprised to do anything except kneel there, frozen. Deborah's blond hair was in disarray around her face as she stared at him. Because of the cold, she wore a thick flannel nightgown, so there was nothing really tempting about her.

But that didn't stop Grady from exclaiming, "Good Lord!" in an awed voice as he stared at her from the tent's opening.

Deborah's head whipped toward him. Her eyes widened at the sight of a strange young man gazing intently at her. She lifted a hand to her mouth, and Simon knew she was about to scream.

If she did, Hog would come bounding in from his cover in the trees, and there was no telling what he might do.

He dropped the Bible and pencil and threw himself across the tent toward Deborah. His hand clapped over her mouth, stifling any outcry. Momentum carried his body into hers and she went over backward in her blankets. Simon landed on top of her.

"It's all right," he whispered urgently in her ear. "It's all right, Deborah. Don't yell, and don't fight me. You hear?"

She had dropped the match when he ran into her. It had gone out when it hit the ground, so Simon couldn't see her face even though it was only a couple of inches from his. He knew she had to be staring at him in utter shock.

She started to writhe underneath him. "Stop it!" he told her. "Quit fighting or you're gonna get us all killed!"

Deborah stopped squirming. She was breathing hard, her chest rising and falling rapidly where his chest was pressed against it. She was either scared or mad — or both. But at least she wasn't frantic anymore, and Simon hoped that meant he could still salvage this situation.

He kept his hand over her mouth but pushed himself up with his knees and other hand so his weight wouldn't be on her anymore. Leaning close, he whispered, "I'll take my hand away, but you have to promise me you won't yell or start fighting again. All right?"

This was a repeat of the same dilemma he had found himself in when Hog grabbed him earlier, he realized. And just like he had seen that cooperation was his only option then, Deborah nodded her head now.

"You promise?"

Another nod.

Simon wasn't sure he believed her, but sooner or later he had to risk letting go of her. He held his breath and lifted his hand.

He heard Deborah's rapid breath. After a few seconds, she seemed to recover slightly and was able to say, "Simon, what . . . what are you doing? Who's that other boy?"

"That's my brother, Grady."

From the tent's entrance flap, Grady said, "Psst! Simon, what's goin' on in there? Hog's gonna get tired of waitin' for us!"

"Brother?" Deborah said.

"You don't remember? My ma took him with her after she left me with your folks."

"It was so long ago . . ."

She sounded considerably calmer now. Simon thought he could risk taking a minute to explain.

"My ma — my real mother — took me and my brother away from our pa. She left me with your family, and I guess she left Grady with somebody else. I don't really know all the details yet. She was going to come back for us, but something happened to her. She . . . she died. So I grew up with

370

you and your folks, and Grady grew up with that other family. But now our real pa has found us and wants us to be with him. I've got to go, Deborah. I've got . . . another family now. My real family."

Those words sounded hollow to Simon even as he spoke them. Blood relations or not, he had considered the Woodsons to be his real family for so long that he couldn't grasp anything different.

Deborah clutched at him, but she wasn't fighting now. She held on to him with desperation. "Simon, you can't go," she said. "You just can't. I don't know if I could stand it . . . all the preaching and hymn-singing . . . without you around."

He had to make her understand, but he wanted to do so without telling her that his real father was an outlaw and that he'd be riding with a gang of owlhoots from now on. Simon could hardly believe that himself. How could anybody's life get turned so completely upside down in such a short period of time?

"Deborah . . ." he started again.

Then Grady exclaimed, "Damn it, here comes Hog! I told you he'd get tired of waitin'!"

Simon scrambled to his feet. He had run out of time. Deborah stood up, too, and he grabbed her by the arms.

"Please don't say anything," he begged. "This man, he's liable to cause trouble . . ."

"Simon, I'm scared! This is wrong!"

It sure was, Simon thought, but it had gone much too far for him to do anything about it now.

"Grady, stop him. Tell him I'm coming right now."

"I'll try . . ." Grady began. Then he grunted as Hog shoved him aside and bulled his way into the tent. Light flared again, striking at Simon's eyes. Hog had just snapped a lucifer to life with his thumbnail.

"Come on, kid," he said. "Time's up." He looked at Deborah, and a leer split his ugly face. "We can take your little sis with us if you want."

That was the last thing in the world Simon wanted, and Deborah's reaction to the suggestion showed that she didn't care for the idea, either. She backed away, stumbling over the blankets, and before Simon could stop her she opened her mouth and let out a piercing scream of pure terror.

This would have been a good night to be sitting in front of a roaring fire somewhere, rather than on the back of his big golden sorrel, Ulysses, Cole Tyler thought as he rode slowly along Grenville Avenue beside the buggy driven by Dr. Judson Kent.

Cole glanced at the Wind River Café as they passed it. The café was darkened now, of course, but the sight of it made Cole think that it would have been really nice to sit in front of that fire he was imagining with Rose Foster. He sighed. Duty came first, and tonight, so had friendship.

The doctor had been called out late in the afternoon to one of the small ranches south of town. One of the rancher's kids was sick with a fever, and Kent wanted not only to treat the ill boy but to try to make sure the sickness didn't spread to the rest of the family.

Cole had happened to be at the doctor's house visiting Billy Casebolt when the rancher rode in to fetch Kent, and he'd offered to come along.

"Man needs company on a night as cold as this one's gonna be," Cole had told Kent. "If anything were to happen — horse run away, buggy break an axle, something like that — a fella could freeze to death if he was stranded out in the open all night."

"As always, I'll enjoy your company, Marshal," Kent had said.

He had done everything he could for the boy, making him comfortable and giving

373

instructions to the mother on how to care for him, along with a warning to keep the other children away until the fever broke. He had promised to drive back out first thing in the morning to see how the patient was doing.

Now the two men had returned to Wind River without incident, and as they drew up in front of Kent's darkened house, Cole said, "I reckon since I'm already out and about this late, I'll take a turn around the town before I turn in. I'm sure Clancy's already made night rounds, but it never hurts to check things again."

"Surely no one is foolish enough to be up to any mischief on a night as frigid as this one."

"You'd think so," Cole said with a smile, "but you never know."

He started to turn his horse, but as he did, someone screamed at the other end of town. Cole sat up straight in the saddle and jerked his head toward the sound.

No shots followed the cry, but even so, he wanted to find out what was going on. He called, "Go on inside, Judson," to the doctor, then turned his mount and heeled the horse into a run. Ulysses was tired but responded immediately.

Somebody yelled. The shout sounded like

it came from a man. Cole headed for the wagon where Brother Franklin Woodson and his wife were staying and the tent pitched nearby. The Woodsons' youngsters shared the tent. Cole was pretty sure the scream and the shout had come from one of those places.

He got proof of that a moment later when a knot of struggling figures spilled out of the tent's entrance flap. In the dim light from the stars, Cole couldn't make out who or how many, but they were fighting, that was for sure.

As he slowed his horse and got ready to swing down from the saddle, the sound he'd been expecting — and dreading — to hear split the night. A gun roared. Muzzle flame bloomed like a garish orange flower in the darkness. Someone cried out in pain.

Cole hit the ground running, his Colt .44 revolver already in his hand. "Hold it!" he shouted. "Drop your gun!"

He didn't know exactly who had the gun, but that uncertainty quickly resolved itself as one of the struggling figures let out a bellow of rage and cast off what turned out to be two opponents with a swing of his massive arm. His other hand came up. Flame spurted from the weapon's muzzle as another report slammed out.

The bullet didn't come close enough for Cole to hear as he dropped to one knee. He still didn't shoot, because the two men who'd been fighting with the big hombre were still close by, maybe in the line of fire.

"Drop it!" he shouted again.

Instead of doing that, the man wheeled around and lurched into a run toward the trees. The other two, much to Cole's surprise, followed him and once again blocked the marshal's shot. Maybe they were just trying to catch him, but what they were really doing was keeping Cole from winging him.

He bit back a curse as he surged to his feet. He was about to run after the three figures disappearing into the woods when someone else stumbled out of the tent, directly into his path. He heard a startled, feminine "Oh!" as the person rebounded from the collision and knew he had just run into a woman. Instinctively, he reached out with his free hand to steady her and keep her from falling.

The three men were gone now, he noted with an angry grimace. A moment later, he heard the swift rataplan of hoofbeats and knew they were fleeing into the cold night.

He still had hold of the woman's arm. She tried to pull away from him as she cried,

"Simon! Simon, come back!"

The voice was too young to belong to Mrs. Woodson, Cole realized. That and the fact that she had come out of the tent told him he had hold of Deborah Woodson, the preacher's daughter. Panicky, she started striking out at him with her other hand.

Cole jammed the .44 back in its holster and caught hold of Deborah with that hand, too. "Settle down, Miss Woodson," he told her. "You're all right. I'm Marshal Tyler."

"Who's there?" a man called. His voice held both anger and fear. "Deborah! Simon!"

Cole held on to both of Deborah's wrists so she couldn't wallop him and turned his head to see that the girl's father had climbed out of the wagon.

"Brother Woodson, it's me, Cole Tyler," he said. "Your daughter's right here." He let go of Deborah and gave her a little push toward Woodson.

The preacher hurried forward and gathered her into his arms. "There, there, child," he said as she started to cry. "What in heaven's name is wrong?"

"He's gone!" Deborah wailed. "Simon's gone! They took him!"

Cole frowned in the darkness. If Simon Woodson was one of the two people he had seen running off into the woods after the varmint with the gun, nobody had taken him. He had gone of his own free will, and from the hoofbeats Cole had heard, all three of them had been together when they lit a shuck away from Wind River. That didn't make much sense, considering that they'd been fighting just a few moments earlier, but that was sure the way it had sounded.

Heavy footsteps approached as light splashed over the ground. Cole turned and saw a tall, bulky shape coming toward the wagon and the tent with a lantern in one upraised hand. The other hand clutched the thick, knobby shillelagh that instantly identified the man as Deputy Clancy Madigan.

"Cole?" Madigan called. "Is that ye?"

"It is," Cole replied.

"I heard a ruckus . . ."

"Seems to be over now." Light from the lantern in Madigan's hand reached Brother Woodson, who stood there fully dressed against the night's chill, holding the shivering, sobbing form of his daughter, who wore a thick flannel nightgown.

Mrs. Woodson peered out from the back of the wagon with fear on her pale face. "Franklin, what is it?" she asked. "Where's Simon?"

That brought a fresh wail from Deborah.

Cole wanted an answer to that question himself. He wanted to know where Simon Woodson was — and what in blazes had happened on a night when folks should have been huddled under the covers, trying to keep from freezing to death.

"I reckon we'd better go down to my office where it's warm," he said, "and get to the bottom of this."

CHAPTER 13

Clancy Madigan tossed another chunk of wood into the potbellied stove and closed the door. The fire had burned down some while Madigan dozed on the cot in the back room, but he had built it up now to the point that it was putting out quite a bit of welcome warmth.

Cole sat at his desk, still wearing the sheepskin coat he'd had on when he rode back into town with Dr. Kent. Mrs. Woodson and Deborah, both bundled in blankets, sat on the old sofa to the left of the door. Franklin Woodson, in an overcoat, stood in front of the desk.

Dr. Judson Kent was the sixth person in the room. After hearing the shots and seeing Cole gallop off, he had disregarded the order to go inside, turned his buggy around, and driven back down here to the marshal's office and jail, just in case his medical services were needed.

"You have to find my son, Marshal," Woodson said. "My wife and I are both frantic. I have no idea who would want to kidnap him, unless it was those freighters we had trouble with."

"I don't know, either, but if anybody does, it'll be your daughter. She was right in the middle of whatever was going on." Cole looked at Deborah. "Miss Woodson, do you feel up to telling us about it?"

Phillippa Woodson tightened her arm around her daughter's shoulders. "Deborah is very upset . . ." she began.

"I . . . I can talk," Deborah broke in. "It wasn't those men who caused trouble at the church. Simon . . . Simon was the one who told me he was leaving."

"Running away?" Woodson said. "I don't believe it!"

Cole said, "Simon was one of the three fellas who were fighting in front of the tent when I rode up?"

Deborah nodded. She didn't seem to want to meet Cole's eyes, but she kept talking.

"I woke up a few minutes earlier, and he was there, writing something in his Bible."

"Writing in the Bible?" Woodson seemed almost as upset by that as he was by the fact that Simon was missing.

"Yes," Deborah said. "And there was

another boy . . . Simon said that his name was Grady and that he . . . he was Simon's brother."

"Oh, dear Lord," Mrs. Woodson said in a hushed voice.

Cole could tell by the startled look on Woodson's face that the preacher recognized the name, too. He said, "Is that true, Brother Woodson? Simon's not really your son?"

Woodson swallowed. "What . . . what makes you say that?"

"Well, if he was, I reckon you and your wife would know if he had a brother. Although, come to think of it, you *did* know that, didn't you?"

Woodson breathed in hard, then said, "Simon is not our son by birth, but we've raised him for more than twelve years, Marshal. Mrs. Woodson and I regard him as our son as much as we would if he were our own flesh and blood."

"But this other young fella, Grady? That's his actual brother?"

Woodson closed his eyes and rested his fingers against his forehead for a second before looking at Cole and saying, "Yes, I seem to recall that was the other boy's name."

Cole thought a moment, then nodded slowly and said, "I reckon you'd better start at the beginning."

For the next ten minutes, while Mrs. Woodson sobbed silently and held her daughter close to her, the preacher explained how Simon — whose real name apparently was Simon Kendrick — had come to live with them.

"It was never a secret among us," Woodson concluded. "Simon was old enough when he came to live with us that he remembered his mother, although I believe the memories were rather vague. He remembered his father, too. For months, he sometimes cried out in his sleep when he had nightmares about the man."

"What happened to Mrs. Kendrick?"

"I honestly don't know, Marshal. We expected her to return for Simon, and when she didn't . . . Well, Phillippa and I feared that something had happened to her. We thought that perhaps she fell ill and passed away, or that something else had befallen her. We had no way to try to contact her, so when I was called to preach the gospel at another church, we simply . . . took Simon with us and considered him a member of the family." Woodson's voice caught a little. "He's been with us ever since."

"Until tonight." Cole looked at Deborah again. "Miss Woodson, did your brother —

I mean, Simon — did he say anything about his mother?"

Deborah shook her head. "No, he said his father had come for him. That he and Grady and their father were going to be together again, were going to be a family."

"You're talking about Blade Kendrick?"

"He never mentioned a name other than Grady's, but that's who it had to be, isn't it?"

Woodson said, "Back in Missouri, the man was suspected of being a criminal, Marshal. I don't know what's happened to him or what he's done since then, but it seems likely he's an actual outlaw by now."

Clancy Madigan spoke up, saying, "Part of bein' a preacher is believin' that folks get a second chance, aye?"

"Indeed," Woodson replied. "But you didn't know Blade Kendrick, Deputy. You never saw for yourself how much fear he inspired in that poor woman, and in his older son. There had to be good reasons for that fear, and I'm not sure such a man could ever change."

Madigan's brawny shoulders rose and fell in a shrug.

"All right," Cole said, "that third fella, the one who took a shot at me, was that Kendrick?"

384

Deborah shook her head. "No. Grady called him Hog."

That made Cole sit up straighter. He opened a drawer in his desk, took out a piece of paper, and unfolded it as he stood up and moved over to the sofa. He held out the paper so that Deborah could see it.

"Did you get a good enough look at him to tell if this was the man, Miss Woodson?"

The paper was the wanted poster on Harry "Hog" Tatum that Cole had taken off the body of the dead bounty hunter, Will Sumner, several days earlier.

Deborah stared at the crude drawing, then said, "I only saw him for a few seconds by matchlight, but I'm pretty sure that's him, Marshal." She shuddered a little. "It's hard to forget a man as big and ugly as that."

Cole grunted. "What happened after he came busting into the tent?"

"I'm afraid I screamed. He . . . he really frightened me. He said that if Simon wanted, they could take me with them. The way he said it . . ."

Deborah couldn't go on, but the bright red flush that stole across her face made it clear what Hog Tatum had been implying.

"That scoundrel," Woodson said. "A man like that should be horsewhipped."

"Strung up is more like it," Madigan said.

"If he's guilty of all the things on this wanted poster, he's got it coming," Cole said. "But you were telling me what happened, Miss Woodson."

Deborah took a deep breath. "When I screamed, that made him angry. He reached for me — God knows what he intended to do — but Simon shouted at him to stop. When he didn't, Simon tackled him. That man, Mr. Tatum, was too big for Simon to force him out of the tent, but Grady grabbed him, too. They were wrestling around, and they all staggered outside, and then I heard a gun go off." She shrugged. "I had to gather up my courage, but I was afraid Simon had been hurt so I rushed out and ran into you, Marshal. That's all I know."

Cole nodded and said, "Thanks. I know you're pretty shaken up. You should go back to your folks' wagon and try to get some rest." He glanced at Kent. "Right, Doctor?"

"That's the best medicine for such a distressing experience," Kent agreed.

"I'm all right," Deborah insisted. "I just want somebody to find Simon."

"Indeed," Woodson said. "I understand that you needed to find out the circumstances, Marshal, but now shouldn't you be out there trying to rescue my son?"

"It sounds to me like the boy left of his

own accord. How old is he?"

"He's seventeen," Mrs. Woodson said. "Only seventeen."

Cole shook his head. "That's considered a man full grown, most places. Besides, my jurisdiction ends at the town limits."

Woodson said, "Even in the short time we've been in Wind River, Marshal, I've heard enough about you to know that you don't always worry about such legal niceties. Besides, I don't believe Simon went with that man of his own free will. I believe he was kidnapped. Kidnapped by a vicious outlaw while within the confines of this settlement, in fact. Doesn't that make it your business?"

Cole could see that Woodson was going to be a bulldog about this. He couldn't blame the man. Even though Simon wasn't blood kin, he had been like a son to the Woodsons for a long time, and of course they wanted him back, wanted to know that he was safe.

"It's too dark to try to pick up their trail tonight," he said. "First thing in the morning, though, I'll ride out and see if I can find some tracks. That's the best I can offer you."

"But you *will* try to find Simon?" Woodson said.

"I will," Cole promised.

Woodson nodded. "And we'll pray for you to be successful. But I'm going to do more than that, Marshal."

"What do you have in mind?" Cole asked, suddenly wary.

"I'm coming with you," the preacher declared.

Grady and Hog didn't pull their horses back to a walk until they had ridden hard for more than a mile. Simon was behind Grady on the younger brother's mount. The horse was tired from having to carry double, especially at such a fast pace, but Hog had insisted they put some distance between themselves and Wind River.

"I don't reckon that damn marshal's likely to round up a posse and come after us in the middle of the night," Hog had said, "but there ain't no use riskin' it."

Simon was glad they had finally slowed down. It would have been difficult enough hanging on behind Grady with two good arms. He had only one because his left arm was sore and throbbing from the bullet graze he had suffered while they were struggling with Hog. The big outlaw's gun had gone off — maybe accidentally, maybe on purpose — and the slug had ripped the sleeves of Simon's coat, shirt, and long underwear and burned a path along his forearm. He didn't think the wound had bled much, but it hurt like blazes and left his arm weak.

Now as they rode along at a slower pace, Hog said, "I ought to thrash you two brats within an inch of your lives. What the hell were you thinkin', fightin' with me like that? Especially you, Grady. We been ridin' together for a while. We're pards, ain't we?"

"Yeah, but Simon's my brother, I reckon. Pa says so, and he wouldn't lie. Anyway, that girl was mighty pretty, and you were scarin' her half to death, Hog. There wasn't any need for that."

"Oh," Hog said. "Now I understand. You took one look at that gal, and you're already sweet on her."

"I never said that," Grady protested.

"You didn't have to. The way you jumped in, thinkin' to protect her from me, that says it all." Hog laughed. "You better ask your brother about that, kid. He's the one who's been sharin' a tent and likely a bedroll with her."

"That's not the way it was," Simon said stiffly.

"Whatever you say. The important thing is, I got the two of you and we're on our way back to Blade. I wouldn't have wanted to face him if anything happened to either of you. He's got his heart set on all of us ridin' together from here on out."

Hog was wrong about that, Simon thought. Blade Kendrick didn't have a heart.

But at least for the time being, the only thing Simon could do was to go along with what his father wanted. That was the only way to keep Deborah and her folks safe. He had no doubt that Kendrick would have tried to take him away from them by force if he hadn't cooperated.

Simon couldn't stop himself from saying, "If you wanted to make sure Grady and I were all right, why did you shoot me in the arm?"

Hog swore bitterly. "I didn't do that on purpose, boy, and you know it! When somebody starts fightin' with me, I just naturally grab for a gun. It's your fault you caught some lead." He paused, then asked, "Just how bad are you hit, anyway?"

"Not bad, I guess." Simon had never been shot before, so he didn't have anything to compare this wound to. "It hurts like . . . like hell."

He never would have been able to say that around Brother Woodson, but he didn't figure Hog or any of the other outlaws would ever tell him to watch his language.

"We'll see to it once we get to camp. Your pa's old partner, Frank Wolters, he's mighty good at patchin' up bullet wounds. Got plenty of experience, I reckon, since he's been ridin' the dark trails for a long time."

Would people say that about him someday, Simon wondered? That he had been riding the dark trails for a long time? It seemed more likely he would be killed before that ever had a chance to happen. He knew he wasn't cut out to be an outlaw. He wanted to think that Grady wasn't, either. He just needed a chance to convince his brother of that.

After a few minutes, he asked, "Where is this camp we're going to?"

"You'll find out when we get there," Hog answered.

They rode on into the night, and after the horses had had a chance to rest a little, Hog pushed them at a faster pace again, although not as breakneck as they had ridden out of Wind River. Simon was cold clear through. He wished he had a hat and a scarf. His ears felt completely frozen, as if they were ready to crack and fall right off his head. He started worrying about frostbite.

The landscape became more rugged as they entered some foothills below a range of small mountains. Hog led them into a narrow, brushy gulch. The outlaw had to have a good sense of direction, Simon thought. Otherwise he couldn't have been able to find the gulch in the dark like this.

The going was slow. Simon's heart sped up as he caught a whiff of smoke. It smelled like a campfire, and sure enough, as they rounded a sharp bend, he spotted a good-sized blaze up ahead. Dark figures stood or hunkered around it, trying to warm up.

They had reached the outlaw camp, he realized. His father's camp.

Blade Kendrick was there to meet them when they dismounted. He must have spotted the bloodstain and the rip on Simon's coat sleeve, because he stepped forward sharply, caught hold of Simon's wrist, and lifted that arm. Simon sucked in a swift breath of pain.

"What the hell happened?" Kendrick said. "How bad are you hurt, son?" Without waiting for an answer, he turned his head to glare at Hog. "Damn it, I expected you to look out for my boys!"

"It was an accident, Pa," Grady said before either Simon or Hog could respond. "There was a little trouble, and the marshal came running up. We traded a few shots with him and Simon got winged. But it's not bad, isn't that right, Simon?"

"Yeah," Simon said slowly. "It hurts, but I'll be fine."

He glanced at Hog and saw the look of relief on the big outlaw's face. With Grady speaking up the way he had — and lying about what happened — Hog hadn't had to tell Kendrick the truth. That was pretty smart on Grady's part. His fast thinking had put Hog in their debt. That might prove to be valuable sometime later on.

Kendrick let go of Simon's wrist, turned to Grady, and put a hand on his shoulder. "You threw down with a lawman?" He sounded almost proud.

Grady shrugged carelessly. "Seemed like the thing to do at the time."

"Did you kill him?"

"No, I don't think he was hurt. But we made him duck for cover while we got out of there."

Kendrick looked back at Simon. "You got what you went after?"

"Yeah."

"Then there's nothing holding you here in these parts anymore. Come morning, we can rattle our hocks and head somewhere else." Kendrick laughed. "In a few days, you'll forget all about that sky pilot and his family. It'll be like you've been riding with us all along, son!"

Simon managed to smile and nod, but he knew what his father said wasn't true at all. He would never forget the Woodsons. He didn't know if things would work out so that he ever saw them again, but he was certain he would never forget them.

"Frank," Kendrick said, "come and take a look at the boy's arm. Patch it up good. It's a badge of honor!"

CHAPTER 14

Cole had no intention of taking Brother Franklin Woodson with him when he set out after Simon, Grady, and Hog Tatum, but he wanted to talk to the preacher before he left, so he rode down to the Woodsons' wagon. The storefront where Woodson had his church appeared to be locked up and empty, Cole noted as he went past the place.

"Brother Woodson," he called as he sat his saddle beside the driver's box on the wagon. His breath fogged thickly in front of his face. It was cold and clear this morning, with an achingly blue sky arching overhead.

Woodson stuck his head through the opening in the canvas cover. "Marshal," he said. "I'll be ready to go momentarily."

"That's one thing I wanted to talk to you about," Cole said. "You won't be going. You need to stay right here in Wind River and take care of your wife and daughter."

Woodson frowned as he said, "I told you

last night that I'm coming with you, and I meant it."

"And I mean what I say now. I'm not in the market for another deputy. No offense, preacher, but I'd rather concentrate on tracking those three than have to look out for you."

Woodson's eyes narrowed. "People who begin sentences by saying no offense usually don't care whether they offend anyone or not. In my experience, that is."

"Well, I'm just being truthful," Cole said. "It'd be better right now for me to go after those three by myself. If I wind up needing help, I can always come back and fetch it."

"Simon is my son. You can understand . . ."

"I sure do, Brother Woodson," Cole said, nodding. "I sure do. But before I ride out, I wanted to ask you about whatever it was that Simon was writing in the Bible. You recall, your daughter mentioned something about that last night in my office. Might be something in it that would give me a clue where to look for them."

"Of course. Wait just a moment."

Woodson disappeared inside the wagon. After a minute, he pushed through the opening in the canvas again and swung his leg over the back of the driver's seat. He climbed onto the box and held out a black-bound book toward Cole, who edged the golden sorrel closer so he could reach out and take it.

"Simon's note is just inside, on the fly-leaf," Woodson said. "I'm afraid it won't be very helpful, though."

Cole opened the book and read what the youngster had written. The letters were very shaky and wandered all over the place, but Simon had written the note in the dark, he recalled. It wasn't signed, because Simon had been interrupted by Deborah waking up and striking a match.

Cole handed the Bible back to Woodson and said, "Doesn't sound like he was being forced to do anything he didn't want to do."

"You don't understand, Marshal. The poor boy was terrified of Blade Kendrick."

"He was that scared of his own father?"

"I'm sure he had good reason to be."

"Well, you might be right," Cole said. "I didn't recall hearing of Kendrick before, but this morning I went through all the reward dodgers that have piled up in my office, and I found a few on him. Nothing earlier than a couple of years ago, but since then he's cut a pretty wide swath between here and Kansas. Mostly bank and train robberies, but he's held up some stagecoaches, too. And there are murder charges against him, so I reckon he's killed some folks while pulling those jobs. But you said it's been twelve years since Mrs. Kendrick left Simon with you. Where's Kendrick been during the rest of that time?"

"I'm sure I have no idea, Marshal. In prison, perhaps?"

Cole thought about it. Woodson might have something there.

"That would explain it. Maybe later I'll send some wires off and try to find out about that. Might stop by our local newspaper, too. The young fella who owns the *Sentinel,* Michael Hatfield, has a big file of papers from Cheyenne and Denver going back quite a few years. Could be something in one of them about Kendrick. But all that's just to satisfy our curiosity. It can wait."

"Indeed it can," Woodson said. "Right now you need to get out there and find my boy."

Cole felt a slight flash of irritation. He didn't need Woodson to tell him how to do his job.

"There's one more thing," he said. "Suppose I find Simon and shake him loose from those outlaws. You want me to bring him back here."

"Of course I do! He's my son."

"What about Grady?" Cole asked.

Woodson frowned at him for a long moment without replying. Then he said, "Are you asking if Phillippa and I want to take him in as well?"

"He's Simon's brother," Cole pointed out. "Even though they haven't seen each other for a good many years, Simon's liable not to want to come along without him."

"Yes. Yes, I suppose you're right. I'll have to talk it over with my wife to make the final determination, and she's still sleeping. She had to take a tonic last night to calm her nerves, she was so upset by everything that happened. But you can't leave a boy in the company of such fiends! He can't be more than fifteen or sixteen years old."

From the corner of his eye, Cole had seen Deborah Woodson appear at the back corner of the wagon a few seconds earlier. He guessed she had heard them talking and had climbed out over the tailgate. She was dressed in a thick coat and long skirt this morning. Her hair looked like she had run her fingers through it, but it was still somewhat tangled.

"My father's right, Marshal," she said as she approached Cole's horse. "You have to bring Grady back, too."

Cole pinched the brim of his hat, nodded politely, and said, "Miss Woodson. How are you feeling this morning?"

"Worried about my brother. Anxious for you to find him."

"He's going to be all right. Kendrick wouldn't have gone to so much trouble finding those boys if he meant them any harm. I'm convinced of that."

Woodson said, "He'll harm them just by having them around him and those other criminals who ride with him. He'll try to turn them into outlaws. They'll probably be killed in some shoot-out with lawmen or honest citizens while they're trying to commit some crime."

Cole couldn't argue with that. There was a good chance Woodson was right.

"I'll do everything I can to find him and keep him safe. I give you my word on that." He nodded solemnly to Woodson and Deborah as he made the promise, then turned his horse and rode out of Wind River in the direction of the swiftly retreating hoofbeats he had heard the night before.

Simon's left arm was stiff and sore this morning, but he could use it. Frank Wolters had cleaned the wound with whiskey the night before. Simon had gasped at the fiery

400

bite of the liquor on raw flesh, but once that pain faded, the arm felt better. Then Wolters had wrapped a strip of cloth around it to serve as a bandage and told Simon to take it easy with the arm for a few days.

"It'll be fine, kid," the dour outlaw had assured him.

"I'll probably wind up with worse," Simon had said. The only response that got from Wolters was a noncommittal grunt.

After spending a cold night in camp, most of the men seemed to be in bad moods this morning. Hog, whose real name was Harry Tatum, Simon had learned, hunkered next to the fire and said to Kendrick, "Now that you've found both of your young'uns, Blade, how about we head for some place warmer than this damn Wyoming? It's probably pretty nice down along the Mexican border." He grinned. "I could do with a bellyful of tequila and a sweet little Mex gal snuggled up against me."

"Heading down to Mexico's not a bad idea," Kendrick said. He sipped from the cup of coffee in his hand. "Got a few things to clear up first, but maybe we'll drift that way pretty soon." He turned to Simon. "You doing all right?"

"Yeah."

"Not missing those folks back in Wind River?"

"I'm fine," Simon replied. "It still seems strange not to be with them, but that'll fade." He knew that was what Kendrick wanted to hear. "Blood's thicker than anything I had with them."

"Damn right. I'm glad that you've come around to that way of thinking." Kendrick grinned and slapped his other son on the back. "Grady took to this life right away. Didn't you, boy?"

"Sure, Pa," Grady said. "It's been a lot more exciting than working from sunup to sundown on a ranch, I can say that."

"You've been taking him on jobs with you?" Simon asked. He tried to keep a note of disapproval out of his voice but wasn't sure he succeeded completely.

"That's right. He's done a mighty good job holding the horses for us."

"I can do more than that," Grady said. "I'm ready to get right in there with you and the other men, Pa. I can use a gun, and I'm not scared of doin' whatever needs to be done."

"Your time's coming," Kendrick said. "Just be patient."

The men began preparing to break camp. Simon had no gear to pack nor a horse to saddle. He would ride double with Grady again until they could get a horse for him. Until they could *steal* a horse, he corrected himself, because he knew good and well his father didn't intend to pay for one.

While the others were getting ready, Simon noticed his father talking intently with Frank Wolters. Wolters nodded in understanding of whatever Kendrick told him. A few minutes later, Kendrick came over to where Simon was standing while Grady saddled the horse they would ride.

"I've got a job for the two of you," Kendrick said. "You're going to ride west ahead of the rest of us and scout out a good trail we can use. I want to avoid the settlement, so we'll travel a ways west first and then cut south." He smiled. "Hog's in a hurry to get to Mexico, you know."

"Why don't we just all ride together?" Simon said.

The smile remained on Kendrick's face, but the jovial expression vanished instantly from his eyes, which turned chilly at having his orders questioned. After so many years, Simon didn't remember particulars, but he knew instinctively how short-tempered his father was.

"The rest of us have something else to do," Kendrick said. "We'll catch up in a day

403

or two. But you'll be with Frank, so you'll be all right."

"We'd be all right anyway, Pa," Grady said. "We can take care of ourselves, can't we, big brother?"

Simon nodded and said, "Sure." He wasn't at all certain of that, and this business of splitting up from the rest of the gang had him confused. But he wasn't going to turn down a chance to be alone with Grady, or at least mostly alone. Maybe they could get away from Wolters and Grady would agree to go back to Wind River with him.

Kendrick motioned to Wolters, who came over carrying a coiled shell belt and holstered revolver. "You can do a better job of taking care of yourself if you're armed," he said as Wolters handed the rig to a surprised Simon. "Strap that on."

Simon looked down at the holstered gun. "You want me to carry this?"

Grady laughed. "You'll get used to packin' iron in a hurry, Simon. I did." He slapped the walnut grips of the gun at his hip.

Again, depending on what happened, it might not be a bad idea for him to be armed, Simon thought. He buckled the gunbelt around his waist, letting it settle slightly on his hips. The holster had rawhide thongs on the end of it that he used to tie it in place.

The gun felt awkward and heavy. Maybe as Grady said, he would get used to it. Simon wasn't sure he *wanted* to get used to carrying a gun. But he might not have any choice.

"Looks good," Wolters said. "We'll get you a hat sometime, and nobody'll be able to tell you haven't been riding with us for a long time."

"Take good care of 'em, Frank," Kendrick said.

"Of course." Wolters inclined his head. "Come on, boys. Let's ride."

A minute later, while the others were still in camp, Simon, Grady, and Wolters rode out, heading west as Kendrick had directed. Simon glanced back.

Something was wrong. He didn't know what it was, but he could feel it in his bones.

"We'll give them a while," Kendrick said to Tatum, "just to make sure they're well away from here before we ride south."

Tatum scratched at the beard on his heavy jaw. "They're bound to hear about it sooner or later, Blade. When a bunch like us rides in, loots a town, and leaves it burnin' behind 'em, they put stories about it in the newspapers."

"By the time they find out, nobody'll be able to prove it wasn't some other bunch of outlaws who raided Wind River. If you and the rest of the men just keep your damn mouths shut, it won't be a problem."

"You don't have to worry about that," Tatum said. "We ain't the sort to flap our gums, and you know it."

Kendrick just grunted.

Tatum ventured to ask, "Are you doin' this just because you're mad about that marshal shootin' Simon?"

"He's got to pay for that," Kendrick said coldly, "but I figure that preacher owes me, too. He helped that bitch of a wife of mine steal those boys from me. There's no telling what sort of poison he shoved into Simon's head along with all the psalm-singing. Whatever happens to him, he's got it coming." Kendrick shrugged. "As for the rest of it, you and Frank both said it looked like the businesses in Wind River were doing pretty well, and there's a bank there. It's been a while since we pulled a good job. We ought to be able to get our hands on enough loot in Wind River to see us down to Mexico in style."

"I like the sound of that," Tatum said with a grin. "And I always like to see the flames

406

leapin' up behind us when we leave a town."

"Yes," Kendrick said. "Let it burn."

CHAPTER 15

Cole had learned how to scout and follow a trail while riding with J.E.B. Stuart's cavalry during the war. He had a natural talent for it — as well as a knack for finding trouble, as the dashing Southern commander had expressed it.

Cole picked up the tracks of two horses on the other side of the woods where the fleeing men had disappeared the night before. The fact that there were only two mounts puzzled him at first, but when he found a place where the hoofprints were a little more distinctive, he could tell there was a good chance one of the horses was carrying double.

That would be the Kendrick brothers, he thought. Hog Tatum had been on the other horse. A frown creased Cole's forehead as he remembered the shooting in which he had killed Will Sumner while Tatum jumped on a horse and raced out of town.

Cole didn't feel any guilt over gunning the bounty hunter. The way Sumner had been throwing lead around, he hadn't cared about any innocent bystanders being in the way as long as he got the man he was after — and the bounty on Tatum's head. He had been about to shoot Clancy Madigan when Cole dropped him. Cole had no doubt he had saved his deputy's life.

But if that whole encounter had worked out differently, Tatum would be in jail and Simon Woodson — Simon Kendrick, Cole reminded himself; he was going to have trouble keeping that straight — would still be safely with his family . . . maybe.

If Tatum had been killed or jailed, Kendrick more than likely would have just sent somebody else after Simon. Things could have turned out even worse.

Cole smiled. Out here on the frontier, things were seldom so bad that they couldn't get worse.

The trail led north toward the foothills and the mountains beyond which lay the valley where Kermit Sawyer's Diamond S Ranch was located. Even if Woodson's suspicions and the wanted posters about Blade Kendrick having a whole gang of outlaws were correct, Cole doubted if they would head for the transplanted Texan's spread. Sawyer had as salty a crew of cowboys as anybody could ever find, and they wouldn't take kindly to a bunch of owlhoots trespassing on Diamond S range.

There was enough rugged country between here and there, however, that Kendrick and his men could have hidden out there while he tried to get Simon away from the Woodsons.

Cole lost the trail a couple of times during the morning, but by casting back and forth he was able to pick it up again. The tracks still led generally northward, toward the foothills. He wanted to find Kendrick's hideout and get Simon away from the outlaws, and Grady, too, if possible. If he couldn't do that by himself, he would head back to Wind River and return with a posse.

For the moment, though, all he could do was keep looking.

He had reached the edge of the foothills and was about to follow the tracks up a slope to a saddle between a couple of rounded, brushy knobs when he sensed something was wrong. A lot of years and a lot of dangers survived had taught Cole to trust whatever his gut told him. He drew back on the reins and turned his horse broadside to the trail.

Just as he did that, he heard a rifle crack

not far off and, at the same instant, the flat *whap!* of a bullet passing close by his ear.

The shot came from somewhere up ahead in that saddle of ground between the two knobs. Cole could guess that much by the sound, but he hadn't spotted a muzzle flash or puff of powder smoke at which he could return fire.

Anyway, he was too much out in the open to put up a fight from here. He jabbed his bootheels into Ulysses's flanks and sent the big horse racing toward the knob that had been on Cole's left as he approached. That was the closest cover.

He bent low in the saddle to make himself a smaller target. Another slug whined past him, close enough for Cole to hear it. He saw a bullet kick up dirt and rocks ahead of him. The bushwhacker — or bushwhackers, because he didn't know how many there were — would be zeroing in on him. Most likely, they would shoot the sorrel out from under him and leave him afoot, so they could take their time about killing him.

He turned Ulysses sharply to throw off their aim, then darted back onto his original course. That cost him a few seconds in his effort to reach the cover of the knob, but since Ulysses wasn't hit and neither was he, Cole figured it was worth it.

Then three men on horseback rounded the south side of the knob and spurred at him. This time he saw the spurts of gray smoke as they opened fire on him with revolvers.

Cole bit back a curse and yanked the sorrel to the right without slowing. Only Ulysses's strength and nimble-footedness kept them upright. Cole pulled his .44 and blasted three shots toward the charging riders, not expecting to hit any of them but hoping to slow their attack.

To his surprise, one of the men went backward off his horse like he'd been slapped out of the saddle by a giant hand. A grim smile tugged at Cole's mouth. He'd take a lucky shot like that any day of the week. And as he had hoped, seeing their companion go down made the other two men ease off some. They kept shooting, though, as Cole galloped toward the knob.

He still had the rifleman to the north to worry about, but caught as he was between enemy forces, the only thing he could do was plunge straight ahead. Ulysses reached the base of the knob and started up the slope. It was steep, and the big horse had to struggle to climb it. The brush and the trees on the knob provided some cover, thankfully. Cole saw a branch jump as a wild shot clipped it off, but that was as close as any of the bullets came.

Unless more trouble was waiting for him atop the knob, once he reached it he would have the high ground. The men who wanted to kill him would have to come to him. He was confident he could hold them off for a while, because he had plenty of .44 rounds for the Colt and the Henry rifle snugged in a saddle boot.

But once he was up there, he wouldn't have any way down. Being generous, you could call it a standoff.

But in reality, he would be trapped.

Simon and Grady had ridden several miles with Frank Wolters when the outlaw's horse stumbled over a rock and immediately began limping.

"Damn it," Wolters said as he reined in. "We didn't need this. I wanted to cover more ground before we turned back to the south."

"We don't have to be anywhere at any particular time, do we?" Grady asked.

"No, but . . ."

Wolters broke off his answer impatiently and swung down from the saddle. He knelt and ran experienced hands over his mount's left foreleg.

"Might not be too bad," he announced when he straightened. "I think he just pulled it a little. He'll need to rest for a while, and then we'll see." Wolters pointed to a cluster of boulders a couple of hundred yards ahead of them. "We'll hunker down in those rocks. They'll cut the wind, anyway."

Even though the sky was clear and the sun shone brightly, it didn't seem to be putting out much warmth. The air was still cold. Simon thought maybe they could build a little fire among the boulders, if they could find enough fuel to burn.

Wolters walked, leading his horse at a slow, easy pace, while Simon and Grady rode the other horse. When they reached the boulders, the boys dismounted. Simon saw that some dried brush had blown up among the rocks, so he pointed it out and asked Wolters, "All right if I make a fire?"

The outlaw frowned. Simon wondered if he was worried about the smoke. Did the Indians in this area still represent a threat? Was that why Wolters didn't want to call attention to them?

Or maybe he was worried that Marshal Tyler or somebody else from Wind River might be looking for them. Simon figured his father would be insistent that they put together a search party.

"Go ahead," Wolters finally said. "Keep it small, though. And don't unsaddle. With any luck, we won't be here long."

Simon piled a few handfuls of brush together and lit it with a lucifer. When the fire was burning, he and Grady hunkered next to it and held out their hands toward the warmth. Wolters walked around restlessly, casting an occasional worried glance back the way they had come from.

After a few minutes, Simon gave in to his curiosity and asked, "What's wrong, Mr. Wolters?"

The outlaw shook his head. "Wrong? Nothing, and I want it to stay that way. Always best to keep your eyes open when you're out on the trail, kid."

That answer was reasonable enough, but something about Wolters's manner made Simon suspect the man wasn't being completely honest. Ever since they had broken camp and ridden off to the west, Simon had had a nagging feeling that trouble lurked right underneath the surface. He wanted to know if his hunch was right, but he didn't figure he would be able to get anything out of Wolters.

The man was Blade Kendrick's oldest friend and partner, after all. Because of that,

Simon would never be able to trust him fully.

After a while, Grady started to get restless, too. He stood up and walked around, lightly clapping his gloved hands together.

Wolters turned to his horse and knelt again beside the injured foreleg. After examining it for a minute, he grimaced and said, "I wish we could just wait here overnight, but we can't. We need to get moving again. I've got some liniment in my saddlebags that might help . . ."

"I'll get it," Grady said. His pacing had carried him alongside Wolters's horse. Without waiting for the older man's response, he unfastened the saddlebag on the side closest to him and thrust his hand in. "Is it in here?"

"Wait, kid," Wolters said as he straightened hurriedly. "Don't go poking around in . . ."

Grady drew his hand out, but instead of a jar of liniment, he held a book. He frowned as he said, "This looks familiar. Where did you get . . ."

He stopped short. Simon heard the sharp hiss of a startled, indrawn breath from his brother. Grady had opened the book, and as he looked up at Wolters, his eyes were wide with shock.

"It's *Ivanhoe*," he said. Simon didn't see

why that would matter, but then Grady went on, "It's Ingrid's favorite book. Where did you get it, Frank?"

"You know I like to read sometimes, kid," Wolters said. "I don't know where I picked that up."

"I do." Grady held up the book in his left hand with the front cover open so the flyleaf was revealed. "It has Ingrid's name in it. This is my sister's copy." His face was drawn and bleak as he asked again, "Where did you get it?"

"Damn it, give me that." Wolters stepped up to Grady and snatched the book from his hand. "You ought to know better than to go poking around in a man's saddlebags."

Grady put his hand on the butt of his gun. "Frank, why do you have my sister's book?"

Wolters gave him a hard look and said, "You don't want to be doing this, Grady. Just forget about it. Anyway, she wasn't your sister. You didn't belong to that family. Your ma had to *pay* them to take you!"

By now the sudden tension in the air had brought Simon to his feet. He looked across the fire at Grady and Wolters. Grady looked like he was ready to draw his gun, and Simon hoped fervently that he wouldn't do that. He didn't know how fast Wolters was, but the man had survived on the outlaw trail for more than a decade, so he had to be more deadly than a green boy like Grady.

Grady's temper was up, though, and he wasn't thinking about anything like that. He said, "You went back there, didn't you? Back to the Claytons' ranch. I remember now. The morning after . . . after I left with you and Pa and the others, Hog and some other men rode back into camp from somewhere. You were one of them, Frank. You and Hog and the rest of them, you went back to the ranch."

"You don't know what you're talking about," Wolters said coldly.

"I know Ingrid wouldn't have given you her copy of *Ivanhoe*! It was one of her most precious possessions. The only way you'd have it is if you . . . if you took it from her after she was . . ."

Grady couldn't bring himself to go on. His face was drained of color and looked like he was as horrified as Simon felt right now.

Wolters's lip curled in a sneer. "What the hell does it matter? They weren't your family."

Grady let out an incoherent cry and yanked his gun from its holster. His draw was quick and smooth, a testament to the hours of practice he had put in since joining Kendrick's gang.

But Wolters was quicker. His gun seemed to leap into his hand. Instead of firing the revolver, he lashed out with it. The barrel slammed into the side of Grady's head before the youngster's gun could come level. Grady's knees buckled.

Simon didn't think about what he was doing. Realization had already burst through his brain. Whatever the motive might have been — sheer cruelty wasn't out of the question — Blade Kendrick had sent Wolters, Tatum, and other members of the gang to wipe out the family that had raised Grady as one of their own for more than a decade. Blood or not, they *were* Grady's family, just as the Woodsons were Simon's.

Kendrick must have recognized that and hadn't been able to stand it.

And if he had been responsible for one such atrocity, that meant he might well have sent Simon and Grady off with Wolters so that he and the rest of the outlaws could ride into Wind River and . . .

All that flashed through Simon's brain in a fraction of a second, and as soon as it had, instinct took over and made him drag his gun from its holster. Grady was still pitching forward, stunned by the blow to his head, and Wolters was turning toward

Simon, the gun in his hand swinging around.

Simon held the revolver in both hands, dragging the hammer back with his thumb as he shoved it out in front of him. He pulled the trigger, and even though he thought he was prepared, the thunderclap of the shot was shockingly loud. He flinched, shutting his eyes, fully expecting that he had missed and any second now, Wolters would shoot him.

Instead, when Simon forced his eyes open again, he saw that Wolters had stumbled back against his lame horse and was pawing at the saddle with his free hand, trying to hold himself up long enough to raise the gun in his other hand. The weapon's barrel had sagged toward the ground, and Wolters acted like it weighed a ton.

That was probably because of the rapidly spreading bloodstain on the front of his coat. As he gasped for air, making a bubbling sound, the gun slipped from his fingers and thudded to the ground. Blood trickled in crimson lines from both corners of his mouth. Simon thought about shooting him again, but before he could do that, the skittish horse danced away and Wolters collapsed. He landed on his face, and except for a momentary, convulsive curling of his fingers, he didn't move again.

Still holding the gun, Simon rushed around the fire and dropped to one knee beside his brother. He holstered the weapon, took hold of Grady's shoulders, and carefully rolled him onto his back. The blow from Wolters's gun had left a bloody welt on Grady's head, but he didn't seem to be seriously injured.

In fact, he was coming around. He groaned and opened his eyes. For a second his gaze wouldn't focus, but then it locked on Simon's anxious face.

"S-Simon . . . are . . . are you all right?"

"I'm fine," Simon told him. "What about you?"

"Head hurts . . . like blazes. That son of a bitch . . ." The memory of his discovery must have flooded back into Grady's brain, because he suddenly clutched at Simon's arm and said, "Ingrid's book! Simon, they . . . they must have killed everybody . . . my folks, my brothers . . . *You're* my brother, but . . ."

Simon put a hand on Grady's shoulder and squeezed. "I know what you mean. And yeah, I think you're right. Kendrick sent them to do that."

He would never call the man *Pa* again.

"And the rest of the gang may be headed

for Wind River right now," Simon went on. "Kendrick thinks he's got a score to settle with the Woodsons, I'll bet, and anyway, they're outlaws. They raid towns all the time."

Grady struggled to sit up. "We got to . . . stop them. Is Wolters . . . ?"

"I think he's dead," Simon said. "I shot him. He looked like he was going to shoot me, and I reckon he might've killed you, too. He would have had to come up with some story for Kendrick about what happened to us, or maybe he would have just ridden on and left us for the buzzards, figuring he'd drop out of sight. But that won't happen now."

"Help me up. We need to . . . head for Wind River."

Simon put his arm around Grady's shoulders and lifted him to a sitting position. Grady moaned. Simon could tell he was dizzy.

"You're not a member of the gang anymore?" The question was painfully blunt, but Simon knew he had to be certain.

While Simon braced him, Grady reached over and picked up the book he had dropped when Wolters buffaloed him. In a voice choked with emotion, he said, "After this . . . I'll never have anything to do with that bastard and his men." He looked up at Simon. "Unless I kill him."

"You won't get the chance today."

"What are you talking about?"

Grady seemed steadier now, so Simon let go of him and stood up.

"I'm taking your horse," he said. "Wolters's mount is still lame. It can't move fast enough. I need to get back to Wind River as quickly as I can so I can warn everybody." Simon drew in a breath. "If there's even still time for that."

"Damn it, Simon, you can't just ride off and leave me . . ."

"I don't have any choice. You can ride Wolters's horse. You'll just have to take it slow."

Grady looked like he wanted to argue, but there was no getting around the logic of Simon's decision. He glanced over at the body sprawled a few yards away and said, "What about Frank?"

"Leave him here. Somebody can come back and bury him later, if the buzzards and the wolves leave anything."

"That don't sound like a preacher's boy talking."

Simon bent, picked up the black hat that had fallen from Wolters's head, and put it on. He went to Grady's horse and took up

423

the reins, then looked back at his brother.

"Maybe it's the outlaw blood in me," he said. "Right now, I don't care what happens to Blade Kendrick's soul. I just want to put the sorry son of a bitch in the ground."

CHAPTER 16

Cole knelt behind the log he was using for cover at the moment and brought the Henry rifle to his shoulder. He cranked off two quick rounds at the man attempting to dart from one clump of brush to another down below on the slope. The outlaw dived to the ground as one of the bullets sent his hat flying. He rolled desperately behind cover.

Cole turned and dashed a dozen feet to a spot where he could spray lead down the opposite slope. He was lucky the knob tapered to a small area. Otherwise, surrounded as he was, he wouldn't have been able to hold off the gang for this long.

As it was, keeping them pinned down instead of rushing him really kept him hopping. His heart slugged heavily in his chest, and he was sweating under the sheepskin jacket. That just made the air seem colder.

He was only postponing the inevitable, and he knew it.

Tied in the midst of several small trees, Ulysses whickered and tossed his head. The horse seemed to know things were looking pretty bad, too.

The shooting from below stopped. Cole wasn't surprised. Several times during the more than half an hour he had been trapped up here, the outlaws had stopped firing. Maybe they were discussing strategy. Or maybe they were just taking advantage of the opportunity to let their gun barrels cool off. Cole didn't care. All that mattered to him was that when one of those lulls happened, he had a chance to catch his breath.

Then he lifted his head as a new sound came to his ears. Hoofbeats. A lot of them.

He cursed, dropped to his belly, and crawled to the end of the log to take a look around it. He couldn't see very well, but he caught a glimpse of eight or nine riders heading south at a fast pace. South . . . toward Wind River.

Cole came up on his knees and brought the Henry to his shoulder. The range was long, even for a dependable rifle. He started shooting anyway, triggering as fast as he could work the Henry's lever.

A bullet from downslope smacked into the log, chewed splinters from it, and sprayed them in Cole's face. He dropped behind the cover again. As far as he'd been able to tell, his shots hadn't had any effect on the men riding away.

It didn't take a genius to figure out what was going on. Blade Kendrick — because it couldn't be anybody else — had left a couple of men posted here to keep Cole pinned down, while he took the rest of his gang and headed for the settlement. The only explanation Cole could think of for that move was that Kendrick intended to raid Wind River. From what Franklin Woodson had told him about Kendrick, the man was loco. He might be seeking revenge on the family that had taken Simon in, or he might just be out for whatever loot he could grab.

Either way, the town was in danger. Clancy Madigan was a good man, and many of the other citizens of Wind River could be counted upon to stand up for themselves.

But the outlaws would be taking them by surprise, and there was no telling how much damage they could do before anybody was able to mount a defense.

He had to come up with a way to bust out of this trap, Cole told himself.

He could see only one way of doing that. Turning his head to look at Ulysses, he said to the sorrel, "I'm mighty sorry about this, big fella, but I've got to distract one of those varmints and fool the other one. That means taking a chance I don't want to take with you, but we don't have a choice."

Ulysses tossed his head again, as if in agreement.

The hastily formed plan had risks for both of them. Cole had to show himself, first on one side of the knob and then the other, and draw the outlaws' fire, so he would know exactly where they were. Their bullets came close enough for him to hear their wicked whine through the air, but each time he threw himself back out of the way in time.

Then he went to the horse's side and looped the reins around the saddle horn so they wouldn't drag. "You're gonna charge right down at that fella on the north side like we're trying to bust out of here," he told Ulysses. "Don't get shot, old son."

The sorrel nudged Cole's shoulder with his nose. Cole gripped the headstall, turned Ulysses the right way, then took off his hat and slapped it against the horse's rump. Ulysses jumped and took off, crashing through the brush and raising a lot of racket as he headed down the slope.

Cole dropped to hands and knees and scrambled quickly back to the log. He raised his head just enough to peer over the rough-barked trunk.

Behind him, the gunman on that side started firing fast, hearing Ulysses charging toward him and thinking that Cole was trying to get past him. On this side, the other outlaw heard the shots and the hoofbeats and leaped to his feet to get in on the kill if he could.

Instead, almost too swiftly for the eye to follow, Cole brought the Henry up and triggered a shot that slammed a .44 round through the base of the man's throat. Even at this distance, Cole saw blood spurt high in the air as the outlaw went over backward. He would be dead in a matter of seconds.

Cole whipped around and dashed to the other side of the knob. The shooting was still going on, but he stopped as he realized he heard the boom of a pistol along with the sharper cracks of the rifle that had been raking the top of the knob. Was somebody else down there now, shooting at him? He didn't hear any bullets slashing through the brush or thudding into tree trunks.

Maybe somebody else had come along and taken a hand in this fight.

Cole started down the slope, darting from cover to cover, eager to find out what was going on. As he neared the bottom, the shooting stopped. So did Cole. He listened intently as the echoes of the gun-thunder faded.

"Damn it, boy," a harsh voice said. "Blade got you and your brother out of the way so you'd be safe. What are you doin' here?"

"I . . . I found out what Kendrick's going to do." That was Simon, Cole realized with a surprised frown. "I had to stop him."

"Ain't nobody can stop him now," the outlaw said as Cole eased forward again. "Looks like I'm gonna have to kill you, but I'll figure out some way to blame it on that damn marshal."

Cole stepped out of the brush and said, "No, I don't reckon you will."

In the next split-second, Cole saw Simon half-sitting, half-lying on the ground as he clutched his upper left arm. Blood seeped between the fingers of his right hand. A bearded, thick-bodied man in buckskins was about fifteen feet from the boy, holding a Winchester. The outlaw tried to whirl toward Cole, but Cole fired while he was turning. The .44 slug ripped through the man's body from left to right, probably going through both lungs. But it didn't knock him off his feet, and momentum continued to bring him on around so Cole's second shot punched straight into his chest. That one put him down.

Cole kept the Henry lined on the fallen man until he was sure the outlaw had stopped breathing. Then he lowered the rifle and called, "How bad are you hit, Simon?"

"I'll be all right, Marshal," Simon replied. The strain in his voice revealed that he was in pain, but he was coherent and didn't appear to be bleeding heavily. "I'm getting a little annoyed, though. This is the second time I've been shot in this arm in less than twenty-four hours."

That comment made a smile tug at Cole's mouth. "I'll take a look at it."

Simon shook his head and said, "There's no time for that. I can tie a rag around it while we're riding. We need to get to Wind River as fast as we can."

"Because that's where your pa's headed with the rest of his gang?"

"That's where Blade Kendrick's headed," Simon corrected him. "My pa is Brother Franklin Woodson. He's more of a father to me than Kendrick ever will be."

"I suspect you're right about that." Cole turned his head and whistled. He was worried about Ulysses. He hadn't seen the golden sorrel for a few minutes, and he wanted to be sure his old trail partner was all right.

Relief went through Cole as Ulysses loomed up in the brush and moved out into the open. Cole spotted another horse grazing about fifty yards away and figured that was Simon's mount. He had a lot of questions for the youngster, but Simon was right: everything could wait except for getting to Wind River in time to prevent Blade Kendrick's raid on the town.

Or, failing that, to make sure that neither Kendrick nor any of the other outlaws rode out of there alive.

Clancy Madigan had the shillelagh cocked over his right shoulder as he moved along the boardwalk toward the storefront where Franklin Woodson had established his church. Madigan wasn't sure anybody would be there on a Monday morning, but he heard hammering coming from inside the building and opened the door to find Woodson working on another pew. Mrs. Woodson and the girl, Deborah, were there, too. They all looked around at Madigan as he strode in and closed the door behind him to keep the cold air out.

"Good morning to ye," the deputy said with a nod.

"Is there any news of Simon?" Mrs. Woodson asked. Her fingers knitted together as she spoke.

"No, I'm afraid not. I haven't seen Marshal Tyler since he rode out earlier."

"Then why are you here?" Woodson asked. The question was curt, even rude, but Madigan knew that was because the man was worried about his son.

"No particular reason," he answered. "I'm just makin' my rounds of the town, heard you workin' in here, and decided to step in and say hello. That's all."

"I'm sorry," Woodson muttered. "We're just worried, and when we saw you, we hoped for good news."

"Nobody can blame ye for that. If I hear anything, I'll pass the word right away, ye can count on that."

"I still wish the marshal had let me go with him . . ."

Woodson stopped in mid-sentence as the door opened again. The man who stepped in was a stranger to Madigan. He was stocky, dark-haired, heavy-featured, with several days' worth of stubble on his face. His thick, quilted coat hung open over a flannel shirt. Madigan caught a glimpse of a gun butt under the coat. He didn't like the looks of the man.

"Franklin Woodson?" the stranger said.

"I'm Brother Franklin Woodson," the

preacher replied. "What can I do for you?"

With a whisper of steel against leather, the man's gun came out fast and leveled. The way it was pointing, the muzzle covered both Madigan and Woodson. Madigan started to bring the shillelagh down from his shoulder, but the stranger's gun swung more toward him.

"Don't do it, mister. You're not packing iron, and I'll kill you before you get close enough to swing that club at me."

Phillippa Woodson and her daughter had both gasped as the man pulled his gun. They started toward Woodson, but he lifted a hand to stop them.

"Stay where you are," he told them. "You're out of the line of fire there."

"Maybe they are," the stranger said with a chuckle. "But I don't think they want to see you gunned down, Woodson, so if they're smart they won't try anything." He glanced at Madigan. "Who the hell are you?"

"Deputy Marshal Clancy Madigan," the big Irishman replied, "and if ye don't put that gun away, you won't just be in jail, my friend, ye'll be *under* it."

A harsh laugh came from the man. "Big talk from a blowhard. But I'm glad you're here, Deputy. Saves me the trouble of having to look you up. Any more lawmen in town?"

"Marshal Tyler . . ."

"Is either dead by now, or still pinned down miles from here," the stranger interrupted.

That bold declaration made Madigan's heart sink, but he was determined not to show that.

"You still haven't told us what you want," Woodson said.

"We're all going to stand right here and wait until my friends get done robbing the bank and whatever else they want to do, and then you and I are going to settle the score between us."

"The score?" Woodson repeated in apparent confusion. "I don't even know . . ." He caught his breath. "My God. I *do* know you. It's been years, but I remember you now. You're . . ."

"Blade Kendrick, that's right. You helped my wife steal my boys away from me. And so my face is going to be the last thing you ever see."

CHAPTER 17

Tying a bandage around his wounded arm proved to be more difficult than Simon expected, so Cole had to help him. The marshal made quick work of the job, though, and it was only a few minutes before they were riding southeast toward Wind River at a fast pace.

"You'd better tell me what all's happened since last night," Cole said over the rattle of hoofbeats. "Who shot you the first time?"

"That was Hog Tatum," Simon replied. "He said it was by accident, but I don't know."

Cole grunted. From what he knew of Hog Tatum, the outlaw had a reputation for brutality. Cole wasn't inclined to give him the benefit of the doubt.

Simon continued his story, telling his version of the incident Cole had already heard the other side of from Deborah Woodson. He explained how Blade Kendrick had sent him, Grady, and Wolters out of the camp this morning, and how Grady had found Ingrid Clayton's copy of *Ivanhoe* in Wolters's saddlebag, setting off a violent chain of events.

"Once we realized Kendrick's gang must have wiped out the Claytons, it didn't take much to figure out that he might go after the Woodsons, and doing that would be a good excuse for them to loot the town, too. So I left Grady to follow as best he could on Wolters's horse and headed for Wind River to warn everybody."

"But you heard the shooting where they had me cornered and decided to look into it."

"I thought it might have something to do with Kendrick, so I had to find out what it was all about."

"I'm glad you did," Cole said. "Sorry you got ventilated in the process, though."

"I'll be all right. The bullet didn't break the bone." Simon laughed humorlessly. "I'm getting used to my arm hurting like blazes."

"You recognized that fella in the buckskins who was shooting at me?"

"Yeah. I don't know his name, but I saw him in Kendrick's camp. He's one of the gang, I'm certain about that. I had my gun out and yelled for him to drop his rifle, but instead he turned around and shot me." Simon shook his head ruefully. "I wasn't nearly as lucky as when I gunned down Wolters."

"You're not lacking for sand, just experience," Cole told him. "Growing up as a preacher's boy didn't teach you anything about fighting outlaws."

They rode in silence for a few moments, then Simon asked, "Do you think they'll kill everybody in town?"

Cole snorted dismissively. "I reckon they'll find Wind River a lot tougher nut to crack than they're expecting. There are plenty of folks there who know how to stand up to trouble. But if they take everybody by surprise, some good people might be killed. I'm going to prevent that if I can."

"I'll help you."

Cole looked over at the youngster. "Even if it means going up against your real pa?"

"The only pa I have is Brother Woodson," Simon declared. Cole believed him.

It was close to midday by the time they came in sight of the town. Cole was a little relieved when he saw that everything appeared normal. No smoke rose into the sky except from the chimneys of the buildings. Nobody was shooting. As far as Cole could tell, peace reigned over the settlement.

He pulled Ulysses back to a walk. The big sorrel was tired. So was the horse Simon was riding. The youngster said, "What happened? You think they decided not to attack the town after all?"

"We don't know for sure that's what they set out to do," Cole said.

Simon's face was grim as he said, "If you'd ever been around Blade Kendrick much, Marshal, you'd know there's nothing he won't stoop to, if it suits his purposes. The man's a monster."

"I don't doubt it, but . . ."

Cole broke off as a new sound reached them and caused both riders to stiffen in their saddles. The reports were unmistakable.

Gunfire had erupted in Wind River.

Inside the storefront, Kendrick had just voiced his threat, causing Phillippa Woodson to cry out and clap her hands over her mouth in horror. Deborah took a step toward the outlaw and exclaimed, "You can't!"

Kendrick turned slightly toward her, bringing the gun with him. Woodson said, "Deborah, no! Stay back."

"That's smart, preacher," Kendrick said. "I'll leave your wife and girl alone if they don't give me any trouble. But they're going to watch you die . . ."

Somewhere down the streets, shots blasted.

Kendrick didn't react much. He would have been expecting gunfire, Madigan knew. But despite that, he turned his head toward the sound, and for a second he could see the big deputy only from the corner of his eye.

The shillelagh was already back, resting on Madigan's shoulder. He whipped his arm forward and threw the club as hard as he could.

Kendrick saw it coming and tried to twist out of the way. The gun in his hand boomed. Madigan felt a hammerblow against his chest that knocked him backward. He was too big and strong for the bullet to drive him all the way off his feet, though. He was still standing as the shillelagh smashed into Kendrick's right shoulder and turned him halfway around. The gun flew out of the outlaw's hand.

An instant later, Woodson tackled Kendrick, crashing into him and forcing him back toward the door. Both men went down. Woodson flailed wild punches at the outlaw.

Madigan's left side was numb, but he was

still conscious and coherent. He swept his right arm toward Mrs. Woodson and Deborah and bellowed, "Get in the back room and stay there!"

Mrs. Woodson caught her daughter's arm and dragged her toward the door at the back of the room. Without waiting to see if they reached that sanctuary, Madigan hurried forward, stumbling only a little, and bent to scoop up the shillelagh where it had landed on the floor after striking Kendrick. Shooting was still going on elsewhere in town, and he was the only law in Wind River at the moment. Determination — some would call it sheer stubbornness — drove him to stay on his feet.

Unfortunately, his big body wasn't equal to the task. He stumbled again, fell to his knees, and then toppled forward as darkness claimed him.

Even tired, Ulysses was stronger and faster than the horse Simon was riding. Cole pulled ahead as they galloped toward the settlement. When he reached the end of Grenville Avenue, he saw that the boardwalks were empty. People must have scrambled for cover when the shooting broke out. Cole was glad for that, anyway.

Guns still roared farther up the street.

Cole knew from bitter experience that the sounds came from the direction of the bank. This wasn't the first time outlaws had tried to loot it.

He had to ride past Woodson's storefront church to reach the bank. As he did, he wondered if Blade Kendrick was with the men trying to hold up the bank, or if he had gone after the preacher. With a gun battle still raging, he couldn't stop to check inside the church.

As Cole neared the bank, several men backed out of its open doors, firing back inside. One of them had a blazing torch in his hand. To be burning that fiercely, it must have been soaked in pitch. He drew back his arm to throw it into the bank and start a fire that would be both a distraction and a deadly threat. Nothing could destroy a frontier town more quickly and savagely than fire.

One of the men heard the sorrel's pounding hoofbeats and turned to throw lead at Cole. Bending forward with a grim expression on his face, Cole ignored the bullets whipping around him and aimed his Colt at the man with the torch. The .44 bucked in his hand.

The back of a running horse was no place for accuracy, but desperation guided Cole's aim. His bullet hit the man in the head and bored through his brain before exploding out the other side. The outlaw dropped like a stone, and the torch flew from his hand to land at the edge of the boardwalk and then bounce into the street. It was harmless, for the moment.

But that left two more bandits on the boardwalk in front of the bank to shoot at Cole. He kicked his feet free of the stirrups and launched himself from the saddle as Ulysses thundered on. His momentum as he landed carried him forward in a roll that took him behind a water trough next to the boardwalk.

As outlaw lead slammed into the trough, Cole came up shooting, too. One of the men doubled over as a slug punched into his guts. The other made a dash for a nearby horse, evidently deciding that he'd rather get away than continue the fight. He was trying to leap into the saddle when Cole shot him out of midair.

Then more shots crashed and bullets kicked up dirt in Cole's face as they struck only inches away in the street. A glance as he scrambled to throw himself into the narrow space between the water trough and the boardwalk showed him more outlaws who had just emerged from the Wind River

General Store. A bullet smacked his bootheel as he pulled his leg behind the trough.

A shot came from back along the street somewhere. One of the outlaws cried out in pain. Cole looked in that direction and saw Billy Casebolt blazing away with his old Griswold & Gunnison revolver. The deputy was hatless and wore a nightshirt that was stuffed into a pair of trousers. Cole knew he had heard the shooting and charged out of Dr. Kent's house like an old firehorse answering the bell.

Casebolt emptied his gun and ducked into an alcove at the entrance to a building. When Cole levered himself up and fired over the top of the water trough, he saw that one of the owlhoots across the street was already down, dropped by Casebolt's fire. The deputy's attack had served as a useful distraction, too, because the other men had turned their guns toward him to drive him back.

Cole triggered twice more, emptying his gun. One of the remaining outlaws folded up as a bullet tore through him. The third man swung his gun toward Cole again, but before he could fire, Harvey Raymond, the manager of the general store, stepped out onto the boardwalk with a shotgun in his hands. The weapon boomed as Raymond squeezed off both barrels. The double load of buckshot caught the remaining outlaw at close range and flung his bloody, shredded body into the street.

Kendrick and his men had underestimated just how much of a fighting town Wind River was.

Cole didn't know what Blade Kendrick looked like, didn't know if he was one of the men who had already fallen. As Cole started to reload, he hoped that was the case. A number of the outlaws were down, but some of the gang might still be at large, and they would be less likely to keep fighting if their leader was dead.

An angry roar, followed by the wicked crack of a rifle, made him look up. Cole recognized the man charging along the boardwalk at him, firing a Winchester. It was Hog Tatum, the outlaw Cole had inadvertantly saved from the bounty hunter, and clearly, he wasn't bent on returning that favor.

Instead he was doing his dead level best to kill the marshal.

Clancy Madigan swam back up out of the dark pool that had swallowed him. He lifted his head and shook it to clear some of the cobwebs from his brain. A few feet away, Kendrick lay on his back, stunned. Franklin Woodson still knelt on top of the outlaw, wearily slugging away at him. Madigan was surprised to see that the preacher appeared to have won the battle. Woodson's ferocity must have taken Kendrick equally by surprise.

Guns still thundered outside. The racket drove Madigan to his feet. He looked down and saw blood on his shirt, but he was still alive and as long as he drew breath, he was going to do his job. He staggered toward the door and jerked it open.

To his left and not far away, a rifle cracked several times. Madigan saw a big, ugly, bearded man running along the boardwalk, firing a Winchester at something or someone to the deputy's right. Madigan didn't recognize the man with the rifle, but he knew an outlaw when he saw one. He didn't hesitate. He launched himself from the doorway and crashed into the man as he started to run past the church.

Cole didn't know if he was going to get his gun reloaded in time to bring the weapon up and snap a shot at Tatum before the big outlaw drilled him.

But then an equally burly figure lurched

out from a doorway and collided with Tatum. The thud as hundreds of pounds of meat, bone, and sinew came together seemed to shake the boardwalk. Tatum's rifle went flying, and both men plunged into the street.

Cole caught a glimpse of what looked like a bloodstain on Madigan's shirt. If Madigan was wounded, he must have overcome the disadvantage by sheer force of will. He came up slugging at Tatum with his right fist. Tatum made it to his feet as well and hammered punches at Madigan.

Cole's gun was reloaded now, but as he stood, he saw that he couldn't risk a shot with the two big men so close together and swaying back and forth as they pounded at each other. He might hit Madigan.

As Cole moved closer, he realized Madigan wasn't able to use his left arm, while Tatum was still hale and hearty. That was taking a toll, because Tatum could block Madigan's punches with one arm and strike with the other, while Madigan had to just absorb the punishment Tatum was dealing out if he intended to get in any blows of his own. Sooner or later, Madigan would be knocked down again.

That would be the best thing, Cole thought, because then he would have a clear shot and could drill Tatum. Maybe Madigan would figure that out and give up the fight.

He should know better than to think that, Cole told himself. Even wounded, Clancy Madigan didn't have any quit in him. But he was a canny brawler, and as Tatum swung a vicious roundhouse punch, Madigan suddenly ducked and went under it. He bulled in, looped his good arm around Tatum's throat, and swung a hip into the outlaw. They went down and rolled over a couple of times in the street.

When they came to a stop, Madigan was behind Tatum and still had his arm around the man's neck. The grip was tight enough so Madigan could reach around and grab hold of his own left shoulder. Tatum bucked wildly as Madigan tightened the hold even more. The Irishman's brawny arm pressed hard up under Tatum's chin and threatened to crush his windpipe. Madigan had swung a sledgehammer countless times during the building of the railroad, and his strength was enormous.

Cole didn't hear any more shooting. Tatum might be the last of the gang still able to put up a fight. People were coming out onto the boardwalks to watch the battle of the titans in the middle of the street.

Tatum tried every way he knew how to knock Madigan loose from him, but he couldn't budge the deputy. Their feet scrabbled in the dirt as they fought for position. With a quick move, Madigan got his right knee planted in the middle of Tatum's back. He reared up and heaved, and Cole heard a sharp crack, like a branch breaking. Tatum suddenly went limp.

Madigan had broken his neck.

Madigan let go of Tatum, who fell facedown. A second later, Madigan followed him, collapsing. Cole would have run to the deputy's side, but from the corner of his eye he saw that the danger wasn't over.

Deborah Woodson stumbled out of the storefront with a stranger right behind her, holding her by the neck with his left arm while he clutched a gun in his right fist. Cole had never seen this man before, but he had to be one of the gang. Considering that he had come out of the church, there was a good chance he was Blade Kendrick himself.

A cold ball formed in the pit of Cole's stomach. He hadn't noticed any shots from inside the building, but with all the powder being burned in Wind River today, they might have blended into the rest of the gunthunder. Woodson and his wife might be dead already.

No. The preacher staggered out after Deborah and her captor, blood running down the side of his face from a gash on his head.

"Stop!" Woodson cried. "Don't hurt her, Kendrick, I beg you!"

"I promised she'd watch you die, preacher," the man said. "It's time."

His gun swung toward Woodson.

Cole couldn't get a shot because Deborah was in the way, but another gun blasted before the outlaw could pull the trigger. He jerked under a bullet's impact and lost his grip on Deborah, and she wrenched away from him and threw herself into her father's arms. The stranger — Blade Kendrick, Cole was sure of it now — twisted slowly toward the person who had shot him.

Simon stood a few yards away, at the end of the boardwalk where an alley cut between buildings. A wisp of smoke still curled from the muzzle of the revolver he held.

"Simon!" Kendrick gasped. "Son . . . I'm your . . ."

"Don't even say it," Simon told him. He pulled the trigger again.

This bullet knocked Kendrick off his feet, driving him backward to sprawl on the boardwalk. His gun skittered away on the planks. He twitched a couple of times and then lay still.

Clancy Madigan was sitting up now, shaking his head groggily as Cole walked over and dropped to a knee beside him.

"We've got to get you to the doctor," Cole said.

"Is it finished?" Madigan asked.

Cole looked toward the church and saw Woodson standing there holding Deborah while Mrs. Woodson came hesitantly from the building to join them. Simon had lowered his gun but not holstered it yet. Between him and the rest of his family lay the body of Blade Kendrick.

"I reckon it is," Cole said. He saw Judson Kent hurrying along the street and waved the doctor toward him and Madigan.

CHAPTER 18

Madigan was sitting up in bed in one of the rooms in Dr. Kent's house, his left shoulder and that side of his chest swaddled in thick bandages. His normally ruddy face was considerably paler than usual, but he wore a grin as he said, "The doc here tells me I'm gonna live."

"Indeed he is," Kent assured Cole. "Our friend is not only as big as a horse, he's as healthy as one."

"That's mighty good to know," Cole said.

Billy Casebolt, who was fully dressed now, including the battered old hat he had thumbed to the back of his head, said, "Looks like you and me have traded places, Clancy. I'm plumb sorry you got shot, but it sure feels good to have my ol' deputy's badge pinned to my vest again."

"I'll be up and around before ye know it," Madigan said. "Then Cole will have to decide who he wants for his deputy."

"Unless the town council can find enough money to pay both of you," Cole suggested as he looked at Kent. "How about it, Mr. Mayor?"

"We'll take up budgetary matters later on, when the time is more appropriate," Kent said. "For now, Mr. Madigan, you can just be thankful that bullet passed on through without damaging anything vital."

Cole left Casebolt sitting in the room with Madigan and followed Kent out to the front porch of the house. "How are the Woodsons doing?" he asked.

"The cut where Kendrick pistol-whipped Mr. Woodson required some stitches, but it should heal. I cleaned and bandaged both bullet wounds on young Simon's arm, and he should be fine as well. They were exceedingly fortunate to come through this with no lasting effects."

Cole nodded slowly but then said, "I'm not so sure they did."

Kent arched an eyebrow. "Oh?"

"Whether he wants to think about it right now or not, that boy killed his father. Now, I'm not saying that Kendrick didn't have it coming — Lord knows he did — but Simon's been raised to turn the other cheek. He took a life, and Kendrick being who he was is liable to just make it worse later on, when everything sinks in."

"And yet Simon's father, Mr. Woodson, I mean, fought more than once in defense of his family. The man clearly does not believe in pacifism at all costs."

"That's true," Cole said. "He went after Kendrick even fiercer than he tackled those freighters yesterday. He thought he'd knocked Kendrick out. That was the only way the varmint was able to take him by surprise."

"Perhaps things will work out for them. Clearly, they're a strong family."

"Simon will have his brother around now, too, since the Woodsons agreed to take him in, so that should help. Still, it wouldn't surprise me if those boys drifted on, one of these days, and tried to put all of it behind them."

"Mr. Woodson's history says that he seldom stays in one place for too long himself. I doubt if the family will settle here in Wind River permanently."

Cole grinned. "I sort of hope they do. Might be a good thing for Jeremiah to have some competition when it comes to preaching. If the town keeps growing, it was always bound to have more than one church."

Kent took a cigar from his vest pocket and put it in his mouth, unlit, as he looked along

Grenville Avenue. The street was busy now in the late afternoon.

"More churches. More businesses. More people." Kent looked over at Cole. "Perhaps it *would* be a good idea if the council found the funds to hire two deputies. A growing town means more and more of a need for law and order. And by that I mean . . . more trouble."

"I never doubted it for a second," Cole said.

ABOUT THE AUTHORS

Lifelong Texans, **James Reasoner** and **L. J. Washburn** have been husband and wife, and professional writers, for more than thirty years. In that time, they have authored several hundred novels and short stories in numerous genres.

James is best known for his Westerns, historical novels, and war novels; he is also the author of two mystery novels that have achieved cult classic status, *Texas Wind* and *Dust Devils*. Writing under his own name and various pseudonyms, his novels have garnered praise from *Publishers Weekly, Booklist,* and the *Los Angeles Times,* as well as appearing on the *New York Times* and *USA Today* bestseller lists. He recently won the Peacemaker award for his novel *Redemption, Kansas.* His website is www.james reasoner.com.

Livia J. (L. J.) Washburn has been writing professionally for over thirty years. Washburn received the Private Eye Writers of America award and the American Mystery award for the first Lucas Hallam mystery, *Wild Night*. Her story "Charlie's Pie" won a Peacemaker award. Her website is www.livia jwashburn.com.

The employees of Thorndike Press hope you have enjoyed this Large Print book. All our Thorndike, Wheeler, and Kennebec Large Print titles are designed for easy reading, and all our books are made to last. Other Thorndike Press Large Print books are available at your library, through selected bookstores, or directly from us.

For information about titles, please call:
  (800) 223-1244

or visit our Web site at:
  http://gale.cengage.com/thorndike

To share your comments, please write:
  Publisher
  Thorndike Press
  10 Water St., Suite 310
  Waterville, ME 04901